Onesimus

The Prince and the Slave

Mark Potter

ISBN:9781520225272
Independently Published

DEDICATION

This book is dedicated to Dr. Paul Potter, my father. Late in life, I learned what an amazing man he is. For many years, he has been a highly-respected professor of communication, and radio and television production, in Texas, Oklahoma, Ohio, and Alaska. He is a man who loves great literature and art. It was a long time before I realized that my love for literature and art came from him. I am indebted to him for that and for so many other things. We both have been on the same road to finding redemption and restoration, like Onesimus, and the journey along that road led us to become friends.

I love you, Dad

CONTENTS

Acknowledgments v
Prologue: Prince 1
Chapter 1: Ephesus 5
Chapter 2: Byzantium 16
Chapter 3: Philemon 26
Chapter 4: An Education 39
Chapter 5: Timothy 50
Chapter 6: A New Philosophy 61
Chapter 7: Marriage 86
Chapter 8: Paul 110
Chapter 9: Artemis the Great 132
Chapter 10: Colossae 140
Chapter 11: Escape 154
Chapter 12: Athens 169
Chapter 13: Corinth 187
Chapter 14: Italy 203
Chapter 15: Reunion 219
Chapter 16: Rome 236
Chapter 17: Stars 256
Chapter 18: Redemption 265
Chapter 19: Runner 281
Chapter 20: Caesar 290
Chapter 21: Brother 301
Chapter 22: Singidava Getae 312
Epilogue: Onesimus 329
Message to the Reader 332
Bibliography 333
About the Author 334

ACKNOWLEDGMENTS

I would like to thank Joshua Ramirez for creating the picture for my book cover. He is a skilled young artist, that I know will one day be discovered. I am so proud that some of his first professional work might be from producing my book covers. He has been one of my favorite students since the first day he entered my class over a decade ago. Thank you, Josh.

And I wish to thank my mother and father, Shirley Pennoyer and Dr. Paul Potter, for their contribution to this novel. My mom is such a mom that anything her baby writes is awesome, but she offered comments and encouragement that have helped me continue, even when I felt that it was an impossibility. My father did much the same, but there are places in this novel that he pushed me to be clearer and more forceful, wanting to make sure I got the message out to you, the reader. Thank you both.

And then there is Virginia Swartzendruber, the Guru of Grammar. I met her thirty-two years ago when I first came to Bolivia. I discovered in her a tough, but loving teacher. It was Virginia that helped me reconnect with friends in Bolivia, ultimately helping me return. She has worked tirelessly making sure that this novel is grammatically correct. I could not have done this without her. Thank you, Virginia.

PROLOGUE
PRINCE

Every morning I run.

I need to be in the forest. That is where I am free. The trees make me feel alive. You can't run fast in the forest. There are fallen trunks of trees, bushes with thorns, and weeds tangling your feet, but I can run faster than others. I run every day and know this forest better than anyone. I know where the fallen logs are. I know the places where a gully suddenly appears. I know my way through the dark corners forgotten by the sun.

On the edge of the village is a great field of grass where the cattle graze. There are also plots of wheat and oats. I can run swiftly through those fields. No one can run as swiftly as me. I am like a deer. Even the wolves can't catch me. One tried once, though the old man who watches over the well said it was just a wild dog. I know it was a wolf. He was jealous because I am so much faster than he is. Not the old man, the wolf.

I run as fast as I can so no one will catch me. I am the fastest. Mother calls, but I ignore her.

Mother calls me Prince. Father calls me Runner. I like to run. When I hear the cock crowing to the village that the day has begun, even before the sun has fully risen, I get out of the house, before Mother can order me to work at some boring task to please her. This day is important to me. I am to be sent to the wise men after Father and the other hunters return. Then I will receive my name.

I want to be called Runner, or maybe Prince of Runners. Just Prince sounds boring.

I am a prince of the Singidava Getae north of the Great River, under the shadow of the purple mountains. There are spirits of our ancestors here who will drink your blood if you do not honor them. Every day I stop on top of the hill that rises above the village and say a prayer of thanks to Rubobostes, my ancestor. I am the son of the son of the son…. Well, I don't know exactly how many sons of, but he was the great chief who defeated the Romans farther back than any in my village can remember. But I stop and remember him so I won't be attacked by my ancestors in the forest.

And then I run again.

I must catch the morning before it catches me. I laugh when I outrun the rabbit at my feet. No one can catch me.

On the edge of the field are the fir and beech and alder trees. To me they look like maidens with slender arms dancing in the breeze. The old man who sits by the well says that some believe they are inhabited by maiden spirits. They wave at me as I pass through them. I wave my greeting to them as I pass deeper into the dark forest.

The forest is mostly oak, but also locust and pine. There is the sharp, clean smell of the pines, but also a musty, old scent of the decaying leaves in the undergrowth. It smells so old here. My bare feet barely feel the cold and damp of the decaying leaves. There is one place I must run to every morning. I want to be there before the sun is high. This time of year, there is usually a mist. If I get there soon enough, the sun breaks through the trees and the mist, and I can see the spirits of the forest welcoming the day. I know the ancestors came from the forest and I know they returned there when they died.

I run but I never feel tired. I run so I won't be caught. And I run so I will discover.

Always I think there is something beyond even my ancestors. I don't know what that is, but I know if I continue running my race through the forest, I will discover it. So, I run and I run. I will be the one to discover what is beyond the forest and who made the ancestors. I will be the discoverer.

It is autumn. The leaves are falling around me, daring me to catch them. I can see better now than in the summer when there are so many leaves. I am faster in the autumn. I like the cold mornings and warm afternoons of autumn. I was born in autumn, so this is my season. And this is my forest.

I am a prince of the Getae, the Singidava Getae, north of the Great River, but within view of the mountains. I am the son of the son of the son of the Great Rubobostes. I don't know how many sons of, but I know he was a great king.

There is a clearing in the forest, with a cold stream. It is a place where the sun shines warmly, even in the coolest autumn day. I always stop for water in a still bend in the stream. I don't know the boy in the water who greets me. He is small, only about five years old. I am too, but I feel older. I know I am smarter than any of the boys who are my age; too smart to play with them. And I am a prince, son of the chief, who is son of the chief before him, all the way back to Rubobostes, so I am better than them too.

It is quiet here. I hear the gentle rustle of the wind in the trees. There are the sounds of frogs and the ever-present crickets. I look around and I am alone.

I sink to my knees in the cold mud by the stream and drink deeply of the cool, refreshing water. I want to examine the boy in the pool. He has yellow hair, freckles, and blue eyes. Is that what I look like? I assume I will never know since I can't see myself. I reach out to touch the boy, but the ripples in the water distort him. I don't know why, but the boy in the stream annoys me. I splash the water with my hands to make him vanish.

I turn from the water when I hear what sounds like a scream. Can I possibly hear my mother this far away? Something in me says I need to return. My race is not half run, but it is time to go. The ancestors around me tell me I must go.

So I run.

I stop on the edge of the forest under the shade of the dancing beech trees and see the smoke rising from the village. The screams are real. I can make out my mother's scream. She is calling for her prince. Is it me or father she calls for?

I run.

I am not halfway across the field when I see the horses. These are slenderer than the horses we use to plow, and they are faster. One horseman sees me and begins the chase. I am faster; I know it. Yet I can feel the pounding of the horse's hooves. I can't see him behind me. Only a fool turns to see who is following him. I feel him getting closer. I can feel the breath of the horse on my shoulder.

I run faster.

A whip entangles my feet and I fall. I can feel the leather cutting into my skin. I am almost under the feet of the horse, but the rider is skilled. I struggle to loosen my feet, but a fist across my face brings darkness. I can't outrun this man.

I never saw Mother or Father again.

CHAPTER 1
EPHESUS

Search me, God, and know my heart. Psalm 139:23

The wine dark sea accepted the spark of gold off the mountains to the east. Slowly the sea turned from deep purple, to orange splashed with gold, to finally becoming the azure for which the Aegean is famous. As the world awoke, on this warm spring day, I could now see the white and gold of a temple, standing above the city of Ephesus, the city of Artemis the Great. As we drew closer, the rumble of a city awakening grew louder.

The *Dolphin*, the ship in which I traveled from Alexandria, arrived shortly after sunrise. Ephesus was one of the great cities of the Empire, some say a third in size after Rome and Alexandria. It looked to me, easily as big as Alexandria, which I had seen many times. Here was the seat of the Proconsul of Asia, the richest province in the Empire. It dominated the business of the Aegean, having eclipsed Athens more than a century ago.

I was afraid. I was unsure how I would make my way here.

As I disembarked from the ship, I realized no one was there to greet me. Why should there be? I was bringing my own letters of introduction. I was not expected.

"Excuse me," I asked one of the men waiting to unload cargo. "Could you direct me to the Bishop?"

"The Bishop?" the man frowned. "Do you mean Useful of the Christian sect?"

I frowned at his question. Though we both spoke Greek, his accent was nearly unintelligible. "The Bishop of the Christians, yes."

"That is Onesimus. Go down the Sacred Way," he pointed. He did not seem to want to continue the conversation, because he stepped away muttering about Christians.

"Thank you," I said, but he was already far away.

I continued in the direction he had pointed. I asked three more people directions to the Bishop and all three said he was Onesimus, a name which means useful, a slave name. I was growing confused. Why did they all say the same thing? The Bishop of the Christians could not possibly be a slave.

I carried a small chest with my money and letters, and over my back was a satchel with my clothes. A porter offered to carry these for me, but I refused the offer. I was growing apprehensive that my meager money would not last. I would need money for the return to Egypt. How long would I be here? A month or two? That would depend on the Bishop.

"Heavenly Father," I prayed. "Let me accomplish my business in this city. Let me find this bishop, and let me make the copies of Paul's letters to take back to Memphis. The church needs this encouragement."

I walked through the crowded, turbulent city as directed. Before me stood the giant Temple of Artemis. I stopped and stared. A man on the steps blew a shrill trumpet, announcing the morning sacrifice. The smell of the burning sacrifice filled the air. The temple was huge, dominating the skyline. Except for the pyramids, I doubt there was a building higher in all the Empire. It's brilliant white marble was painful to the eye. It was surrounded by a dark grove of pines and oaks.

The Festival of Artemis had just ended, so the city was empty of tourists and pilgrims. I had been told that the city was filled with shops selling souvenirs of Artemis, but I only saw a few. At the dock, a few told me I was too late for the festival. When I said, I was seeking the Bishop of the Christians, most frowned, though some smiled. All of them told me to seek Useful. Who was this Useful? Who was this slave they were sending me to?

"Excuse me," I stopped at a bakery. The sign over the door said, "The Bread of Life" in both Latin and Greek. There was also a fish drawn under the sign. It looked very much like the symbol the Christians, the followers of the Way of Christ, used in Egypt to identify themselves as fishers of men.

"Excuse me," I asked a middle-aged woman, whose arms were dusted in flour. She smiled at me, revealing several missing teeth. I would guess she was in her forties. She appeared to have lived a hard life, though she never lacked bread. As a baker, she ate daily, maybe a little too much. "I'd like to buy some bread and need help finding someone."

Her brilliant smile encouraged me. But it was her eyes that captured me. They were an amber color, like honey. There was a sparkle in them that I recognized. This woman knew Christ. She knew real joy. I sighed with relief, knowing she would help me.

"You are a traveler?" She handed me a small loaf of bread, still warm from the oven. The smell caused my mouth to water. "You are not from around here by your speech."

"No, I have traveled from Egypt to meet someone in this city," I said with my mouth full of bread. "This is delicious."

She smiled her gratitude and handed me another as I finished the first. "I have lived all my years in this city. I know almost everyone and can tell you where they live."

"Do you know the Bishop, the leader of the Christians? I was told to search for a slave named Useful."

"Yes, Onesimus is our Bishop." I frowned. Something was wrong with this. Maybe she did not understand my Alexandrian Greek accent.

"Are you a Christian, young man?" Her warm smile comforted me.

"I am indeed."

"I also follow the Way of Christ. We meet in the Bishop's house each morning of the first day of the week to pray and study God's word." She wiped her hands on the apron tied around her waist. "There are prayer meetings with several of the ladies on other days of the week. He allows us to meet in his courtyard."

"His name really is Onesimus?" I was sure she did not understand my accent.

"He is a great man. I will send my son to guide you to his house. It is a short walk from here." She shouted into the back room of her bakery, "Phyllo, come out here, please."

A skinny youth of maybe fifteen years appeared. Like his mother, he had flour on his apron and all over his arms. He had white smudges on his face, and even some in his hair.

"Phyllo, this man has come from far away to see the Bishop. Stop what you are doing and guide him to his house. And take a few loaves to share with the Bishop's household."

The youth wiped his face and arms with his apron, then gathered up half a dozen loaves and wrapped them in his apron. Without another word, he headed out onto the street. He was quick, so I had to walk fast to keep up.

"I didn't pay for the bread," I said looking back at the shop.

"Don't worry about that. My mother believes that if she feeds enough strangers, she might feed an angel one day." He laughed merrily.

Show hospitality to strangers, because some have entertained angels without knowing it. That is what our church taught. It was taught here too, meaning these people were my brothers and sisters in the faith.

"Tell me about this bishop," I said devouring a third loaf.

"He is the head of our church and he oversees several other churches in the area." He slowed down to allow me to catch up with him, just as we turned a corner onto a quiet street.

"But what is he like?"

"He is nice. He teaches me to read a few afternoons a week." With a laugh, he added, "though honestly, I am not very good at studious work like that. I am a good cook though. I made the bread you were eating." He smiled a broad happy smile. Life was good for this boy.

A few moments later, he stopped in front of a villa with a gate of intricately wrought iron bars. The door was opened behind the gate, and I could see a courtyard full of pots of flowers and small trees, and a fountain that sported a bronze nymph.

"Sophia," the youth shouted. A girl about the same age as Phyllo came to the gate.

"What do you want, Phyllo?" she asked opening the gate.

"Mother sent these loaves for the Bishop, and he has a visitor." He pointed his chin in my direction.

She looked at me curiously. She appeared to be an Egyptian like me, maybe a slave. Her hair was dark with thick curls and her eyes were black.

"Wait here while I tell the Bishop." She took the bread from the boy.

"I must go back to work," he said smiling and blushing. It was obvious to me that he liked the girl.

"Tell your mother thank you," she said bending forward to accept a kiss on the cheek. The boy disappeared down the street, almost skipping in delight, and the girl entered the house.

I waited in the courtyard, admiring the beautiful tile on the floor and walls, the bronze fountain, and the colorful flowers. This was not the house of a poor man. Inside I could see a large house, with a second, much larger courtyard beyond. How did a slave get a house like this? What must the Christian community of Ephesus be like to afford a house like this for their bishop?

I thought of the importance of my visit, the reason I needed to see the Bishop. In Egypt, we have the sermons of Peter, written down by the Evangelist Mark before the mob in Alexandria killed him by dragging him through the streets. We have meticulously copied these writings and shared them with every church in Egypt and Cyrenaica. I had two copies, written by my own hand, to give to the Bishop. Though now I wondered if I was on a fool's errand.

The church was well established in Ephesus. Paul, who was recognized as God's messenger, spent a lot of time here. The followers of the Way respected his teachings as God's word. The Apostle John was here until recently imprisoned on a nearby island, it was said. When he came to Ephesus, he brought Mary, Jesus' mother with him. She was reported by some to still be alive and by others to be dead. I would learn which. We could not ignore this city that is at the heart of our religion. I had to find out all I could, even if that meant dealing with a slave.

"He will be out shortly," the girl said reentering the courtyard. "He invites you to wait in the library. Would you like something to eat or drink?"

"Thank you very much," I answered following her. "I have only had some bread since I arrived this morning."

She motioned me to a door. "I will bring you something."

I was stunned by the beauty of the room I entered. There were shelves built into the wall and stacked from floor to ceiling with books, scrolls written by every conceivable author a library would want. It was the largest private library I had ever seen; larger than even the public library of Memphis. I could only guess how many books were here. A thousand? Or twice that? I walked up to the shelves and carefully took down a scroll to read *Thucydides* on the cover. Another said, *Commentaries on Homer. The Oresteia*, by Aeschylus. There were a dozen plays of Euripides. My fingers caressed the title of another that said, *The Complete Works of Plato.* It was impossible that a library like this could exist. I don't know how long I stared at the books surrounding me, longing to spend hours searching the knowledge contained in them.

"Good morning, young man."

I was startled back to reality by an old man standing in the door. I don't know how long he had been observing me. He seemed kind, like a grandfather; and he was old, but I have never been good at estimating ages. Maybe sixty. His hair was only partially gray, so maybe as young as fifty. He was dressed in plain, unbleached wool, not as richly as someone who owned such an extensive library would be expected to dress.

The girl came back with a tray of cheese, bread, olives, and figs. She poured two goblets of watered wine. The old man motioned me to sit.

"I was told a visitor has come to see me. I always enjoy meeting new people." He sat down with some difficulty, almost stumbling. The girl tried to help but he waved her away. "I am fine, my dear. Thank you."

Not sure that this was the man I sought, I hastened to stage my mission. "I was sent by the church in Memphis to find the Bishop of Ephesus."

"Please sit, young man," he again motioned me to sit. "I am too old to stand and it would be impolite to speak to you while you are standing."

"Thank you, sir." Maybe this gentleman could explain the tales I had heard since entering this city about a man with a slave name. I cautiously sat on the edge of a chair.

"You said Memphis? What is your name, young man?"

"My name is Cedronus. I am originally from Alexandria, where my family became followers of the Way of Christ, but for most of my life I have lived in Memphis."

"Why did your family move to Memphis since Alexandria is such a rich city and the center of a thriving church?"

The old man seemed more interested in my personal history than my mission.

"My father was killed the day after Mark the Evangelist," I continued, fearing I would choke telling my story. It was uncomfortable to talk about my father, though I was proud of his life. My errand was important, so I knew I must endure his questions. "He stood up to the authorities and demanded the body of Mark so the church could give it a proper burial. The magistrate gave the body to the church, but demanded my father's life in exchange. That same day the church sent my mother, my younger sister, and me into hiding in Memphis."

"I am sorry to hear about your father," he said with sincerity. "Now, young man, why are you here?"

"In Memphis, I learned to read and write in Greek, Hebrew, and Coptic. I am honored that the church has hired me to copy the letters and gospels important to our faith. That is why I am here."

I pulled a pair of scrolls from my small chest. The squeaking of the lid made me nervous, but the old man ignored it. I handed him the two letters. "The first is from the Bishop of Memphis. He is sending me to the service of the Bishop of Ephesus, for as long as he has need of me. The second is a copy of the Sermons of Peter written by Mark, which we call his gospel."

I kept one hidden, in case this man was not the Bishop I was to meet.

"I am indeed the Bishop of Ephesus. Thank you for the letters." He ignored the letter of introduction, placing it on the table next to him, and began to read the gospel. I waited patiently while he read for several minutes. "This is well-written and quick. I like his style."

He set the scroll down and from memory quoted, "After me comes the one more powerful than I, the straps of whose sandals I am not worthy to stoop down and untie." His eyes were closed as he said this, as if reliving a memory. "He is quick and precise. He gets to the point without wasting time. I think he might have been a runner." He said that with almost a laugh.

"I don't know about that."

He smiled at me, seeing my nervousness. "What can I do for you, young man?" He placed the scroll on a table beside him. "Did your Bishop send you all this way just to give me this book written by Mark?"

"No sir. He knows you have in your possession several letters to the churches written by Paul. He hopes you will allow me to copy them and carry them back to Egypt where we will treasure them."

"That is easy to arrange." He stood and walked to the shelf. He handed me a scroll that read *To Colossae* on the cover. "Here is one you can copy while you are here. There are others too. I have a dozen letters written to the church and to Timothy, when he was Bishop of Ephesus."

"I was also told I might be able to meet Apostle John and the Mother of Jesus."

"John is being held captive on an island called Patmos. He stirred up a crowd when he stood in the door to the Temple of Artemis and commanded a demon to leave the place." The old man laughed. "It must have worked. Since he has been imprisoned, the visitors to the temple are less and less each season. Half of the shops that sold souvenirs of the goddess closed this year alone." He laughed to himself some more, as if reliving a memory of long ago.

"And Mary, the mother of Jesus?"

"She came here with John, but was already very old." His face became sad. "She spent her last years in bed. When she was awake, she told stories about Jesus as a child. She went to be with the Lord only a few months ago."

"I am sorry to hear that she has passed away." I was a little more at ease with this kindly old man, so I felt it was the time to be brave and ask, because it did not seem he would clear up my confusion. "And sir, I don't know your name yet."

"I apologize," he smiled. "My name is Onesimus." He sat down again.

"Maybe I am tired from the journey, but I am confused. You are Onesimus, and you are the Bishop of Ephesus?"

"I am the Bishop of Ephesus and my name is Onesimus. Paul gave charge of the church to Timothy before he died in Rome. Before Timothy was martyred he gave me charge over the church. When John came here, I asked him to take charge, because he had walked with our Savior and knew him better than any man alive. But he declined. So, to this day, I am still the Bishop of Ephesus."

"I don't mean to be rude, but isn't Onesimus a slave name? It is in Egypt, but maybe not here."

"It is very much a slave name. It is not the name my mother gave me, but it is the name I was given by my first master. Before you ask the next question, yes, I was a slave."

"But you are Bishop of Ephesus."

"I lived in Rome with Paul before he died. One of the things he told me many times was that there is neither Jew nor Gentile, neither slave nor free, for we are all one in Christ Jesus."

"Are you still a slave?"

"I was given my freedom."

"How did you come to live in this house, with these books? Your library is magnificent!"

"My brother gave it to me before he died."

"Your brother? Forgive me, sir, but I am so confused. How did a slave come to own the house of a rich man, who is his brother, and how did that same man become bishop of one of the greatest churches in the Empire?"

"That, young man," he answered with an enigmatic smile, "is a long story indeed."

CHAPTER 2
BYZANTIUM

Before you were born, I set you apart. Jeremiah 1:5

“Useful, bring me more blah-blah.” I was still learning the language, but I guessed he meant madder, because he was making a red dye. I hurried to the store room to bring a package of madder, the plain yellow flower I had seen some women at home turn into a red dye. This man did the same work that women did at home, but somehow, he was respected for doing women’s work. I resented being his slave, but I knew he was my only way out. I would learn as much as I could from him.

He took the package, so I must have reasoned correctly.

“Maddur, maddur,” I said quietly a few times.

“What are you mumbling about, Onesimus?” My master asked.

“Learning word,” I answered.

“Learning ‘a’ word,” he corrected. He never praised me, but he also did not beat me. I could not be angry with him when he corrected me, because it helped me to learn. He was old. He would not always be here, so I wanted to learn as much as possible before the old man died and I was sold. I knew little of this crazy land devoid of trees, but I knew that to be successful, one needed to speak the language. I learned that in my first days here. Somehow, I would get home, but I had not reasoned how I would accomplish that.

"And the word is madder," he held the flower up to my face.

"Madder." I said clearly, imitating him. And I whispered, "Learning a word."

My first days as a slave were a blur. I had no idea what had happened. There were twenty of us from the village that were taken. All of us were young. There were five girls who were all very pretty, and fifteen boys who were all very strong. The boys were older and stronger than me. I was faster, but as we walked to the river, we were chained together, so I could not have run if I wanted to.

For two days, we walked. The slavers did not stop to let us rest. They did not stop to feed us. When one girl asked for us to stop so she could take a piss, it became obvious that they would not stop for even that. Every day the forest became thinner and the grasslands larger. Why had the ancestors abandoned me? I could no longer hear the whispers of the ancestors. Their home had been my home and now we were far away.

On the morning of the third day, noise of a hunting party grew closer. We were forced to run. But we didn't have to run far. Over a small hill was the River.

Now I understood why those who had seen it called it the Great River. It was too wide to swim across. It was blue, the color of the night sky just before the sun disappears. It was like an immense path cut through the plains on either side. On the southern side, was higher land, though on the north it was almost flat. Along the shore were reeds and swamps. We had difficulty making our way through the swamp land, but our captors were in a hurry.

There were boats in the middle and a few near us at the shore. We ran toward those boats. Our chains were partially released so we could enter the boats in pairs. I was with, Teudila, the girl who cried the whole way and complained about not getting to piss. I wanted to be away from her.

"You can piss now," I said to Teudila as we sat on the floor of the boat. She began to wail even more loudly. What did it matter? The floor of the boat was already covered in filthy water.

The oldest boy in our group, Zoltes, the son of the wood cutter, began to fight with our captors. Over the top of the hill were Getae soldiers approaching quickly, so the captors beat him till he died. He was chained to Duras, a shepherd. They didn't unchain him when Zoltes' body was thrown in the river. Duras drowned before my eyes, struggling to keep his head above the water. I was too little to fight, so I did not try.

We were in the middle of the river before the soldiers came close to the shore. I couldn't see who they were. Maybe they were of our tribe, but what did it matter? The ancestors had deserted me. My family was dead and I was floating on a river, probably destined for the Realm of the Dead. When once I asked the old man by the well what death was, he said it is a journey on a black river to the Realm of the Dead. He said there would be days of wailing and moaning, followed by a dark chasm, darker than the night. When the dead reached their destination, if they were evil in life, they would sink in the inky waters, never to be seen again. Who was I? I had never done anything good in life. The inky waters were my destination.

We floated on that river for days. Teudila never stopped crying. I could not sleep with her at my side. They didn't feed us. How I longed for a piece of bread and bowl of beans from my mother. Maybe a slab of meat off a boar my father hunted, smothered in onions and garlic. And a bowl of milk fresh from the cow. The more the girl cried, the more I dreamed of food and the wilder my imagination became. I was so hungry that my stomach was yelling at me. She would not stop her crying. Why were girls like that?

And then one day, Teudila stopped crying. We had arrived at a city on the coast. For the first time, I saw the Sea. When the old man by the well had told me about the Sea, I laughed. There could not be that much water in the world, I told him. Yet there was more than he said. It was black and frightening. I looked at Teudila to see why she had stopped crying. She looked like she was asleep. Her golden hair partly covered her face. Her cream-colored skin was almost white. There was a slight smile on her face. Sometime during the night, she had died.

As they were taking us off the boat, the chain that attached me to Teudila was undone. For a moment, I was free. I could jump off the boat and run. But where would I go? Where was home? I was lost. There were no trees here, only scrubby bushes and reeds by the water. This was not my land.

I'm not sure exactly, but there were about thirty of us who were forced out of the boat. About a dozen had been picked up a day before and a few more a day before that. None of us were as old as Zoltes. He was fourteen, I think. I was easily the youngest.

I could not understand anything these men said, but I listened closely for words they repeated often. One was the word slave. I had heard that Greeks would raid our land for slaves, but we raided theirs too. It was why our tribe had moved away from the River to live closer to the mountains. It was safer, at least they supposed it to be. Now I was one of those slaves. Masters beat their slaves for no reason. A master could kill his slave for no reason. What would my life be like as a slave?

We were herded to a building near the dock. If one of us was slow or stopped, a whip was there to wake us from our stupor. I was not slow, but the others around me were. I felt the whip aimed at them more than once. My left shoulder, the shoulder facing the man with the whip, became more bloodied and more painful with each crack of the whip. I hated these slow people next to me.

The building we were sent to was dark and smelled of dung and piss. There were moans coming from the dark. I imagined this was the very gate of Hell itself that the old man had talked about. But the darkness lessened, just as it did in the dark forest once the eyes became accustomed to the lack of light. It was not Hell, but a cage for children like me.

We were stopped in front of an old man who looked us over. He had a sour look on his face, like he was about to vomit. But I learned two new words from him; boy and girl. The girls were sent to one place, while the boys to another. The old man, still with the boys, began to talk to several other men. We were ordered stripped and our clothes were raked into a pile like trash. Naked before these men we now stood. One of the boys next to me began to cry like the girl had cried.

"If you cry," I whispered to him, "you will die."

The only proof I had of that was that Teudila had died. But from deep within the sorrow hit me. My mother was dead. Zoltes and Duras were dead. Teudila had died at my side. There was too much death. I was hungry. My shoulder was bleeding and ached. I started to cry too, but quietly to myself.

The crying boy looked at me. "I guess you are going to die too," he said. Maybe I was. What did it matter?

Money was exchanged and ten of us were separated from the group. Crying boy was not with me. None of the boys with me were from my village. I knew none of them. We left the building that looked like Hell and were again by the docks. We were pushed into a cage too small to stand up straight in. As the littlest in the group, I was pushed to the back, my shoulder smashed into the wooden bars of the cage.

None of the group hid their sorrow anymore. They all cried through the hot hours of the afternoon. Even boys of fourteen or older cried for their mothers. I cried too.

Sometime in the night I woke and saw the moon overhead. I wanted to be free to run in the forest under that moon, but if I were free I would not know the forests here, if there were any. I had wondered what was beyond the forest. Now I knew. The ancestors were not powerful enough to save me. Was there anyone who could?

"If you can hear me, help me," I cried out to the darkness. I was hungry. My body was in pain. I missed Mother. "I don't know what I have done to anger you, but help me."

It was quiet. There was no answer. Except that I saw a golden spark out over the Sea. It was the sun. It was still too dark to see anything, but the sun would soon rise and welcome a new day.

I heard footsteps as the gravel was being kicked near me. I looked up to see a man dressed in a white, unbleached robe come close to the cage. He knelt beside the cage and reached from inside his robe to show me a small loaf of bread.

"Have faith," he said handing the loaf to me. "There is a plan for your life."

I grabbed the bread and devoured it. When I looked back up, he was gone. A plan for my life? What did he mean by that? Suddenly I realized he had spoken the language of the Getae, even with the accent of one from my mountain home, though he did not look like one of us. Who was that man?

The next day I looked for him. I was still hungry, but I felt braver. I was no longer crying. If I saw him again, I wanted to ask him what he meant and wanted to beg him to buy me. But I never saw him, or anybody like him.

We were put on a ship that day, larger and capable of going out onto the Sea. The old man who sat by the well called it the Black Sea. Its name made sense to me; it was black like the night. What was below the surface, I could not fathom. Were there monsters of a size that would engulf the ship? Or were there men punished to dwell in its depths after an evil life?

After boarding the ship, we were led to a cell below the deck and chained to the wall. The others with me vomited because of the rolling of the Sea. I did not. I was glad I did not, because twice each day they gave us a piece of bread. Several were too sick to eat, so I took their bread. I was going to be healthy wherever we were going. One day I was going to be free and I would return home.

It was four or five days, I don't remember exactly, until we arrived at a new city. We arrived at night, so I could not see my new home.

A few hours later, the sun came up, and we were led to a cold, stone building. We had been bathed, but still not given anything to wear. We were given a piece of bread and a bowl of something that smelled like rotting fish. I am still not sure what I ate, but I felt refreshed. I decided I would not let despair rule me and ate it all to regain my strength.

The day was long. We stood and waited. Men passed by to examine us, sometimes as a group, and sometimes individually. They argued back and forth. I learned new words that day; money, strong, weak, and fool. The seller often called someone a fool who didn't like his price. They called some of the boys strong and bought them. Others they labeled as weak and passed them by.

Around noon, a man, who looked a lot like the man who used to sit by the well at home, came by. He ignored the seller and looked at several boys. He asked me a question, but I couldn't understand him, so I just shrugged my shoulders. The seller spoke rapidly; I assume telling him what a bargain I was. The old man held out a small bag with coins in it. Whether gold or silver, I never knew. Quietly he said something to the seller, who argued back. The old man held out his hand for the seller to give him back his coins. The seller instead pocketed the coins and unshackled me from the others.

Still naked, the old man led me out of the auction house. The sun burned my naked skin. My new master threw a rag around my shoulders and began to talk with me as we walked down the street. I understood not a word. I wanted to run, but there was the dark sea to one side and to the other an impenetrable, terrifying city. I wanted to flee, but I was also curious about this quiet man who bought me.

The next years were difficult, but never grueling. The old man was a dyer of cloth. One day we would work with madder, dying things red; another we would work with sweet smelling saffron to make things shine yellow like the sun. Rarely we worked with murex, rock snails, to die things purple. The murex always stunk, but the color it made was amazing. Other minerals or plants could be mixed to make a host of colors. I began to see that beauty could come from something ugly like murex or plain like madder.

The man talked to me every day. He did not talk a lot, but when he did, I listened. I was not his friend, but his slave. I worked all day, before the sun came up and after it set. At first, I went with him to the market and carried his purchases, but after I learned what to do, he sent me to the market for things.

Usually his requests were written on a scrap of paper. I studied the paper, trying to decipher the symbols. After a while, I assumed some of the groups of symbols, those repeated often, were words another could understand. That made sense and those symbols stayed in my head.

I cleaned the old man's house, and rinsed the dye pots. My arms were now a reddish orange from working with the dyes. But he did talk to me and I listened.

Daily I tried to learn new words. Sometimes I would hear something repeated day after day and month after month, before it would suddenly make sense. Everything the man knew how to say, I soon learned to say. Somehow the words he wrote on paper made more sense. One day, looking at the paper, I read, "One pound of salt, two bags of madder." He was surprised I could decipher the words.

I never learned his name the entire stay there. To me he was always master. He never told me about himself. I did not know how old he was. I did not know why he worked in dye. I did not know why he always looked sad.

Much of my day would be spent in a tedious exercise with the dyes or cleaning his shop and store rooms. That was when I was left alone. I could remember the forests and dream about running in them. That would make me smile. In my mind, I would retrace my race from the village through the forest. Slowly the order of places became jumbled. I no longer knew where the logs were, or the mist covered hill, or the stream, and I could not remember what my mother looked like, or the sound of her voice.

"Master," I asked one day. "Where am I from?"

"Dacia, they told me when I bought you."

"Where is Dacia?" I wondered what this place was he called Dacia. I was a Getae and had never heard this word before, but after so many years, I had begun to forget the words of my people.

"It is to the north across the Sea."

"Can someone get there by walking?" Or running I thought.

"Are you planning on running away?" He stopped what he was doing and looked at me. I saw in him a tired, old man. He had bought me to ease his work in his old age. I wanted to be free, but I could not leave him. There would come a day in the future when I would try to run, but today was not that day. At least not yet.

"You came here by ship and to get home you would have to go by ship."

That night I dreamed of running through the forest, a stag running beside me. I was free, jumping over logs and ravines in my forest. But in my dream, I fell and that woke me. I was not free and never would be.

"Father, I am closing the shop," the man's son told him. The son often came around and argued with his father. If I had argued that way with my father, I think I would have been killed by him long ago.

"I don't want to close the shop. I have customers who depend on me and orders that must be filled."

"Father, it is not your choice. You thought you had to have this expensive slave. When you borrowed the money from me to buy him, you gave me the deed to the shop."

The old man sat down and looked at his son. They did not understand each other and never would. I did not understand either of them, but I knew the old man lived for his work.

"Your miserable little shop is not profitable. The land is worth more than your cloth. There is a Jewish dyer who will buy all your supplies and take over any outstanding orders you have. Your neighbor wants to buy the shop to enlarge his house since his son is marrying soon. Both will more than cover the expenses of this slave." He pointed to me. "What do you call him?"

"Useful."

"Look at him, he is useless."

"What will you do with him?"

"I am going to sell him. He doesn't look like much, but at least he has learned to speak Greek. He can possibly make a decent house slave. There is a buyer that is looking for slaves to sell in the province of Asia. I think I can sell him for enough to recoup my losses.

"Do I have a choice in the matter?"

"No, Father."

Later that day, a man came to the store, bound my hands and led me away. I never knew what happened with the old man.

CHAPTER 3
PHILEMON

A brother is born for a time of adversity. Proverbs 17:17

I was back in the same building where I was bought by the old man. No one seemed to want me. I don't think the son got the price he hoped for, because he was angry when he left.

As he walked away, he turned back to me and said, "Useless."

Was I useless? Running did not matter anymore. That was the only thing I had ever been good at. Maybe I was useless. I was unable to defend my mother from attack. I could not outrun the slaver. I had not helped the old man that much. I just did a few things to make his life easier. If he had been younger, he would not have needed me. I was useless.

For several days, I don't know how many, maybe ten or more, people came by and looked at me and other boys. Few gave me more than a glance. The pits of the slave seller were filthy. I was naked and because it was winter, I was cold. I tried to attract the eye of a few buyers, but I was skinny. I must have looked underfed. They could not imagine me being strong, but I knew I was.

One day, I was bought, but not how I expected. The seller had given up on me and sold me to another merchant along with a dozen other boys. We were given cheap robes to wear and herded to the docks. Again, I was placed on a ship.

This journey was nothing like the one before. The weather was stormy for days and the ship rolled heavily, not able to make progress against the wind. We continued in the same direction for a week, until one day the ship turned a different direction. As suddenly as it changed direction, the sea seemed to calm. The roll of the ship, because they always roll on the sea, was mild, more like when a mother gently rocks her baby in her arms because he is crying.

I felt the arms of the sea wrap around me. I felt secure and at peace. Through the open hatch above my head, I could see the sun as it came and went. I lost count of the days. In the mornings, the sun rose on the port side of the ship. In the evening, it sank into the sea on starboard side. I slept long hours each day. At night I imagined myself journeying the world on a ship while looking at the stars through the hatch.

But one day it ended. We changed direction again, heading toward the rising sun. On noon of that day, we arrived in my new home, a great city with magnificent buildings. Even the warehouses on the dock were greater than any I had seen in Byzantium.

We were again herded like animals to pens to be sold. It was cleaner than Byzantium and the seller fed us well, so we would not look sickly, but we were forced to stand for long hours. And the days passed.

I was so tired. All I wanted to do was sleep. My legs ached from standing so long. I was thinking I could not endure this torture any longer, when I was awakened from my stupor.

A lady was looking at me. Her eyes were amber, with a ring around the iris of dark green. She studied my face. I was unaccustomed to someone looking me in the eye. It had been years since someone had done that. My mother used to do that. The lady's look was gentle. It seemed as if she was asking me something with her look. I did not know how to answer. The pain in me softened. I was lonely. I missed my mother. I missed my master, the dyer. I felt as if I would cry.

"What is your name, boy?" she asked in a gentle voice. I felt wrapped into that voice, as if my mother were calling me. She spoke Greek, the language I learned from the dyer, but it had a different ring to it.

"I am Onesimus," I barely got the words out, not realizing how dry my mouth was.

"Are you useful?" she asked, a slight smile emerging on her face. I could tell she would be a gentle person to be around.

"I think I am." I felt secure explaining myself. "I worked for an old man who dyed cloth. He got too old, so I was sold." With a bit of hesitation, I added, "I think I was useful to him."

A boy walked up to her. He was my height, but I thought he was a bit older than me. I think I was ten years old, but I had lost count. He had thick brown hair that needed cutting. His eyes were amber like his mother's. I knew she was his mother by his eyes and how she slipped her arm around him. He studied me differently than his mother. She was studying to see if I would be useful to her. With him, I had the feeling he wanted a friend to go running through the streets with. She was searching my heart, to see if I were trustworthy or not. He was looking for a playmate.

"I am Philemon, son of Archippus of Colossae, a tribune of Caesar's legions in Spain."

Why would a boy introduce himself to a slave? That was peculiar to me. How should I answer that?

"I am Onesimus." I smiled, because I knew he was not a bad child.

The boy laughed. I had not yet received my name when I was taken, nor did I remember my father's name. The Singidava Getae was my tribe, but where they were, I did not know.

"I want this one, Mother," Philemon said. Already the mother was paying the seller. She did not haggle over a price; something I could not imagine her doing. Nor did I think the slave dealer would dare to cheat her.

I was unchained and given a rough robe to cover my nakedness. It only came to a little above my knees, but I was glad to no longer be naked. The lady was accompanied by a hefty guard who warned me not to run away and two female slaves. I was curious about this new life, so I decided not to risk flight. Besides, where would I go? I did not know where I was.

Philemon chatted incessantly. I could barely hear him over the roar of the city around me. Thousands crowded on the wide avenue that went through the middle of the city that he called the Sacred Way. The road was paved with smooth white stone, with gutters along the side for the water to drain. Magnificent buildings, whose purpose I could only wonder, and shops of every sort lined the road. The smell of freshly baked bread and grilled meat made me hungry. Stalls of fresh fruit and aromatic spices crowded next to each other. Many shops sold small statues of the goddess of the city. Above many shops were houses of three or four stories, some with girls watching the passing crowds, or women hanging laundry to dry.

We turned a corner and I saw a building that was beyond my imagination. I stopped, unable to move as I looked upon a vast white marble building, surrounded in white marble pillars, as high as trees. A garden of dark green pines surrounded the building, but it was built higher on the hill, so it towered above them. The sun glinted off its golden roof. What kind of people were these that built places like this?

"That is the Artemesium," Philemon said tugging my arm. The hefty guard pushed me from behind. "It is the Temple of Artemis. The Romans call her Diana. I have a sister named Diana. The goddess is why Ephesus is the most blessed city in the world, beloved of the gods."

I had yet to learn about the gods of these people. Maybe they were great. The spirits of my lands that lived in the trees, the spirits of my ancestors, had abandoned me, unable to protect me from these people whose gods lived in palaces of stone.

We soon arrived at a beautiful villa, a veritable garden of flowers and color. We entered an iron gate, to a tiled atrium, open to the sky. A fountain with a statue of a nymph bubbled nearby. Blue and yellow tiles were under my feet. Dozens of pots and urns were filled to overflowing with roses, geraniums, jasmine, and more flowers.

I followed the boy, Philemon, further into the villa and a second patio. In the middle was a pool, about waste deep. Surrounding it was a colonnade of rose colored marble. Many rooms were beyond, most open to the fresh air. I could see walls painted with beautiful scenes of merry people enjoying life. The floor of the entire villa was inlaid with marble of different colors, creating pleasing patterns. Like the atrium, the interior patio was filled with pots of flowers. One rose bush wrapped around a pillar and continued to the second floor, dropping its red petals on the white marble below. A dark girl, a little older than me, swept the petals into a pile. She eyed me curiously.

Philemon headed to the back of the villa. Here was a large room with a desk, a few chairs, and shelves with books, paper, and musical instruments. He pushed open a double door to another room.

"This is my room."

I didn't know what to say. It was messy. Clothes, pillows, toys, and books were strewn about the room.

"You'll live here with me."

An elderly woman followed us into the room and pointed to a small room off the boy's room. "You'll live in there."

"He can stay in my room," Philemon countered.

"Your mother commanded me to teach him his duties. You are to go to your father in his library, Young Master."

"I don't want to go. I want to play with my slave."

"It is not I who commands you; your father commands you."

Philemon bit his lip and fidgeted with his feet, but within a moment, he hurried out the door.

The old woman stared down at me; as if she did not approve. She walked around studying me as she shook her head.

"You are a mess. What is your name?"

"They call me Onesimus."

Her disapproving stare angered me, so I whispered, "Balaur." It was a word from home that came to my mind meeting her.

"So, I am a dragon?" She stopped walking and stood looking directly in my face. Her bony hand raised my chin, forcing me to look at her. She said some words that sounded familiar, but in my confusion, I did not at first recognize that she spoke the language of my home. I had not heard it spoken in years.

"You are Getae?" She asked in Greek. Her voice softened.

"Singidava Getae." I said with relief. "I was little when I was taken."

"How old are you?"

"Ten," I answered, then I added in almost a whisper, "I think. I don't know exactly."

"I am Agata. That is my slave name. I was born Amalusta of the Sucidava Getae. I was sold when I was thirteen because my family had no money for a dowry."

"I am a prince of the Singidava Getae, as were my father and grandfathers before me." I proudly stuck out my chin.

She sighed. "Today you are the slave of the young master, Philemon, son of the Tribune Archippus. I have lived in this house since I was fifteen, serving the Mistress, Abigail of the House of Abijah. Now she is married to the Tribune Archippus. Like me, you will forget you are Getae. You are a slave. You will grow old in this house. You will never see your homeland again, nor will you ever mention its existence. As far as you are concerned, the Getae are all dead. Your life will center on the young master." She sounded sad, but she had her duty, which was to make me as subservient as she was. "Wipe your tears, Onesimus. You have much to learn."

The slave who had been sweeping the rose petals entered, carrying three clean robes; one was a beautiful sky blue and the other two were plain white.

"The blue robe is for special occasions. Do not wear it unless told to do so." As Agata spoke, she folded it and placed it on a shelf in my small cubicle. "The other two are for daily wear. You are responsible for keeping them clean. Zoe," she indicated the girl who brought the clothes, "will show you where to wash them. Don't wear a robe for more than three or four days at a time before washing it." She handed me one of the white robes. "Now put it on."

"I am naked under this," I said. Zoe giggled, but Agata pushed her out of the cubicle leaving me momentarily alone. Quickly I put on the robe. It felt good to be in clean clothes.

"Zoe will also show you the bath for the servants," she said as I came back into Philemon's room. "The master doesn't want to smell his slaves, and you smell."

Zoe giggled again.

"Your job, Onesimus, is to keep the young master's room clean. He can be untidy, but it is your job to keep him tidy. Find a place for all his things. If his clothes are dirty, take them to be washed. Be ready to wait on him always. If he wants something, get it, and get it quickly. And this, Onesimus," she said pulling a pot out from under the bed, "is the night water pot. You must empty it first thing every morning. Do not wait an hour. Do it immediately."

I was confused. What was the purpose of this empty pot? There was no water in it. When I wrinkled my forehead, Zoe giggled again. I wondered if this girl could do anything but giggle.

"And wash as soon as you can."

Agata left me to be further instructed by Zoe. I discovered that until my arrival, she had done for the boy the things I was now assigned.

We walked to the front of the villa, where there was a stair case that led to the servant quarters below the villa. Besides workrooms, there were a dozen cubicles that the slaves slept in, and an enormous kitchen. As Zoe showed me the kitchen, the cook gave me a small loaf of bread about the size of my fist, stuffed with goat cheese and herbs. I revealed how famished I was by eating it too rapidly. The cook had mercy on me and gave me another loaf of bread. Zoe showed me where things were kept and who I was to ask to use them as I cared for Philemon. Then she left me to make my way on my own.

There was a basin of water and I washed as well as I could. I was not as clean as I had been with the old man, but at least I did not I smell so bad. I would soon figure out how to be clean.

I found my way back to Philemon's room. He had not returned. At first, I looked around sizing up my task. The clothes that smelled, I threw in a pile. The ones that did not smell, I folded neatly, glad I had learned how to do that in the shop of the old man. There were a dozen scrolls, a few even torn. I reasoned that the open room next to his, somehow belonged to the boy, so I neatly placed them in the shelves above the desk. The toys found a place on a shelf in the corner. Most of his toys consisted of tiny ceramic or carved soldiers. Because he did not care for them properly, some were broken. The sheets and pillows on the bed were rumpled, so I arranged them as neatly as I could.

I stopped for a moment and considered what else to do. The floor needed sweeping, so I looked for Zoe to find a broom. She followed me back to the room and watched as I swept. She giggled again.

"Why do you do that?"

"Do what?" she giggled.

"Laugh all the time."

"Sweeping is my job. If you keep his room neat, I will sweep it every day." She giggled again, "Unless you want to do my job too."

At that moment, Philemon returned. "Come with me," he said, tugging on my arm. I handed the broom to the still giggling Zoe.

I followed him through the villa to some stairs on the opposite side. There was a second floor with more rooms. I could not fathom the purpose of all of them.

"My three sisters have rooms here. Sometimes relatives come to visit and stay here too." He kept walking until we found another flight of stairs. "Come," he said pushing me up the stairs. On the roof of the house was a wide terrace. There was a place for clothes to dry, but mostly it was empty. "This is where I go to get away from the women. This is where we can play."

His face held unconcealed joy.

Play? I didn't know how to play. When I as young I did not play with the others because I thought I was better than them. I had run in the forest alone. This child expected me to play with him? I thought I was to be his slave.

"I am glad you are here," he put his arm around me as we looked out onto the city. The glowing white temple in the distance was changing to a salmon pink in the afternoon light. "You are the brother, I have always wanted."

Philemon pointed out buildings of the government officials, temples, other villas, and the synagogue, which I was soon to learn was a place of worship and learning. He was proud of his city.

While we were talking, his mother, Abigail, came up to the roof. "Philemon, I wish to talk with your slave."

"Mother, I haven't had a chance to show him everything."

"You will have plenty of time, my child," she said, gently caressing his head. "Now it is time for me to speak with him. When I am done, he is all yours." Gently, she nudged him away. "Now go."

Philemon walked down the stairs, Abigail watching until he was gone. Then she looked at me, again with those eyes that studied me.

"I bought you because I thought you would be good for my son." I bowed my head out of respect. "He is surrounded by women and girls. His father is busy. It is time that he spends his day with another boy. You must remember this, Onesimus," she reached out and stroked my cheek. I looked in her eyes. I felt the warmth of a mother's touch and it felt good. "You are not his friend. You are not his equal. You are his servant, his slave. You will serve him all the days of your life."

She took the hand away. That was painful.

"Yes, Mistress," I dropped my gaze and looked at my feet. I wanted to cry. All the hope and joy I had experienced on this day washed away with the miserable knowledge of my future.

"Go find him, Onesimus, and make him happy," she said as she walked down the stairs.

I looked out over the city and saw the walls surrounding it. In the distance were hills, dotted with farms and vineyards. This was not my land. Yet now it was my home.

That night I heard Philemon cry, so I left my pallet in my cubicle to check on him.

"Philemon," I whispered. "Are you sick?"

"I don't want to sleep alone. Sleep in my bed."

He was my master, as his mother said, so I obeyed, coming into the bed to lay next to him.

"No, not like that." He pointed to his feet. "You sleep there," he added cheerily. So, I slept at his feet.

Sometime in the night, I heard him again. I looked up to see him peeing in the pot. He was sloppy and missed. Now I understood what night water was, and why Zoe giggled about it.

I awoke before Philemon. I remembered the instructions to take care of the pot first. It smelled and fly buzzed around it. I looked around and saw one of his undergarments and used it to wipe the floor clean, all the while disgusted at him for being so messy. I took the pot, and dirty clothes and went looking for help.

"The clothes go in there," said a slave about ten years older than me, who I soon learned was named Thestius. He was using a rag to wash himself in a pool in the slave quarters next to the kitchen. "Wash it thoroughly or it will smell." He sniffed the air at me, "and wash yourself too. If the master smells you, he will not be happy."

I dumped out the pot and washed it as best I could, making sure there was no smell. By that time, Thestius had gone. I looked around and no one was there, so I took off my robe and sank into the pool. The water was cold, but it felt good to be clean. It was a new life, a new beginning. I did not know what it held for me, but at that moment, I felt fresh and clean.

As I was returning to Philemon, I almost ran into a man I was soon to learn was the master of the house, Archippus. I was so frightened I almost dropped the pot.

"And who might you be?" he asked with a stern look.

"I am Onesimus."

"And are you useful, Onesimus?"

"I hope to be, Sir."

"Do you know who I am?" I looked at him directly in the eye.

"I think you might be the master of the house, the Tribune Archippus."

"I am. What makes you think you can look at me in the eye as an equal?" Quickly I dropped my gaze to the floor. "Do not ever call me by my name. You are not my equal. Do not call me *sir*; you are not a freed man. You will address me as *master*, because if you are in my house, I am your master. Do you understand me?"

"Yes," I started to say sir, but quickly corrected myself. "Yes Master."

"How did you come to be in my house?" he asked angrily.

"I bought him, Archippus," Abigail walked up from behind him and put her hand on his arm as if to restrain him.

"Why did you waste my money on this boy?"

"We have discussed this the last few weeks. You agreed that Philemon should be waited upon by a male slave his own age. He is a little younger than our son, so he can expect to be here his entire life."

"What are you waiting for, boy? Get back to your duties."

I hurried off as the master and his wife discussed my purchase. I did not feel welcome, so I knew I would have to prove myself to the master and his mistress. As for Philemon, he only wanted a playmate.

CHAPTER 4
AN EDUCATION

Teach me knowledge and good judgment, for I trust your commands. Psalm 119:66

Days turned into weeks. Weeks turned into months. Months turned into years. I grew taller and my voice deeper. My yellow hair faded to brown. I became a fixture in the house of Tribune Archippus. Everywhere that the tribune's son could be found, there was also his slave, Onesimus.

Daily life with Philemon did not vary much. I woke before him, sometimes having slept at the foot of his bed, but most nights in my own bed in my cubicle. I cleaned his pot and the mess he left on the floor. Sometimes I told him to aim better. He always responded with a laugh, but never tried to get better. I even tried to find a wider pot, but then he still managed to splatter his piss everywhere.

When I was in the slave quarters, washing the pot and taking my own bath, I always ate something. The slaves ate well, though not nearly as well as the masters. There was always freshly baked bread and a gruel of beans or oats. Sometimes there was an egg, or leftover cheese, or meat from the master's table. But always I had enough to eat.

By the time I returned, Philemon was usually awake, though at times I had to wake him. He was unable to decide what to wear each day, so quickly I assumed the responsibility of choosing the appropriate clean clothes for the day. He ate with his family shortly after he awoke. His mother and sisters were always there. Archippus was frequently missing about half of the mornings.

The family ate meat, cheese, eggs, olives, hot bread, and butter for breakfast. There was fruit, but no matter how often his mother encouraged him, Philemon never touched it. Zoe was reassigned to care for the girls. She and I brought platters of food for the family, while Agata oversaw our work and continually instructed us. At times, we would snatch a piece of cheese or some fruit, but never when the master attended breakfast.

Archippus was my only fear in the house. He was a warrior, having been stationed in Spain for many years. Briefly he fought in a campaign on the German frontier. Already from a wealthy Roman family from Capua, his time in the military enriched him even more. Before he married, he settled three hundred of his soldiers in Macedonia, near the Thracian border. After that he bought a large cattle ranch in Colossae, married a girl from a wealthy Jewish family, and settled into life in Ephesus.

Abigail was the eldest daughter of Abijah of Colossae, a wealthy Jewish merchant with familial connections throughout the Province of Asia. Archippus was a soldier not a businessman, but at the encouragement of his father-in-law, he invested heavily in various business deals. He was now one of the richest, if not the richest, man in Ephesus. He maintained not only the house in Ephesus, but a dozen more that he rented. Upon the death of his father, he inherited a small estate in Capua, that his Jewish business relations managed for him.

Archippus was frequently not home. Sometimes he journeyed to Colossae or to Lystra or to Pergamum, taking care of his growing business interests. Sometimes, when in Ephesus, he visited with friends of a military background. Sometimes a soldier would come asking for advice or help with an investment. He did not often have visitors in the home, but usually visited others, and then early enough for breakfast. When he ate with his family, Zoe and I dared not sneak a bite of food. Food for the family was different from food for the slaves. He was also critical of the way his children dressed. If one of the girls, Alyx, Xanthe, or Diana, had a stain on her clothes, Zoe would be blamed. The same held true for me. If Philemon, who could stain a new robe in the first few minutes he wore it, was seen with a stain, I was blamed. For that reason, I carefully chose what Philemon wore. If something had not been properly washed, I made it my duty to clean it thoroughly, rather than blame the slave who washed the clothes.

After breakfast, Philemon had lessons in Greek. There was a freed slave, with the lofty name of Aristotle, who came to the house every day. He taught lessons in geography one day of the week; philosophy another; readings in Homer and the Greek playwrights on other days; but daily taught oratory and grammar. Though sometimes I was sent on errands to fetch something from the library or to bring food and water for Philemon, I was allowed to attend the lessons. I sat for hours learning about the vastness of the world around me, how the Empire of the Romans worked, ideas from philosophers and poets, and my mind grew.

Philemon went to the gymnasium to learn how to handle a sword or spear on two different afternoons a week. He wasn't good at either, and as a slave, I wasn't even allowed to touch the swords or spears, so I could never help him practice. Mostly he went to the gymnasium to play war with other boys near his age.

Two other afternoons a week, we went to the Hall of Tyrannus, a Latin school near the Artemesium. As the son of a Roman from Italy, Philemon was expected to learn Latin. He was the only boy who was accompanied by a slave, but the others did not seem to notice or they did not care. The boys learned Latin grammar and practiced reciting Julius Caesar and Cicero.

On the other afternoons, we went to the synagogue, where he was expected to learn Hebrew, the language of his mother's ancestors.

All three languages were different and all three languages had their own unique alphabets.

I discovered something about myself listening to the lectures. At first it amused me, but soon it terrified me. Anything I saw on paper I could memorize in a matter of moments. In my head, I could correct Philemon's recitation of Plato's Republic, because I could see it written, word for word. I could see the correct conjugation of *amar*, even when he could not. I could recite the Song of Solomon, even when Philemon could not pronounce the Hebrew words correctly. In a matter of months, my Greek was better than the Greeks living in Ephesus. Aristotle commented one day that I sounded like I was from Athens. I could understand every word spoken by Archippus when his Roman friends came for the rare visit, and I would recite verses of the Talmud to myself when taking a bath. What would these people think if I learned everything better than their son? I tried to keep it quiet, but at times I could not help myself and would correct Philemon.

"*Ero, eris, erip,*" Philemon said as we were walking to the Latin tutor. He nonchalantly kicked a rock in front of him, ignoring his recitation.

"*Erit,*" I corrected. I carried a satchel with his stylus and writing board, as well as scrolls he was supposed to have studied.

"*Erimus, eritus, erunt.*"

"*Eritis.*"

"How do you know you are right?" He asked indignantly. He kicked the rock fiercely, hitting the wall.

"I listen to your teacher."

"Well, you are a slave and you don't know anything," he quipped.

To myself I thought of him often calling me his brother. I don't think he truly understood the concept of brotherhood any more than I did. I was not his brother. I was his slave. But I did know the proper conjugation of *sum*.

Moments later he was reciting to the tutor. "*Ero, eris, erip, erimus, eritus, erunt.*"

"Third person singular is *erit*," Marius corrected. "And *eritis*, instead of *eritus*."

Philemon eyed me angrily.

Later that day, I stood in the library while Master Archippus completed writing a note, then handed it to Thestius. While I stood waiting, Thestius eyed me occasionally rolling his eyes at me. He had more than once commented to me that I had yet to learn my place. I hated when another slave tried to put me in *my place*. Who was he, a slave, to tell me, a slave, my place?

"Have it delivered to Marius, the Latin tutor, immediately." Thestius hurried away. I continued looking at the floor.

"I have heard complaints about you, Onesimus." Terrified I did not know what to say. "Do you have an answer for me?"

"I don't know what the complaints are, Master."

"You are mocking my son, your master." His face held no mercy. He was angry.

"I would never do that," I had difficulty breathing, terror seizing me.

"He says you corrected him on his Latin conjugations this afternoon. And he says it is not the first time." I winced, because what he said was true. "Do you have an explanation?"

"Yes Master," I said tentatively. If I was going to be beaten, I would at least be beaten for doing what was right. "He was reciting the future active conjugation of *sum*, but was getting some of it incorrect. He had been told to memorize it for today's class. I wanted him to get it correct, so I was just trying to help him."

"When did you learn Latin? You are not from Italy."

"No, sir, I mean Master. I am from Dacia, I think. I was too young when taken to remember exactly."

"So how does a Dacian slave learn Latin well enough to correct his master, the son of a Roman tribune?"

"I listen to his tutor."

"And my son does not?" He raised his voice.

The terror overwhelmed me, enough that I was shaking. "No, I didn't say that. It's just…"

"It's just what?"

"Philemon studies and studies well, as well as any of the other students. It's just that if I see it written, I don't forget it. I can't explain it."

"What?"

"If it is written, I remember it."

"Are you saying to me that you don't forget anything you see that is written?"

"Yes, Master."

He studied me for a moment, seeming to soften. He turned to the shelf and pulled out a scroll. He looked for a place then thrust it in my face.

"Read this."

I read it and wondered what would happen next. He rolled up the scroll and carefully placed it back on the shelf.

"Tell me what you read."

"Oh, the torment bred in the race, the grinding scream of death and the stroke that hits the vein, the hemorrhage none can staunch, the pain, the curse no man can bear."[1]

Archippus sat down considering me. For an eternity, he said nothing.

"You can memorize anything in Latin and Greek just by reading it?"

"And Hebrew."

He laughed. My terror began to ease. "Let me tell you about my son, Onesimus," Archippus said with the softest voice I had ever heard from him. "Look at me, Onesimus."

I did not look up, but said, "You commanded me not to look you in the eye."

"Now I am commanding something different. Look at me, Onesimus." I looked into his eyes. They were dark green and looked very tired. "I want my son to be well-educated. I want him to be able to converse with the intellectuals not only of Ephesus, but of Athens and Rome. I even want him able to converse with the intellectuals of Jerusalem, those of his mother's religion. I probably am asking too much of him, learning Greek, Latin, and Hebrew, but he needs this to survive in this world. He is not a soldier and never will be. He needs to use his mind. Do you understand?"

"Yes, Master."

"I am giving you a new command. Correct him. If he makes a mistake, correct him. Help him learn what he needs to learn. In addition, listen to what is being taught. Learn what he learns. Later in life you will be invaluable to him."

"Yes, Master."

"If you have spare time, I give you permission to read some of my books. Maybe you can quote some of the great Athenian playwrights to me, from time to time."

I hesitated, still looking him in the eye. I thought now was the time to lower my gaze. "Master, may I borrow the book you just had me read?"

"*The Oresteia*, by Aeschylus. A son who kills his mother." He took the scroll off the shelf and handed it to me. "Yes, you may read it."

I felt the meeting was over so I bowed and said, "Thank you, Master."

He did not acknowledge my thanks as I left.

That night I read and read, absorbing the sad tale of Orestes. I had been given a freedom I never expected, to explore new worlds.

Now the teacher could ask me questions, since I had been given permission to learn whatever Philemon was learning.

"Onesimus," the Hebrew teacher asked one day. "Do you remember what I taught yesterday?"

"From the Proverbs of Solomon. A wise son brings joy to his father, but a foolish son brings grief to his mother." I felt proud that I knew these words.

"It seems the slave learns better than his master." The rabbi looked at Philemon with scorn.

"Why do you do that?" Philemon asked as we walked home.

"Do what?

"Make me look foolish by remembering things better than I do." His voice was sad rather than angry.

"I don't try to make you look bad, Master. I just remember things easily."

He knew I had been given permission from his father to learn and he knew that I remembered everything I learned. As a freeborn man, he was supposed to be superior; but in this was one thing I was undeniably better. I felt proud of this accomplishment.

Philemon put his arm about me. "I have a smart brother who makes me look stupid." He then started running. "Catch me if you can."

Carrying his books, stylus, and writing tablet, I could scarcely keep up. He knew that, but when we got home and his things were put away, we could run, or wrestle, or play games, and occasionally I let him win.

The family went to the Temple of Artemis for festivals or special occasions. As his personal servant, I could enter with the family, wearing my blue robe. The towering white marble columns made me think of the trees of my forest. I could close my eyes and imagine myself standing on the hill ready to run deeper into the forest. But this goddess disturbed me. She was called the goddess of the hunt, but I could not see her as a huntress. The statue in the middle of the temple was of a goddess with dozens of breasts. These breasts would get in the way, flapping about, if ever she were to hunt. When I told this to Philemon he could not contain his laughter. The priestesses looked disapprovingly at the two laughing boys.

Abigail never entered the temple, like me, she was uncomfortable with the goddess. There was a place she would sit in the shadows of the Temple. When I saw her sitting like that, I felt a deep sadness. She did not seem happy. I had completely forgotten what my mother looked like. Abigail was the closest I had to a mother in this world. I wanted her to be happy.

Every Sabbath we went to the synagogue, though Archippus purposefully avoided joining his family, saying he was too busy. I was allowed to enter, but was relegated to the back wall. The mournful recitations from the Jewish scriptures lulled me into a trance. I imagined myself standing on the hill of my forest wrapped in the love of my ancestors. When I was here, listening to the chants, I remembered wanting to discover what was beyond the forest. I had discovered that beyond the forest was a great world, bigger than I could have imagined. I discovered that the world of Asia Province lacked the great forest of my homeland. I started to forget what being a Singidava meant. Standing on that hill in the forest, I wanted to run, but my legs would not move. I would never see that place again, but here, I could dream my sad dreams.

As Philemon's sisters grew older, they eventually gained their own personal slaves. Diana now claimed Zoe, who still giggled, and Xanthe had a girl named Helena, who was as chubby as her new mistress. Alyx, when she was seven years old, was given a slave they called Rhoda who was about my age.

She did not know what her name was originally, nor where she came from. She was given the name Rhoda because of her red hair. Rhoda means from Rhodes, but also implies roses, because Rhodes is the island of roses. Her hair was red, a dark rosy red. Her skin was white like milk. No one in the house had skin as white as hers, not even the Master's daughters. Her eyes were dark brown, but if you looked closely, there was a hint of green. They reminded me of a dark forest with the browns blending effortlessly with the greens. I imagined her being from my homeland and dreamed that we might be freed one day and allowed to return.

I could never disguise my feelings for her. Philemon laughed at me more than once when he was talking about some mundane topic and I was looking across the patio at Alyx and Rhoda sitting in the shade under the rose vine.

Because she accompanied her mistress everywhere, like I did with Philemon, we were often in the same room together, especially for meals. When I smiled at her, she smiled back, sometimes blushing. I made a point to pass platters to her, so I could brush my hand against hers.

I looked for opportunities to be alone with her, which was difficult to do. One day during breakfast, she took a bowl of berries that was almost empty, saying she would return with a full bowl, because the girls loved to eat berries.

I was holding a jug of milk. The jug was half full, but I quickly said to Agata, "I need to refill this jug. I'll be back."

I walked beside her, noticing her smile.

"You smile at me, Onesimus, but you rarely speak to me." I blushed. What do I say? "Well, go ahead and speak." She stopped at the top of the stairs, waiting for me. She laughed; a sweet sound.

"Your laughter has indeed stirred my heart. Whenever I look at you, even briefly, I can no longer say a single thing."[2]

"What a beautiful thing to say."

"From the poetess, Sappho."

She leaned forward and gently kissed me on the cheek. Never had I been so glad that I could memorize anything I saw in front of me as I felt that moment.

CHAPTER 5
TIMOTHY

You stretch out your hand against the anger of my foes; with your right hand, you save me. Psalm 138:7

My life continued relatively unchanged for years, until one day, Abigail's sister, Eunice, came to visit with her son, Timothy.

Timothy was my age, two years younger than Philemon. He was short, but had a boxer's build. He liked to run, so he and Philemon often raced each other, forgetting to include me. He had sandy-blonde hair that his mother said was getting darker each year. His eyes were blue, but dark like the river of my homeland.

He was always laughing and making the family laugh. He complimented Abigail till she blushed. He asked Archippus to tell stories about his campaigns in Germany; asking questions to encourage him to add more details. He teased the girls, eliciting giggles. The slaves, on the other hand, were unimportant to him. He did not note their presence unless he wanted something, then he ordered them around as if they were his own. Sometimes I saw that his eyes lingered too long on Rhoda. He was more gentle to her than the others. He smiled at her and looked her in the eye. That made me jealous.

Mostly, he was in the company of Philemon. He told him stories and said things to impress his gullible cousin, who would praise him as the most amazing young man he had ever met. When he said that, Timothy would get a smug look on his face. I knew he was trying to get praise from his wealthier and more influential cousin. I had no proof, but I felt Timothy wanted to use his cousin to better himself in the future. He was always speaking softly to Philemon, bringing him into his confidence. I felt jealousy in a different way when those two were together, their heads bent in quiet conversation.

For years, Philemon had been my brother. True, he treated me like a slave, having me wait on him in every way possible. But often we were walking to or from one of his tutors and he would share his dreams for the future. He dreamed of going to Rome and expanding his father's businesses and doing things to make his family proud. Always, I was included. I would go to Rome with him. Together we would build a financial empire that would make us the envy of the most influential people in Rome. Now, all his time was spent with Timothy.

With me, Timothy demonstrated that he had a sense of status that Philemon lacked. To Philemon I could be a confidant in private, but not so with Timothy. I was a slave and he made sure I knew it. He would send me on an errand for fruit, or water, or a book from the library. When I returned, he complained that I took too long. Now the water was too warm to drink. The fruit tasted like it was on the verge of being spoiled. I had brought the wrong book. He would tell Philemon that slaves were unreliable these days.

Philemon did not know how to respond. I was his slave, but he liked my company. Timothy was his cousin and he found him to be brilliantly intelligent and funny. He would look at me sadly, as if I had embarrassed him in front of his beloved cousin.

Timothy joined Philemon for his morning lessons in Greek,

insisting that I stay outside the study, in my place as a slave. When I told him I had been commanded by Archippus to attend Philemon's lessons, I could see the anger simmer in him. He would not contradict his uncle, but he hated being corrected by a slave.

He had seen my affection for Rhoda, so he devised a cruel plan to make me jealous. When he was talking with the girls and Rhoda was present, he would praise her for the things she did, always saying she was the best slave in the house. He would tell Alyx that she had a slave as beautiful as she was. When Rhoda would blush and say her thanks, Timothy always looked at me to see my reaction.

He stayed at the villa in the afternoons, except on the days that we went to the gymnasium. I hated the thought that he would be alone with Alyx and Rhoda, but the afternoons gave me time with Philemon that had been lacking since Timothy's arrival.

"Timothy told me about a beggar who sits outside the walls of Lystra. He is lame from birth and cannot walk."

"Oh?"

"Once he played a trick on the beggar, making the man cry."

"Your cousin is cruel."

"Don't say that. Timothy is funny."

"A nice person would not make a person cry, even a beggar."

"It was only a joke." Philemon shrugged his shoulder. "He is kind to me and appreciates me."

"He only fawns on you to make you like him."

"Of course, I like him. He is my cousin."

"He does not like you. He only does the things he does and says the things he says, because he wants to impress you."

"What makes you think that?"

"Because he doesn't like anybody but himself."

I realized I had just said too much, but once the words came out, it was impossible to take them back.

Philemon did not say a word the rest of the way home. Upon entering the house, he immediately went to find Timothy. They talked for minutes, while nervously I cleaned Philemon's study, organizing the books and putting everything in its proper place.

"Slave, look at me." Timothy entered with his fists clenched at his side, turning white in anger. I defiantly looked at him. "You rude, base animal. How dare you imply things about my character?"

"I only spoke what I saw." His palm struck my face and I stumbled. Angrily I stood and was close to striking him. He stood up straight. He was not taller than me, but the look in his eyes showed no fear.

"Hit me," he said coming closer. His eyes blazed in their anger.

"Don't, Onesimus," Philemon said, standing beside his cousin.

"Hit me," Timothy repeated. The anger seethed in me. I wanted to beat him; to prove I was better than him.

Philemon put his hand on my chest and pushed me back. "I command you to stop."

"I will report your insolence to Archippus. He needs to know what his slaves do in his house. You should be beaten."

Philemon turned to his cousin. "Timothy, he is my slave. I should not have told you what he said. It is my duty to punish him. I ask you to keep silent."

Timothy turned his stare from me and looked at his cousin. He shrugged his shoulders, as if none of it mattered, but the look he gave me promised that he was not finished with me.

"We are leaving tomorrow anyway. He is a slave and nothing he says matters. But if he insults me again, I promise I will beat him myself." Timothy growled as he walked away.

Philemon let out a breath, as if he had been holding it for too long.

"I apologize, Master. I should not have said the things I said."

He looked at me, eye to eye. "You are my brother."

Inside I screamed, "I am not your brother. A brother would never do what you just did, revealing things said in confidence. A brother would never command his brother not to beat someone who had just hit him. A brother would never have his brother clean his piss every morning. A brother does not act like you."

But I bowed my head and said, "Yes Master."

There was a lot of confusion the next day. Timothy and Eunice had a conversation with Archippus and Abigail in the study, with the doors shut tight. I was sure they were reporting me.

Shortly after the meeting, they were gathered in the atrium saying their goodbyes. Alyx was crying and Rhoda did not accompany her.

After Timothy had said his goodbyes to Philemon, he walked to me. For a moment, he stared at me, almost challenging me to insult him. I stood stoically, saying nothing. I looked past him, keeping my place. "Remember, Onesimus. You are a slave and always will be. I am better than you. Don't forget that."

He walked away and moments later, they were gone. I thought it was over and done with.

Alyx cried all afternoon and did not come down to dinner. The next morning, she appeared, but looked as if she had cried all night. Rhoda was not with her.

When I had a moment, I pulled Zoe aside. "Where is Rhoda?"

Her lip quivered.

"Is she sick?"

"She has been sent away to be sold."

"Why?"

"The Mistress' sister, Eunice, accused her of taking liberties with her son."

"What do you mean?"

"He said she asked to return to Lystra with him, offering to be his personal slave."

"That's not true."

"I know. That is what Alyx said too. Alyx insisted they never once were alone together."

"Where is she?"

"Thestius and another slave took her to the auction house, with a letter to sell her."

Timothy could not get even with me directly, so he got even by destroying the woman I loved. I looked back at the dining room, where the family seemed unconcerned about the loss of Rhoda, a girl more beautiful than any person in this house. I looked at Zoe who was crying. My chest ached. My vision blurred.

I dropped the tray I was carrying and started to run.

I was out of the gate before the slave at the gate even noticed. He yelled something to me, but I did not hear him.

I ran.

I weaved through the crowded streets of Ephesus, knocking over a woman's basket and bumping into an old man. A barking dog chased me. People shouted at me for nearly hitting them, but I didn't hear. I had to be away from that house.

I ran.

I imagined the forest enveloping me. I was a runner, a prince of the Singidava Getae north of the Great River, under the shadow of the purple mountains. I was not a slave. The spirits of my ancestors ran with me this morning. I honored them by proving I was a runner. As I ran, I said a prayer of thanks to Rubobostes and begged him to save my Rhoda. I was the son of the son of the son of Rubobostes, the great chief who defeated the Romans, these people I hated, farther back than any in my village remember.

I had to find Rhoda before it was too late. I jumped over a cat and he screeched. Dogs chased me, but I ran faster. No one could catch me.

In my mind, I saw myself on the edge of the fields, with the fir and beech and alder trees; the trees inhabited by dancing maiden spirits. But this was not my forest. Ahead of me was a crowded city that smelled of waste and filth. I pushed through people, carts, and shops, as if I was fighting the branches and brambles of the forest. I had to find her. There was one place I had to be before it was too late, before my sunshine was gone forever. This place was not the forest of my ancestors.

Always I thought there was something beyond even my ancestors. I did not know what that was, but I knew if I continued running my race through the forest, I would discover it.

I had discovered what was beyond the forest. It was a dirty, evil world where people were enslaved. It was a crowded city that could be beautiful, but filthy with the stench of too many humans. It was a world where innocent girls were sold because of a lie of a free man.

I arrived at the slave auction house. It was almost empty. There were maybe a dozen slaves for sale.

"Where are the female slaves for sale," I asked one man near the entrance.

"Yesterday was the day for selling the female slaves. There are none left."

"A girl, about my age, was she here? She had red hair and brown eyes."

"I remember her. There were many bidding on her."

"Who bought her? Where is she?"

"She was sold and placed on a ship. I don't know where she went from there."

She was gone. Archippus had arranged to have her sold, because of Timothy's lie. He had destroyed her. He had destroyed me. The weight of it caused me to stagger to the floor. I could not stay here any longer. I had to leave Ephesus. I lurched to my feet.

I had never been beyond the walls of Ephesus, but I ran toward the gates now. I had discovered what was beyond my forest. I hated it. I had to find my forest again. I had to be gone from this detestable place and the stench of humanity.

"There he is," a man shouted.

I turned to see a group of men coming after me. I knew I was faster so I ran. I knew I could outrun them.

Suddenly before me was the eastern city gate that led to the mountainous interior. The gate was closing. I tried to run faster, but it was closing even faster. The guards at the gate started running toward me. I stumbled. Rough hands grabbed me. One man struck me across the face.

"A runaway," he laughed.

Five men brought me back to the home of Tribune Archippus. My face was bloody and bruises covered my body. I didn't care. If I couldn't be free, I wanted to die.

I was tied to a pillar in the inner courtyard. Abigail gathered her daughters intending to take them away. Philemon ran to his room. Thestius brought a whip and handed it to Archippus.

"Uncover his back," he ordered Thestius. He walked to me and ripped my clothes apart, revealing my back. The whip struck my bare skin. Unimaginable pain tore through my body and I screamed.

"Answer me," Archippus bellowed. "Why did you run from my house, after I treated you so well?"

I felt another sting of the whip, as it tore my flesh. I screamed in pain.

"Answer me."

"You sold Rhoda," I wept through the pain. "Timothy lied to you."

"What concern is it of yours what I do with one of my slaves?"

"I love her." I heard the whip crack and again the whip tore into my flesh.

"Stop father," Philemon shouted.

"Go away Philemon, this is not your concern."

"He is my slave; he is my concern."

"He is a slave in my house."

"You are wrong. He is mine!" Philemon shouted. I heard a scroll being unrolled, but could not see what was happening. "On my birthday, you gave me this document. It says that Onesimus is my slave. I am seventeen. I am almost an adult. This is my slave and I do not wish him harmed anymore."

"He must be punished."

I felt a pressure against my back. Philemon was leaning against me, standing between me and his father. "He is my slave. You will not punish him."

"Father," I heard the voice of Alyx pleading.

"I loved her," I whispered. Only Philemon could hear me.

"He is my property. I will not have him damaged." Quietly he added, "He is useful to me. He helps me in my studies."

The whip was thrown to the ground, breaking a pot nearby. Archippus stormed out of the villa.

"Untie him," Philemon ordered. Nobody moved. "Untie him," he shouted at Thestius.

Thestius untied me, and Zoe and Helena came to me. They helped me stagger to my cubicle. Zoe stayed by my side, while Helena brought water to wash my back and herbs to place on my wounds.

I didn't look at them, but could hear Zoe crying. After a few minutes, Philemon quietly ordered them to leave.

I turned my head so I could look Philemon in the face. He did not look angry; rather there was a deep sadness.

"You are my slave and useful to me." Always when we were alone, he had called me his brother.

"You are my brother, Philemon." I said.

He did not move, but I saw a change in his face. He was no longer a boy. This incident had turned him into a man.

"You are a valuable slave to me. Prove to my father that I am not wrong." Looking down at me, he said, "You will rest today, but tomorrow you will perform your duties as expected. You will forget this slave and serve me."

And he was gone. I cried, thinking of Rhoda, but more I cried because I was a slave without a brother. At that moment, I hated Philemon and everyone in this house that destroyed Rhoda and caused me so much pain.

I dreamed I was in the forest. I was running. As I approached the hill, the trees vanished. My hill was barren, a burned-out desert wasteland. My ancestors turned their faces away in shame.

I am a slave.

CHAPTER 6

A NEW PHILOSOPHY

When the crowd saw what Paul had done, they shouted in the Lycaonian language, "The gods have come down to us in human form!" Acts 14:11

I grew numb. I felt no joy when things should have brought me pleasure, such as the weddings of Diana and Xanthe, when even the slaves could participate in the celebrations. I felt nothing. I did not smile; I did not complain. Nothing could ever make me feel again.

I was useful to Philemon. I did everything he asked and more. Even Archippus could see that I had changed. Philemon left his studies so he could learn more about the family's investments, often spending time with his grandfather, Abijah, in Colossae. I regained their trust, but I did not accompany him on trips to Colossae. I was trusted to deliver documents to government offices in Ephesus, take delivery of stock at the port, or deliver money to the bank, but I was never allowed out of the city.

After many years, I was allowed to accompany a merchant in Archippus' employ to Pergamum and permitted to return on my own. My return surprised Archippus. He assumed I would run once I was finished with my duties. I think he expected it and hoped for it. But I did not. I had nowhere to go. My life meant nothing. All I had left was my duty to Philemon.

I remember Archippus looking at me curiously when I reported back on time and gave him the documents in my satchel. My face was like stone. Emotion was gone. I had done my duty and returned.

"Thank you, Onesimus."

I did not answer.

Timothy had not been here since the time he had lied about Rhoda. Philemon had seen him many times on visits to Colossae, when I stayed behind in Ephesus to take care of his business investments. Now Timothy was again in Archippus' villa in Ephesus.

Yet I could not feel anger. I felt nothing.

"You wrote that you have encountered that Jewish sect that is doing so much damage in Judea."

"Yes, I have, Uncle Archippus," a smile radiated on his face. He looked handsome behind that smile. He had grown taller; now taller than Philemon. He was slender, because he still ran each day and competed in races across the province of Asia. His face was clean shaven; making him look more Greek than Jewish. Because of what he had done to Rhoda, I could never look at him with anything but distrust.

"I've heard in the synagogue that they worship a dead man, claiming he is not dead," Philemon said joining the conversation. Philemon was now a confident man, soon to take over the family business. He was well-educated and made sure everyone knew it. "They should not waste their time on dead men, but search the scriptures to learn how God wants them to live, such as the teachings of Solomon, in the Proverbs."

"Is it true, Uncle, that you have begun visiting the synagogue?" Timothy asked, ignoring Philemon's comments.

Archippus said nothing in reply. In fact, he had been going to the synagogue regularly. At times, he invited the rabbi to talk to him in his study. In the past, he had always bought scrolls in Greek or Latin. Now he was buying scrolls of the Hebrews, especially the prophets, and commentaries of rabbis, such as Gamaliel of Jerusalem. Something had happened to him, as he grew older. It was never discussed, but Archippus was ill. I think I might have been the only one who noticed him holding his stomach in pain. He hid it from the rest of the family. Maybe he felt he was dying. I don't know, but I know he was searching for something, but never openly discussed it.

"I am glad you are," Timothy continued, not waiting for an answer. "I have been witness to some amazing things, Uncle. That is why I came here. I want my family to share in my joy."

"Tell us, Nephew," Abigail commanded, leaning forward. As an aging matron, she was still beautiful. Her hair was now salted with white, with a streak of white over the forelock, which always tended come loose from her braids and fall over her eyes. She never ceased to be a kind woman. She was not a mother to me though. Rarely did she acknowledge my presence in the room. I was like any other useful household furniture.

I saw they needed a refill of wine, so while Timothy talked, I quietly went around the table refilling their goblets.

"Remember, Philemon, I once told you about the beggar that always sits at the gate in Lystra."

"Yes, I remember," Philemon looked at me as if reminding me of a conversation, of years past. I ignored the look and went back to standing quietly by the wall.

"One day two men came to town. They were standing at the gate telling people about Jesus, the dead man you were talking about." Timothy closed his eyes as if he were trying to remember everything. When he opened his eyes, there were tears in them. What new trick was he playing, I asked myself?

"It was a market day, so it was busy. Always the entire town gathers at the gate, where we have our market. It was the beginning of spring and many booths had garlands in preparation for the celebration of the rebirth of Persephone. It was just two days away, so you can imagine that the market was filled with the scent of flowers. Two men were standing on the steps of the temple of Zeus, which is just outside the gate. One of these men, who I soon learned was named Paul, was talking about how Abraham went to Mount Moriah to sacrifice Isaac."

"But he didn't," Philemon added. "Instead God substituted a ram at the last moment, just as Abraham was about to plunge the knife in his chest."

"That is always one of my favorite stories," Abigail said, placing some olives on a plate and passing them to Timothy.

"Unfortunately, I never paid much attention to that passage," Timothy took an olive and ate it before he continued. "Paul quoted a verse, that I had never noticed before. Remember when Isaac asked where the sacrifice was? Abraham said, 'God himself will provide the lamb.' Paul was saying this was not just a story from Israel's past, but a prophecy."

"What prophecy?" Archippus asked. When he met with the rabbis, he was always asking about prophecy, though when they left, he was always more confused and frustrated.

"That verse, he said, was a prophecy."

"I've never heard that spoken of as a prophecy," Philemon said. Of all at the table, he seemed bored.

"Nobody was paying much attention to Paul and Barnabas," Timothy continued, not explaining how the verse was a prophecy. "I was only because I was bored. I was accompanying Mother, who was buying garlands for the upcoming spring festival. And there was the beggar, sitting on the steps of the temple. He was watching Paul as he spoke, enraptured by every word said. Suddenly, Paul stopped what he was saying and looked at the beggar. He reached out his hand and said, 'In the name of Jesus of Nazareth, stand on your feet.' The beggar grabbed Paul's hand and stood up. The crowd began to hush, seeing the beggar stand. I looked at his legs, which had always been nothing more than sticks and covered with sores. Uncle," Timothy said looking directly at Archippus, "I watched the muscles grow on his legs. They filled out and were quickly the legs of a normal, healthy man. And the sores disappeared."

"That's impossible," Philemon said. He had a cup of wine halfway to his mouth.

Both Archippus and Abigail had stopped eating and were listening. Alyx had her hand over her heart, as if frightened.

"I was stunned and could not move. The crowd saw the miracle and for a moment they were in silent awe. Then one by one they began to murmur about him being Zeus. I was close enough to hear Paul tell the beggar that Jesus of Nazareth, the Messiah, was the one who healed him. But the crowd started going insane. A few ran in fear, but others began to grab garlands from the stalls, red and purple cloth, and someone brought a white bull. They threw the bolts of cloth at Paul's feet and strewed flower petals on the improvised rugs. The white bull was brought forward and forced on his knees, and several women placed garlands around Paul and Barnabas' necks."

Timothy stopped, considering his words. The table was silent. It seemed no one breathed.

"Please continue," Alyx encouraged. Since the sale of Rhoda, Alyx, once the happy, fun-loving member of the family, had become quiet and introspective. She rarely smiled; she never laughed.

"Paul shouted to the crowd, 'We are not gods. We are men like you. Stop what you are doing,' he said preventing the men from cutting the bull's throat. He went back to the steps of the temple, now that he had everyone's attention. 'We are here to bring you good news, telling you to turn from these worthless idols to the living God who made the heavens and the earth and the sea and everything in them. In the past, he let all nations go their own way. Yet he has not left himself without testimony: He has shown you kindness by giving you rain from heaven and crops in their seasons; he provides you with plenty of food and fills your hearts with joy.'

"Some listened, but many wanted to sacrifice the bull. Paul's friend, Barnabas, forced his way through the crowd to stop them. Paul seemed to grow stronger before my eyes. He told the crowd about Jesus of Nazareth, the Son of God, who had been crucified in Jerusalem, but rose from the dead."

"I've heard of this Jesus," Philemon added. "Many say bad things about his followers."

"I am now one of his followers, Cousin." Timothy looked intently at Philemon, to make his point clear. For the first time, Philemon stopped eating and listened. "I know what you have heard in the past, because we have discussed these very same things. Everything you heard is false. They worship Jesus, who claimed to be God."

"How is it possible that a man can be God?"

"Jesus is God. He left His home in Heaven to live here as a man. That was His purpose. He lived like you and me, but led a sinless life. No one has ever been able to find a single sin that he committed, even minor sins, like lying to his mother, or exaggerating when telling a story."

"Yet he claimed to be God," Philemon countered. "Is not claiming to be God a sin?"

"Of course, that would be a sin. But he is God! That is what we believe. That is what Paul teaches. This man, Jesus, died in exchange for my sins."

"What do you mean?" Archippus asked. He was breathing rapidly and the color had washed out of his face. He looked like he was becoming sick, so instinctively, I added fresh wine to his cup.

"As God, He did not have to die. He could have struck dead the Romans and Jewish leaders. But He willingly died. His followers didn't understand at the time, but three days later, He rose from the grave and spent forty days meeting believers and teaching them, before He ascended to heaven, an event witnessed by five hundred people. This is not hearsay, but a witnessed event."

"Finish the story," Abigail implored. She had also seen her husband and quietly placed her hand on his. He gripped her hand as if in fear.

"The Jewish leaders asked Paul to speak later that week at the synagogue. Some Greek leaders asked him to come and speak at the gymnasium, and allow the students and teachers to ask him questions.

"I was bold and asked if they had a place to stay while in Lystra. Paul said he did not. By then mother was with me and repeated my invitation. We escorted them home, where Paul and I talked till the late watches of the night. He shared with me what the scriptures said about this Jesus, prophecies that never made sense before, as if they were mumblings of insane men. Now they are so clear to me. I don't know how I never saw them in the past. Like the one I just mentioned. Not only did God provide a lamb for Abraham, he provided his Son, the Lamb of God for the children of Abraham." Timothy looked around the table at each one seated there. "So, Uncle, Aunt, Cousins, I am now a follower of this Jesus."

"I would like to meet this man Paul one day," Archippus said.

"That is one of the reasons I am here. He wrote a letter that he plans to be in Ephesus soon, with two of his associates, a Roman couple from Corinth. I don't know exactly when they will be here, but I expect them any day."

"If Archippus agrees," Abigail added, "we will ask them to stay with us while they are here."

"Of course," Archippus said. "And until they arrive, maybe you could share everything you have learned with me. I would like to know more about this Jesus."

Timothy looked at me for a moment. I thought he was going to say something. I instinctively dropped my gaze. His look quickly returned to the family at the table, the people who mattered as far as he was concerned.

The next several days, Timothy and Archippus stayed locked in the study, discussing prophecies of the Jews. Sometimes Philemon joined them, but he seemed skeptical.

"Onesimus," Archippus called one afternoon. "Come in here." I entered and stood at the door, waiting for instructions. "Where is the book of Malachi?" Archippus asked.

I looked around the room for a moment and saw it on a shelf with poets. "Here Master," I said handing him the scroll.

"It is close to the middle," Timothy said. "It says a man will come before Jesus."

I remembered the passage, so I spoke up. "I will send my messenger, who will prepare the way before me. Then suddenly the Lord you are seeking will come to his temple."

Timothy looked at me annoyed, "Yes, that is the passage."

Archippus unrolled the scroll and was looking for the quote. He did not read Hebrew well, so I pointed to it. Like every book in the library, I knew it by heart.

"Thank you, Onesimus." Without looking at me, he added, "that will be all."

Less than a week later, news reached us that Paul had arrived. Philemon, Timothy, and I hurried to the dock. Timothy approached a man, who physically was not very impressive. He was of average height and sported a limp when he walked. He had chestnut brown hair that had recently been cropped short, but with a large bald spot growing on top. His beard was thick, though recently cut short, with bits of white here and there. His arms and legs seemed strong. Though his chest was broad, he looked like there were times that he went without food. Why would anyone imagine this man as Zeus, the King of the Gods?

Timothy greeted him effusively. He introduced his cousin, Philemon, but not me. Of course, not, I was nothing more than a mere slave. Paul introduced the couple, a middle-aged man named Aquila and his wife, Priscilla. He was from Rome, though a Jew originally from Pontus. Though both had Roman names because of their Roman citizenship, they were very much Jewish. When Claudius had expelled all the Jews from Rome, they had moved to

Corinth and there met Paul.

After the many greetings and arrangements were made for porters to carry their luggage, Paul met my curious gaze. His eyes commanded my attention. They were grey, with a hint of blue in them when the light hit them just right. Maybe it was the way the sun hit his eyes, but they seemed to sparkle. He wanted to greet me, but I assumed he kept silent because I was just a slave. There was a slight smile on his lips, almost as if he were going to laugh at a joke only he knew. Who was this strange man?

Soon we were at the villa. Paul looked around at the rich surroundings, but did not comment on the wealth, which the normal Jew, Greek, or Roman would have done. He did not seem impressed. Archippus greeted Paul and immediately invited him into the study.

"Sit, Rabbi," Archippus motioned Paul into the study. "I have so many questions."

"I would be honored, Tribune." Paul looked at me, speaking to me for the first time. "Might I have some cool water to drink? What is your name?"

"Onesimus, Master," I said lowering my eyes.

"I am not your master, Onesimus," Paul was smiling. I wondered if there were some amusement I was about to be the target of.

"We have some good wine," Philemon added.

"For now, just some cool water, Onesimus." A few minutes later, I returned with cups for all five men, a pitcher of cool water, and another of wine, in case the others desired it. I poured Paul the water and left the wine for the others.

"A little wine, Onesimus." Archippus requested. As I handed him the cup, he added, "Stay please. You know the library better than I do."

"You are a literate slave, Onesimus?" Paul asked.

"I have been Philemon's personal slave for more than ten years. When he went for his studies, I accompanied him, and yes, I learned to read."

"He not only can read, he can memorize everything he sees," Philemon laughed. "It annoyed me when we were children, because he knew every answer to every question my teachers asked."

"Is that so?" Paul asked me.

"Yes, that is true."

"Tell me how that is possible."

I looked around, knowing as a slave I should be silent. Timothy, as always, looked annoyed at me. Archippus and Philemon showed no real emotion. If I went too far, Timothy would tell them. Later I would be punished or maybe just corrected. I was asked to speak by a guest. My duty was to answer.

"I don't know, Master," I began. "You said not to call you master, but then I don't know how to address you."

"My name is Paul. Call me by my name."

I could sense it was wrong, but he was a guest and asked me to call him by his given name.

"Paul, nobody taught me how to read. My first master, a dyer of cloth in Byzantium, would write things on paper and send me to select merchants. I studied the papers and eventually could decipher what words meant. A few years in his house and I could read basic Greek. Then I came here and accompanied Philemon to his studies of Greek, Hebrew, and Latin. I listened and saw what was taught. I discovered one day that I never forgot anything that was written. It stuck in my head as if written there. Beyond that, I cannot explain it."

Paul asked Archippus, "You said you have many scrolls of the Hebrew prophets. Do you have Isaiah?"

"Yes, I do." He stood to look for it. Without thinking, because I had done it hundreds of times, I reached for the scroll of Isaiah, a large one near the bottom shelf and handed it to Paul. He laid it on the desk and began to unroll it from the back. I stood by the door waiting, because I had not been dismissed.

"You have read Isaiah before?"

"Yes."

"He had no beauty or majesty to attract us to him," Paul read. He paused and looked at me. "Finish it."

I cleared my throat. "Nothing in his appearance that we should desire him. He was despised and rejected by mankind, a man of suffering, and familiar with pain." I stopped there. I was familiar with pain.

"Go on, please, Onesimus."

"Like one from whom people hide their faces he was despised, and we held him in low esteem. Surely, he took our pain and bore our suffering, yet we considered him stricken by God, stricken by him, and afflicted. But he was pierced for our transgressions, he was crushed for our inequities; the punishment that brought us peace was on him, and by his wounds we are healed." I paused. The words seemed to sting, but I didn't know why.

"You may stop there, Onesimus," Paul said quietly. I could not decipher the look on his face.

"This man is a marvelous addition to your house, Archippus," Aquila said smiling.

"He is the most valuable piece of property I own," Archippus said. Property, I thought, but not a man in his eyes.

"He has been like a brother to me since I was a child," Philemon added. "Thank you, Onesimus, you may go."

I heard no more of the conversation. Though a valuable piece of property, I was not a man, nor a brother. Though I could memorize any work of literature, I was just a slave, a curious oddity who could memorize any written work. As a slave, I could not engage in meaningful discussions with these men who were free. I was angry and could not afford to reveal my emotions, so I walked back to Philemon's rooms.

Zoe was sweeping the room. I never forgot Rhoda. Her face was always before me, her red hair, her brown eyes, her milk white skin dotted with freckles. Zoe was older than me and almost as tall as me. Her hair was dark brown, almost black. Her skin was dark. I asked her once why she was so dark and she said she wasn't sure, but was told she was probably born in Egypt. Her eyes were dark brown and always looked sad. When she saw me, she always stopped what she was doing and, if we were alone, teased me. At first, I hated that about her. Now, as the years passed, I loved that about her. She was the closest I came to having a friend in this house.

"Onesimus," she looked up smiling.

"Hello, Zoe."

"What is he like?" She asked excitedly.

"Paul?"

"Yes, I only caught a glimpse, before the mistress and I took the lady, Priscilla, to her rooms. She is nice."

"Paul is on the ugly side, I guess. If you saw him in the street, you'd turn the other way. But…" I could not describe how I felt with him around.

"But what?" She came closer, as if we were sharing a secret.

"He makes me feel strange. It's like he is studying me. I am afraid he is going to ask something of me that I will be punished for doing. Yet he is a guest in the house. How can I refuse?"

"Ask what kind of thing?"

"I don't know."

Zoe quickly forgot what I said, because she had other matters of interest. "I overheard the mistress tell Priscilla that we would have other guests in a few days."

"Who else is coming?"

"Lady Junia, Mistress Abigail's cousin, and her daughter, Apphia."

"Oh?" I asked. Philemon had told me a few days before that his mother wanted him to marry his cousin, Apphia, from Colossae. I had listened, but didn't pay much attention. "That isn't Timothy's sister?"

"No, she is a cousin of the mistress and Timothy's mother, Eunice. I think this couple, Aquila and Priscilla, will go to Lystra with Timothy soon."

"Good. I will be glad for Timothy to leave."

She laughed. As Zoe left the room, she stepped close to me and kissed my cheek. I blushed and that caused her to giggle. I had never thought of another woman since Rhoda. It felt wrong to be unfaithful to her, but I would never see her again. For all I knew, she was dead. If Philemon were to marry, then I would not be allowed to sleep outside his door. Would he let me marry? Surely, he would; he always said that I was his brother.

I left Philemon's room, knowing I should be near the study in case I was needed. As I arrived, the group was leaving.

"Onesimus, show Paul to his room," Philemon said, his hand on Paul's shoulder. "He is tired from his journey. Give him whatever he needs."

"Of course, Master."

"I want to talk more about this with you, Paul." Philemon added.

As I passed by the study door, I could see that Archippus was studying the scroll of Isaiah. He had a look of surprise and fear. Why should he be afraid, I thought?

We went up the stairs to the second floor. I noticed that Paul's limp bothered him on the stairs. "If the climb is difficult for you, I will ask my master to make different room arrangements."

"No, no," he said with difficulty. "Wherever they put me is fine."

When we got to the top of the stairs, he took a deep breath. He was not tired, but an injury made the climb difficult. I waited for him. He signaled to go on and I led him to a fine room that had two windows. One opened to the patio below and the opposite window opened to city, with a fine view of the Artemesium.

"May I ask you some questions, Onesimus?" Paul sat on the edge of the bed. His inquisitive look bore into me. I wondered what he could want from me.

"I am your servant while you are here."

"Pfff," he waved his hand as if getting rid of a bug. "I am not looking for a servant, but just want to ask you some questions." He indicated I should sit at the only chair in the room, but I did not. "Were you born a slave?"

"No, I was born free." I looked out the door to make sure nobody was looking.

"Where are you from and how did you become a slave?"

"From Dacia, I think. We called ourselves Getae, though the Romans call that area Dacia. I don't know how old I was, maybe five. Men came to our village early in the morning. They destroyed everything. I was taken with others. All of us who were taken were children. I don't know if they killed those in the village or not. I never saw them again."

"Your master calls you his brother."

"Yes, he does."

"Well?"

"I don't know your question."

"Is Philemon your brother?"

"Of course, not. I am his slave." I knew he could detect the anger behind my answer.

"Then why does he call you his brother?"

"He is my master and can call me what he wishes. I am still his slave."

"Tell me what you think about what you read in Isaiah?"

"He is an interesting writer."

"I mean what did you think of what he wrote."

I heard footsteps and turned to see Timothy had just come up the stairs and was coming this way.

“I am just a slave and my thoughts don’t matter.” Before he could respond, I left the room and headed for the stairs.

“Onesimus,” Timothy stopped in front of me. I feared looking directly in his eyes and again being accused of insolence, so I kept my eyes on the floor. “Look at me.”

Though he requested it, I dared not, but I raised my head a little, keeping my eyes lowered. He waited, maybe waiting for me to say something.

“Don’t bother Paul. He is getting old and tires easily. Don’t waste his time asking foolish questions.”

“Of course, Master Timothy.” I had never addressed him as master, though I knew it was what he expected.

“What were you talking to him about just now?”

“I was making sure he was comfortable. He will not be bothered by me.”

“Good.” He waited again. There was something he wanted to say, but he didn’t. “You may go.”

“Yes, Master.” I left seething inside, hating Timothy. I wanted to sneak into his room and kill him in his sleep. Everyone would know it was me. I would be beaten and then sent to the arena to be brutally killed by gladiators. It would be worth it. If I couldn’t be free, I would rather be dead.

Paul stayed for almost a month. Every Sabbath he spoke in the Synagogue. It had been a long time since I had been allowed in the

Synagogue, so I stood outside and waited. The first week, as people were leaving, they commented on his interesting ideas. By the last week, some left angry.

We learned in the first few days that Aquila and Priscilla were staying in Ephesus to work with the few Christians that were here. I did not know there were Christians in the city, but it seems there were about a dozen before Paul arrived.

Philemon was asked to find them a suitable place to live. There was a rental house nearby, owned by Archippus. It was small, but roomy enough for the two. For them, the most important room was a large gathering room that opened to the street. Originally it was meant to be a storehouse or shop, but Aquila wanted to use it as a place to gather with the other Christians here as quickly as they were situated. Archippus insisted they live there for free.

Archippus met privately with Paul almost every day. A few times I was there to look for books, but mostly I was doing errands for Archippus or Philemon somewhere in the villa or in the city.

When I was there, Paul was always expounding on some verse in one of the prophets, telling how it related to Jesus. I remembered many of these prophecies. He was to be born of a virgin. He was a Nazarene, but born in Bethlehem, and to live in Egypt as a child. He would be spat upon, beaten, and left to die, though none of his bones would be broken. He would heal the sick and raise the dead. Paul told how Jesus had fulfilled all of these. This Jesus was an amazing man, if all these stories about him were true.

Philemon asked if the stories were true many times. Paul repeatedly reminded him that so many had witnessed his ministry, his death, and met him after his resurrection. Already some, a man named Stephen and another named James, had died for their beliefs. They believed he had risen from the dead and refused to recant their beliefs even when threatened with death.

Many times, Paul tried to talk to me alone. I avoided him. I don't know why, but he scared me. I think it was fear that he would cause me trouble. I don't know exactly, but he wanted something from me I wasn't ready to give.

Then one day, Archippus was ready to take the next step.

"Paul," he started. "I know you are leaving soon, but before you leave, I want to become a follower of Jesus."

"Then what is stopping you?"

Archippus laughed, "Nothing I suppose."

"Archippus," Paul said leaning closer to him. "You are not required to do anything to become a follower of Jesus. If you believe that He lived a sinless life, died in place of you, and rose again so one day you will rise to meet Him in Heaven, then you are one of his."

"You don't have to do anything else?"

"You spoke of baptism recently," Abigail added. "Is this a requirement?"

"It is not required, but it tells the world that you are his follower. When you are baptized, symbolically you are buried with Christ. When you come out of the water, it is like you are raised with him. You bury the old life and are resurrected to a new life."

"Like Father," Alyx added timidly, "I want to be a follower of Christ. Will you baptize me before you leave, so I can tell the world I am one of His followers?"

"I can do it today," Paul indicated the pool in the middle of the patio. Alyx laughed.

"And me, Paul," Abigail added.

Paul looked at Archippus, "May we use the pool in the courtyard?"

"I am head of this house. You may use the pool, but under one condition. I ask that you baptize me first, so I can lead my family in their walk with Christ."

Philemon had not said a word. Paul looked at him.

"I would also like to be baptized." He said finally.

"I want to pray with you and your family."

"Pray, like we do in the synagogue?" Archippus asked.

"Not a formal prayer, but something more personal. I want you to repeat what I say, but I want you to think about the meaning of what I say and say it from your heart." Paul looked around the table. "Will you do that?"

They all nodded their heads in agreement. Abigail took Archippus' hand.

"Father God," Paul said.

"Father God," they repeated, as they repeated every phrase of the prayer.

"I have searched for your truth my entire life, only to discover that I am a sinner, unworthy of your grace. You have shown me that Christ provided a way for me that I never could when he died on the Cross. By faith, I accept Christ's gift of salvation. By faith, I choose you as my Lord. By faith, I will follow you the rest of my life. Thank you for bearing my sins on the Cross and giving me the gift of eternal life. Come into my heart, Lord Jesus, and be my Savior, Amen."

"Amen," they all repeated.

"Now, if I am going to baptize you, you will need to change into something you don't mind getting wet."

Alyx laughed and was first to leave. As Abigail was leaving, she stopped to kiss Paul on the cheek.

When we were alone, Paul looked at me. Before he could ask me anything, I said, "I should go help Philemon."

But I pondered the words of the prayer. It moved me.

All four quickly changed into simpler robes. When they returned, Archippus had the slaves gathered to watch the ceremony. Many had listened to Paul, Aquila, and Priscilla speak and had talked among themselves about what they said. Some were curious and wanted to know more. Now they were seeing something they never imagined. All four members of the house were standing in the courtyard pool. When the children were little, they were never allowed to play in the pool, but now the adults were waist-deep in the water.

Archippus stood by Paul and addressed the household. "I have been a searcher all my life. I traveled to many corners of the Empire as a soldier and businessman. I have wondered what the secret was to true happiness. I never found it. Growing older, I feared death more and more. Had I done right in the eyes of the gods? I began to search the Hebrew scriptures, the religion of my wife. I discovered I am a sinful man, who does not merit favors from God. These past few weeks, my nephew Timothy, and my new friend Paul," he put his hand on Paul's back, "have taught me that I am hopeless. I cannot do anything that pays my way into God's favor. I have come to see that the man, Jesus, died in my place, so that one day, if I just have faith, I will see God face-to-face." He looked around at his many slaves. "I am this day, giving my life to Christ." He indicated that Paul take over.

"Archippus, because of your testimony of faith, I baptize you in the name of the Father, the Son, and the Holy Spirit." Gently Paul lowered him into the water and then lifted him out.

With each of the others he asked why they wanted to be baptized.

"I follow my husband in believing that Jesus has died for me," Abigail said.

"Because I love what Jesus has done for me," Alyx said, "I do this to show that I love Him in return."

"At first, I doubted what you told me about Jesus, but as the weeks have passed, I see that it is true. I want, like my father, to lead this house into following Jesus."

Paul, repeated what he did with Archippus, gently lowering them into the water and saying, "I baptize you in the name of the Father, the Son, and the Holy Spirit."

Some of the slaves stared, uncomprehending. Some clapped. A few cried. I was unsure what to think. To me it seemed like a strange religion that only the rich could participate in. As a slave, I could only do as told. I could not follow this god of theirs. They would never want me to participate in their religion as an equal.

Two days later, as Paul was preparing to leave with Timothy, who was taking him back to Lystra where he could continue his journey to Jerusalem, Paul requested that I come to his room and help him pack. Dutifully, I went.

"Onesimus, I wanted to speak with you before I leave," Paul said when I entered. He indicated I should sit.

"It would be improper," I said.

"I don't care about propriety," Paul said. "When I am speaking to someone, I want to look at them in the eye. I am becoming an old man and sometimes it feels better to sit. So sit!"

I looked hesitantly out the door, but did as he instructed.

"Don't worry. If one of them comes into the room, I will say I ordered you to sit."

I took a deep breath, unsure how to respond.

"Onesimus, I can see you are a good man, obedient to your masters, but you are not happy."

How should I respond to that?

"My masters are good to me. I am as happy as I should be."

"That is an obedient answer, from a slave, but as a man, you are not happy."

No one had ever considered me to be a person, except this man, Paul. My happiness had never been anyone's concern.

"I don't know how to respond to you, Paul. The things you say to me would create problems for me if they overheard us. How do you expect me to respond? I am a slave. I have been beaten once for trying to escape. I was always told I should appreciate what they have given me. What is that? I am not free. I cannot walk out that door and be a man like you. I cannot say what I think. If I am better at something than my master, I must hide it. My ability to memorize makes me a valuable piece of property, not a man of worth."

"The day I met you, Onesimus, I heard a voice." Paul reached out to put his hand on my shoulder. The touch of friendship made me shudder. He pulled his hand back with a look of sadness on his face.

"I have heard the voice of God. I don't say this as a way of saying I am superior to you or others, but it is a voice I recognize."

"What did he say?"

"He told me that I was meeting you for a reason. I believe that I came here to lead Archippus' household to Christ, but never has a day passed that I do not believe that I was sent here for you."

"What do you mean?"

"God has a plan for your life, Onesimus."

I remembered long ago, while I was a child locked in a cage, crying for my mother, a man saying the same thing to me.

"Paul, I will grow old and die in this house. I was told this on my first day here. Nothing has changed."

"I do believe you will die in this house one day, but you are still destined for more."

"What?" I asked sarcastically.

"You will travel as many miles as I have. You will see places you have never dreamed of. I believe you will know Christ, the man I am a witness to, and be his witness to lands far from here."

I stood and looked out the door nervously.

"Paul, I respect you. You are a kind man, and wise. I see the things you have taught my master's household. It is good for them, but not for me." I took a deep breath. "But you are wrong about me. I am a nobody. I am a slave."

I removed the robe from my shoulder, so he could see the scars on my back from the beating. "I have been beaten. I have learned my place."

I left with him calling for me to come back. What insanity? I would travel the world? I would never leave my master's house, except to be buried.

Paul left that same day.

CHAPTER 7
MARRIAGE

This is now bone of my bone and flesh of my flesh; she shall be called woman, for she was taken out of man. Genesis 2:23

We soon learned that Archippus had negotiated a marriage contract for Philemon with Apphia, the daughter of Abigail's cousin, Junia.

Junia was the widow of a wealthy Jew from Colossae. Her money was in investments at Archippus' banking firm, with a regular return that provided her and her daughter a life of luxury. The house in Colossae was willed to Apphia, the daughter, with the stipulation that Junia could live there the rest of her life. Normally a house would be willed to a son, but Apphia had no brother. In Greek society, it was expected that she would marry and the house pass to her husband. It was a villa easily as luxurious at Archippus' villa in Ephesus, though a little smaller.

On visits to Colossae, Philemon had met them more than once. When Eunice, Timothy's mother, had suggested the idea of a union between the two, Philemon always smiled. He liked the idea, but said nothing. Several months ago, it had been suggested that the mother and daughter visit Ephesus. Archippus had already begun making marriage plans.

What Philemon did not know is that the mother and daughter had become Christians. Paul had visited Colossae on his journey between Ephesus and Lystra. Junia and Apphia had been in the market when Paul arrived and were immediately drawn to his teaching. Over the next few days, they had sat at the feet of Paul, listening to him speak. Before Paul left, both had begged to be baptized. Colossae now had a growing group of followers of Christ, being taught by a young man named Demas. The Jewish rabbis would not let them meet in the synagogue, so Junia had volunteered her villa. Neither Junia and Apphia, nor Philemon and his family, knew that the others were leading very similar lives.

Apphia, however, was frightened, not that she didn't like Philemon, but afraid that he might not approve of her new found faith in Jesus. For months, she had worried about coming to meet her distant cousin, Philemon again. There were days she did not eat because of worry and often seen crying when she was alone.

"Mother, can't we get out of this arrangement?" She begged in tears as they approached Ephesus in their private carpentum, a carriage that Philemon had bought for the express purpose of transporting Junia and Apphia to Ephesus.

"We signed a contract. The only way we can get out of it now, is if both sides agree." Junia looked nervously out of the window, frightened for her daughter.

Apphia bit her knuckles as she looked out the opposite window of the carriage. How would her future husband, reputed to be a devout Jew, react to her new religion?

Philemon had been discussing the same thing with his mother only days before. He feared that Apphia would react the same as his sister Diana had to the news of the family's new religion.

Three weeks before, Diana had arrived one morning, asking to meet with her mother. Things began cordially enough, with Diana kissing her mother's cheek. She had brought her mother a bolt of dark pink silk decorated with burgundy and yellow flowers.

"Thank you for the gift," Abigail said examining the silk. "This will make a lovely dress for Apphia when she arrives."

"You are welcome, Mother," Diana said uncomfortably waving away a slave's offer of sweetened wine.

"You seem upset, dear," Abigail said, putting the silk to the side.

"I am, Mother."

"Tell me what the problem is."

"Mother," Diana said, her cheeks flushing with anger. "Is it true what I have heard said around Ephesus?"

"What have you heard?"

"That you have been entertaining the teachings of that 'dangerous sect' of the Christians."

"What do you mean entertaining?" Abigail folded her hands in her lap and became very still. She noticed her daughter's attitude and wondered to herself how she should react.

"Some are saying that you have become a follower of that sect." Diana shook her head, indicating that such a thing could not be possible. "You are a reasonable person. I know the rumors must be false."

"I am a Christian, Diana," Abigail said softly. "I am a follower of the dangerous sect you speak of."

"Why would you do that?" Diana asked aghast. "You know that will only create problems for our family. This sect is causing disturbances throughout the Empire. Many have been arrested and a few have even been executed because they follow this Jesus."

"I am aware of this, but I have listened to the teachings of Paul. It answered in me a longing I have had my whole life."

"Mother!" she exclaimed in exasperation.

"For years," Abigail explained, "I have wondered why there was such an emptiness in my heart. I wondered about the suffering in the world. I wondered if the answers I was always given in the synagogue were sufficient. Now I know that Christ has died for my sins."

"Sins? We give a yearly donation to have a lamb sacrificed in Jerusalem. What more is needed?"

"King David said, 'You do not delight in sacrifice, or I would bring it. You do not take pleasure in burnt offering. The sacrifices of God are a broken spirit; a broken and contrite heart.'"

"You are embarrassing me and my husband in front of the governor. He asked my husband about this the other day."

"Jesus is the Messiah, Diana. He is God's lamb, who was sacrificed for my sins. I cannot deny him."

Diana stood and smoothed out the wrinkles on her dress. "If you will not desist, Mother, then I can no longer acknowledge you as family. That is what my husband, Quintus Tertullius, has decided. This is why I came today."

"My Savior told his disciples, 'What good is it for a man to gain the whole world, yet forfeit his soul? If anyone is ashamed of me and my words in this adulterous and sinful generation, the Son of Man will be ashamed of him when he comes in his Father's glory with the holy angels.'"

"Your decision is to continue following this Christ?"

"Yes."

"Even if it means losing your daughter?" Her voice was shrill.

Tears began to stream down Abigail's face. "I will not deny my Christ. Even for you."

"Then I am no longer your daughter."

Diana walked out of the villa, never to return.

That was the situation when Junia and Apphia arrived.

It was a sunny spring morning, with flowers blooming and birds singing. What more could one ask of a love story? Abigail had insisted on everything being above reproach, so had Junia and Apphia placed in a rental house. It would be more comfortable in the villa, but some might talk, because people always do. Before the marriage, because of where she lived, I rarely saw Apphia unless she was visiting for dinner or I was delivering something to their house.

But I saw her that first morning. She was not exactly beautiful, but I was prejudiced against any woman, after being in love with Rhoda. She had the normal brown hair and brown eyes of most Jewish girls. Her complexion was good, without blemish. Her skin was white, because like most women of the upper class, she did not venture out of the house much. When she arrived, her head was modestly covered.

Abigail was overflowing with cheer as they entered the villa.

"Junia," she said kissing her cheek. "It has been years since I last saw you."

"Abigail," Junia returned the kiss. "We were both young. Now look at us!" Junia gripped both of Abigail's hands. "We have both aged, haven't we?"

Both women laughed. "I already have two married daughters," Abigail continued. "Both are older than we were when I last saw you."

"This is my daughter, Apphia," Junia said pushing her daughter forward. The girl was shy. She didn't look at Abigail in the eyes. There was a quiet terror in those eyes.

"Don't be afraid, dear Apphia." Abigail lifted her chin.

"Abigail, my daughter wishes you to know something important before we go any further with plans for the marriage." Abigail looked concerned. "I heard that Timothy has been here recently. Knowing him, he told you about his new faith."

Abigail smiled. "Yes, Timothy has been here. And Paul."

"Apphia wants you to know that she is a follower of Christ."

"My dear," Abigail wrapped Apphia in her arms. "We have listened to Paul and we also believe. We are followers of the Way of Christ and were baptized by Paul before he left. He left two of his disciples here, Aquila and his wife, Priscilla. They are teaching us more about Christ. We are not afraid to let the world know we are believers in Jesus Christ."

"Philemon too?" Apphia asked in a whisper.

"My son too." Apphia sighed in relief.

Philemon appeared. Abigail greeted him with the joyful news that Apphia and her mother were also followers of Jesus.

Philemon's joy was complete. He saw before him a woman who was not only beautiful, but also a believer. He would be proud to present her as his wife.

She averted her eyes. I wondered about this. Was she shy? As the years passed, I realized she was not shy. She was raised differently than girls in Ephesus. She was demure, a modesty taught to her as the way a woman should behave in a world of men.

She was small. Philemon had grown and was now tall. He towered over her. He bent down to kiss her on the cheek.

"Welcome to Ephesus, Apphia. Anything you desire is yours for the asking."

Quietly she responded with a "thank you."

Alyx was excited, seemingly more so than the others. "Welcome, dear sister." They were the same age and looked much the same. They could have been sisters. "I am so glad you are here," she kissed her cheek and then hugged her tightly.

Apphia laughed.

"It has been so boring in this house without my sisters."

"I hope you and I will grow to become like sisters." Apphia smiled as Alyx took her on a tour of the villa.

Agata was still Abigail's personal slave, but did not get around as easily as in the past. The mistress decided that Zoe, who had been Diana's maid before her marriage and knew the intricacies of the house as well as Agata, should be her personal slave. But while Junia and Apphia were in a house down the road, Zoe was instructed to attach herself to Apphia, to make her feel at home, and to teach her how things were done in Ephesus.

With an upcoming marriage, things would change in the villa. Alyx still had her rooms on the second floor. She had a new slave since Rhoda had been sold, but she never became attached to Selene.

Archippus had long shared a room with his wife, but recently he was restless most nights. I suspected he was ill, but it was not my place to say anything. Most nights, he stayed in the library reading throughout the night. Next to the library was a small room, barely large enough to fit more than a bed and night table. Archippus had made it his sleeping room, so he would not disturb his wife when he had a sleepless night.

Abigail thought it was fitting that her son, who would one day be master of the house, should have the master suite. This included a bedroom, a room for the mistress' use, which would now be Apphia, and private bath. There was another bath for the family and in the basement one for the slaves, but this bath was exclusive to the master. There was also a room for personal storage, and two small cubicles for personal slaves. The master's suite covered the entire southern side of the villa. Abigail moved into what had been Philemon's rooms.

Before a marriage would happen, the rooms were repainted with new frescos, tiles were replaced, and newer, more appropriate, furnishings were bought or refinished for each room.

There was another bedroom on the ground floor, but it was not used often. Before Eunice was widowed, if she visited with her husband, this became their room, but she did not visit often enough to make a claim on it. Now Philemon decided he needed an office where he could conduct business, separate from his father's library.

There was a small cubicle connected to this room. It was now my sleeping room. It was larger than what I had had since I arrived in the house. Not only did it have room for a bed, but also a table. Since I was often doing business for Philemon, I needed a place to write. It was also a place where I could read in the evenings. Since I was allowed access to the library, I read everything. There were fantastic stories, love poems, philosophy, and dramas. I loved them all. I remembered them all. I could roll out the scroll to the exact phrase that moved me the most.

Aquila was a regular visitor in the house. I rarely heard his discussions with Archippus, but I slowly learned that the master was searching the scriptures of the Jews because he was afraid of his mortality. I remember one day I was there. Philemon was on the other side of the city, so Archippus asked me to sit in on a meeting, so I could find scrolls for him.

"I have been wondering about something I read in Isaiah about men perishing."

"Can you locate that, Onesimus?" Aquila asked, as he sat down.

I unrolled the Isaiah scroll to the place Archippus referred to. "Read it for me," he instructed.

"The righteous perish, and no one ponders it in his heart; devout men are taken away, and no one understands."

"What does this mean?" He asked faintly. In the past, Archippus could walk all over Ephesus and seemed filled with energy. Lately, he could hardly walk from one room to another without being out of breath. His eyes had dark circles around them, though he slept half the day. Archippus put his hand over his stomach, because lately his stomach always seemed to pain him. He took a drink of water. He could no longer tolerate wine without becoming ill. Still the water made him cough.

"As with much written in the prophets, some deals with issues at the time of the prophecy." Aquila leaned forward to look at the passage and I backed away. "At the time he wrote this, King Hezekiah had just died. He was a good king who supported the devout in his country. And now Manasseh, his son, was king. He would prove to be an evil king who led his people away from God and persecuted those who remained faithful."

Archippus was quiet, pondering the scroll. He touched the spot where the verse was written, as if the touch would make it real in his mind.

"What are you thinking, my friend?" Aquila asked.

Archippus coughed again. "Is it possible that he is warning us of some future event?"

"What do you mean?"

"You said that King Manasseh was an evil king who persecuted believers. Is this something we, as believers, can look forward to today or in the near future?"

"The scriptures clearly say that the righteous will be persecuted." Archippus looked at his friend with a deep sadness.

"Making this choice to become a follower of Jesus could mean persecution for my family?"

"It could mean that."

"My son-in-law has ordered my daughter, Diana, to have nothing to do with us. My wife is heartbroken."

"I have heard this about Diana. I am so sorry, my friend." He paused before continuing. "Jesus told his disciples that the servant is not greater than his master. Jesus suffered much." Aquila looked at me when he said that. "Jesus told his disciples that they should expect to be persecuted like he was persecuted and the prophets were persecuted. It is the cost of being a disciple."

"What have you lost, Aquila?"

Aquila put his hands on his knees and looked at the floor. "I had a profitable business in both Rome and Capua that my family ran for four generations. We were more Roman than Jewish. My wife and I accepted Christ at the same time Claudius issued the decree to banish all Jews from Rome. My son gained special permission to stay because he rejected Judaism, as well as rejecting his parents and their new faith in Christ."

"I did not know this."

"We have not heard from our son in ten years. Our grandson should be sixteen years of age now. Priscilla cries many nights, longing for her son and grandson."

The sad expression on Aquila's face was different from the man I had come to know. Usually he was laughing and smiling. Nothing seemed to faze him. If someone insulted him in the market, calling him a fool, he would smile and say he is most certainly a fool. When someone insulted him like that, he usually repaid them with an act of kindness, forgetting that an insult was ever given.

"I fear the same thing might happen to my family."

"What will you do if this happens?"

Archippus spoke up immediately. "I will never forsake my Savior."

With the new religion of my masters, my duties were becoming a strange mix. I helped Philemon with business paper-work, or delivering messages, contracts, and money from one place to another. He knew I could remember, word for word, anything on paper, so copying contracts and such filled a great part of my day.

Philemon had another slave who took care of his clothes and cleaned his rooms. I had learned that Apphia did not like a night water pot in her room, so Philemon was learning to take care of that business in the bath room. I could not change his bad behavior, but a woman did.

About half of my day involved being a servant to Archippus and to Aquila. Archippus relied on me to keep his library organized and to help him find where things were. Most mornings I organized the previous day's readings and searched for new things he wanted. If he mentioned a subject, I could find it in a dozen different books.

Helping Aquila, Philemon felt, was his Christian ministry. He had the financial means to support one who shared Christ with the masses of Ephesus. Lending his slave was as valuable as money. At first, I helped Aquila become familiar with Ephesus, where things were located, who could make this or sell that, which vendor could be trusted and which would cheat you. Aquila tended to ignore the part about who would cheat; that was the vendor he usually sought out.

Aquila spent a part of his day making acquaintances with people in the city. He was a tent maker. That meant he made tents and awnings for shop owners and vendors in the markets, or repaired those that became damaged by wind or use. His prices were cheap, because he was not in the business for profit, but to become acquainted with the people of Ephesus.

He walked around the market, asking about a sick relative, a sad child, a widowed mother, or an upcoming marriage. He surprised everyone because his concern was real. He never asked about someone's problems without saying a prayer. He never asked them if he could pray, he just did.

After a woman would tell him her problems with her husband and sick child, he would counter with, "Let me take a moment and pray for you."

He told people, men, women, and youths, about Jesus. He always shared how Jesus had changed his life. People asked questions and he always asked them to come to his house on the first day of the week to learn more. For those who said they could not take off work that day, he made a point to visit during the week, usually telling them what he had shared at his house. After a few weeks of this, they could usually find time to visit on the first day of the week. Early on that day, he would sit with whoever showed up and teach them about Jesus.

Philemon attended the synagogue with regularity. Archippus never missed a Sabbath, even if he was sick. The rabbis knew he was a Greek, but he gave regular offerings that they coveted, so they did not discourage him from being there.

As the weeks turned into months, Aquila rarely asked me for help navigating the city. He used me, like Philemon, for my ability to accurately memorize what I saw written. When I was with him, in the market, he would ask for a passage from Isaiah, Zechariah, or Jeremiah to help lend credence to his explanation. At first, it seemed like he tested me, but soon, he knew I would be accurate.

For me, personally, Isaiah was just another writer. Some of what he wrote seemed confused and out of order, while some of it was the most beautiful poetry ever written. But it never changed who I was, a slave of the House of Archippus.

Because of Aquila, there were now two groups of believers that met each week. There was a small community that had been here before the arrival of Paul. Aquila taught that community and had enlarged it by several dozen. This group met early in the morning, shortly after sunrise, in Aquila's house.

Aquila was invited to teach the group at Philemon's house later in the day. Those who came were mostly Jewish, stirred by Paul's teachings and wanting to learn more. There were also a few prominent Greeks and Romans of Ephesus that had business dealings with Philemon. They knew nothing about Jesus, so tended to ask many questions and seemed filled with doubt.

"How is it that Jesus had to die, as you say?" Alexander Rufus, a Hellenized Jew from Pontus asked one day.

"You are quick to call him the Messiah, but that is not how we were taught about the Messiah." Aristarchus, a Hellenized Jew added.

"What do you mean by Messiah?" Brutus Gallicus, a Roman bureaucrat living in Asia, asked.

"Messiah is a term the Jews use for the man who would deliver his people, the Jews, from their oppressors and captors," Philemon explained.

"To answer your question, Alexander," Aquila responded. "We Jews have only been told half of the story. The Messiah who is to come and put an end to all Israel's enemies, is still expected, but at some future date."

"So, what is it that makes Jesus the Messiah?" Leonidas, the ship captain asked.

"Paul explains that the prophecies are layered with things of the time of the prophets and things of the future. There are prophecies of Jesus, as the Messiah who will put an end to Israel's enemies. But among those layers are the prophecies only recently fulfilled by Jesus as the one who suffers for the sins of his people."

"Such as?" Brutus asked with a bit of irritation.

"A lengthy part near the end of Isaiah talks about the Messiah, being a man who was not attractive, who was despised, who was stricken by God, who was punished and wounded, and took upon himself our sins."

When Aquila said something like this, they always wanted to read it directly from the source. That meant I would find the Isaiah scroll and open it to the selection.

Some of these men were won over by these arguments, but most just came week after week to participate in the debate.

One hot summer day, as I was returning from the dock, I noticed a man standing at the entrance to the Temple of Artemis. He was speaking to a small crowd gathered around him. At first, I ignored what he said, but then I caught his words.

"Jesus is the man the prophets spoke of the voice of one crying in the wilderness." I remembered what the prophet spoke of; the voice was John the Baptist who prepared the way for Jesus. That is what Paul said, and I had heard Aquila say the same thing repeatedly.

This man seemed to know a lot about Jesus, but some of his facts were off. He confused something written by David with something written by Zechariah. I pondered what to do. My master would want to meet this man. I was on my way to Aquila's house, so it seemed right to take this man with me.

"Excuse me, Sir," I said to him when he had finished.

"What do you want?" he asked defensively.

"I am Onesimus," he frowned at my name.

"My master is Philemon. He is a believer in this Jesus you speak about." Now he looked at me curiously. "I am on my way to the home of Aquila, a man trained by Paul."

He did not seem impressed upon hearing the name Paul.

"I would be remiss if I did not invite you to their home. They would expect it of me."

"I have many things to do, young man."

"Knowing Aquila's wife, Priscilla, she will feed you a hearty meal."

The man must have been hungry because his countenance changed immediately. Soon this man, whose name was Apollos, was seated with Aquila and eating like he had been deprived of food for weeks.

Apollos was from Alexandria in Egypt. He was dark, showing he was more Egyptian than Greek. After an encounter with Peter, a disciple of Jesus, he felt he was supposed to travel beyond his home and share the gospel message. He had a good heart, but was not well informed.

"I intend to go to Corinth, in the province of Achaea, as soon as I can afford passage."

"We are well acquainted with Corinth."

"That is where we were before we came here with Paul," Priscilla explained.

"Then you can give me a letter of introduction?"

"We can, but first we want to make sure you fully understand about Jesus."

"I don't need to know more. I am excited about my faith in Jesus and am ready to tell as many people as I can about him."

"If you don't have your facts straight and misquote the prophets, then you do need some training."

"Why do you assume I don't know what the prophets said?"

"Because you were quoting them wrong," I spoke up.

"And how do you, a Greek slave know that?"

"I am not Greek by birth. But I have sat through the training of my master, Philemon, as he studied Greek, Latin, and Hebrew."

"Onesimus also has an uncanny gift from God. He can remember anything he has ever read. Have you studied Hebrew?" Aquila asked.

"I can read it, but have not studied it much. I heard Peter quote from the prophets often."

"If you are going to share information from the prophets, then you need to be prepared to share them correctly."

"I don't see how that matters. I just want to tell others about Jesus."

"It matters for two reasons. One, you need to accurately know what the prophets said about Jesus and be able to quote from them correctly. A well-educated Jew might catch your mistake and decide not to follow Jesus because of your errors." Apollos shrugged his shoulder at that. "Two, I will not write you a letter of introduction to the believers in Corinth if you do not agree to stay and learn."

"We have a nice guest room," Priscilla added. "And it looks like you need a little more food on a regular basis."

"But I should be about my business," Apollos insisted less defensively.

"Jesus waited many years till he began his ministry. He took time to get alone with God in the wilderness. Paul, our teacher, spent the years of his youth learning the scriptures under Gamaliel. And then he spent more years learning from the Holy Spirit in the wilderness. A few months will not hurt you, but will make you stronger."

So, the fiery Apollos became a new fixture in the Christian community of Ephesus. Like the others, he quickly learned that I knew the scriptures by heart. When he quoted one wrongly, I showed him the exact place where it was found. Humility was something he learned slowly.

The villa's restorations were complete. According to custom, Archippus said they were ready for the new bride. The marriage was upon us. It began at sunset on the summer solstice. It was a hot and still night, that caused the smell of jasmine to fill the air around the villa.

A dozen of Philemon's friends and relatives, all as young as him, joined us as we set out for the synagogue. I and six other slaves were carrying torches. We entered the synagogue and the rabbi read a psalm of blessing for the marriage.

"May God be gracious to you and bless you and make his face shine upon you, that his ways may be known on earth, his salvation among all nations. May the peoples praise you, O God; may all the peoples praise you. May the nations be glad and sing for joy, for you rule the peoples justly and guide the nations of the earth. May the peoples praise you, O God; may all the peoples praise you. Then the land will yield its harvest, and God, our God, will bless us. God bless us. God bless us, and all the ends of the earth will fear him."

"Amen," Philemon said.

"Amen," chimed in Philemon's party.

"May God bless you on this, your wedding night," the rabbi said smiling.

The men cheered and led Philemon out of the synagogue, singing a passage from the Song of Solomon.

"We rejoice and delight with you, we will praise your love more than wine." Some were already drunk and laughed loudly.

Timothy walked next to Philemon, whispering in his ear, making him laugh nervously. I couldn't hear what was said, even though I was on Philemon's other side, carrying the torch.

Some people heard the ruckus and looked out their windows or doors and shouted after us.

"Have fun tonight, Philemon." One man called from his stoop.

"God bless your house." A woman said leaning out her window.

"I hope the girl is as pretty as they say." A youth said in passing.

Soon we stood at the front of the house of Junia and Apphia. Philemon walked to the door alone and stood for a moment, looking nervously at the door.

"Go on. Don't be nervous," Timothy said.

Philemon knocked.

For a moment, there was silence. Then a voice from within asked, "Who disturbs us at this time of night?"

"I, Philemon, of the House of the Tribune Archippus."

"What do you want with us at this hour?"

One of the companions laughed.

"I have come to claim my bride, the Lady Apphia."

Philemon's companions laughed.

The door opened with a squeak. Junia's face was the first we saw, lit by a candle. She was dressed in her finest silk and brocades, with gold around her neck and in her ears.

But she paled to the beauty of Apphia when she emerged. She was in a dark red gown with milk-white brocade work on the breast and sleeves. Her head was covered by a diaphanous white veil. The jewels on her wrists, neck, and ears sparkled in the torchlight.

Philemon offered his arm. She lowered her head, and knowing her, she probably blushed, but it was too dark to know for sure. She lightly placed her hand on his arm and Philemon's chest swelled with pride.

Again, the men began to sing as we started down the road. We made quite a raucous parade with Apphia and her attendants added to Philemon and his young men.

"How beautiful you are, my darling! Oh, how beautiful!" The young men sang. "Your eyes behind your veil are doves. Your hair is like a flock of goats descending from Mount Gilead. Your teeth are like a flock of sheep just shorn, coming up from the washing. Each has its twin; not one of them is alone," Apphia put her hand to her face in embarrassment. "Your lips are like a scarlet ribbon; your mouth is lovely. Your temples behind your veil are like the halves of a pomegranate."

Apphia's attendants began to sing their own song.

"Awake, north wind, and come, south wind! Blow on my garden, that its fragrance may spread abroad. Let my lover come into his garden and taste its choice fruits." This caused the men to laugh more. "My lover is mine and I am his; he browses among the lilies. Until the day breaks and the shadows flee, turn, my lover, and be like a young gazelle or like a young stag on the rugged hills."

As they finished the song, we arrived at the villa. Standing in the courtyard was Archippus. At his side was Thestius carrying a basin of water. Abigail was on his other side, with Aquila, Priscilla, Apollos, and other guests behind them.

"Why do you break the silence of the night, Son?" Archippus asked.

"I bring you my bride, Apphia."

"Why do you carry these torches?"

"To light our feet as we traverse the city. We want our deeds to be revealed honestly before all mankind. Our God is light; in him there is no darkness at all. We come at night to celebrate, but we want the world to see that we follow God in all things. So we come to you bearing torches."

"Step forward daughter," Archippus commanded.

Abigail removed her veil and kissed her cheeks already wet with tears. "We greet you in our house, Daughter," she said.

Archippus took some water in his hand and poured a little over her head. "From this day forth, you are a member of my household. You will be protected, fed, and loved as one born in our house." He kissed her on the cheek and whispered, "Don't cry."

"I am so happy, I cannot help myself." She answered in a mixture of laughter and tears.

The guests began to laugh, shout, and cheer.

The patio had been arranged with dining couches, enough for all the guests. Tables had been arranged in front of the couches, with cloths covering them that made them look like one long dining table. Already there were cups ready for wine, platters filled with fruit, sweets, and hot bread.

I placed my torch in a sconce. The patio was already covered with torches and sweet-scented candles were on the tables. The room sparkled with brightness.

Before the guests sat, Aquila had the couple stand before him. Abigail put a white shawl on her son. Aquila began to read another psalm, "Unless the Lord builds the house, its builders labor in vain. Unless the Lord watches over the city, the watchmen stand guard in vain. In vain you rise early and stay up late," he said looking around at the guests and raising his voice. "Toiling for food to eat; for he grants sleep to those he loves. Sons are a heritage from the Lord, children a reward from him. Like arrows in the hands of a warrior are sons born in one's youth. Blessed is the man whose quiver is full of them. They will not be put to shame when they contend with their enemies in the gate."

"Thank you, Aquila," Philemon said.

Priscilla took the shawl and extended it over the shoulders of Apphia.

"By covering her with your shawl," Aquila continued. "You show that you will protect and care for Apphia, as you would your sister or your mother."

"I will do so," Philemon promised.

"Apphia, being a part of this family means you will serve them and care for them as if they were your own blood family."

"I will do so," Apphia promised.

"Then let us celebrate the union of these two!"

Many of the guests shouted. Some came forward and greeted Apphia with a kiss. Abigail began directing guests to places to recline for the meal.

I quietly slipped behind a pillar, where Philemon would be eating. I was not required to serve at the feast, but as always, I would be there in case he needed me. As he was sitting, Philemon noticed me and smiled at me. Politely, I bowed my head.

"She is pretty, isn't she?" I did not know that Zoe was standing next to me.

"Welcome back to the villa."

"I am glad to be home." She hugged her body, as if she were cold. "I am so happy for them. I hope they have many children."

"Oh?"

"Yes, I miss having children running around this place."

I didn't say anything. I just watched the festivities. She was quietly studying me.

"What makes you happy, Onesimus?" She asked in barely a whisper.

"Why do you ask that?"

"We have known each other for years, but I don't know what makes you happy. Some days you seem content, but others you have a look of anger or sadness about you."

"What makes you happy, Zoe?" I asked deflecting the question.

"Thinking that one day I will be allowed to marry. Having a man hold me in his arms at night and one day giving him a child. Those thoughts make me happy."

I didn't respond. I looked at her, realizing all these years, I never knew her. She had lived in this house, just like me, and had her own dreams. She was as alien to me as any other person.

"You never answered me."

I didn't answer right away. I thought about it, though I knew exactly what I would say. "I dream that one day I will be a free man, walking through the hills and forests of the land of my birth."

Zoe leaned forward and kissed me on the lips. I responded by kissing back, a pleasure I had never felt before. When she pulled away, she smiled at me and left me trying to take it all in.

Junia left a few days later for Colossae. Nervously, Apphia began taking over the duties of running the house. Abigail seemed glad to relegate the duties to her, but she was equally glad to explain how things worked and the duties of various slaves. The two became close friends.

The slaves were happy. Apphia was the kind of woman who thanked slaves for doing something well or if they went beyond what was asked. Since the household was so happy, I felt it was time to make my own request.

Philemon was in his office, reading a manifest from one of his ships that arrived the day before.

"Master, may I ask a favor of you?"

"Of course, Onesimus?" He did not look up from his reading.

"May I sit?" This was something I never asked. He was surprised. He stopped what he was doing and motioned for me to sit.

"What is this important request?"

"The house is very happy with the new mistress."

"Yes, she is a special woman I am discovering every day."

"Because of this, I was thinking it is time that I married."

At that moment, Timothy walked in the room. He didn't say a word, but listened.

"What?"

"I would like to marry Zoe."

"What?" he repeated. "Zoe, my mother's slave?"

"I have been here many years, serving you faithfully. I no longer must sleep outside of your room. I have a room of my own now."

"Why do you want to marry?"

"Zoe and I have known each other since we were both children. We are friends and…"

He interrupted me. "Onesimus, you are like a brother to me, but this is an outlandish request."

"It would be good for me and for her."

"And what if she were to become pregnant?"

"Then she and I would raise this child as a loyal servant to this house, like we both are."

"No, Onesimus."

"But Master…"

"That is all I have to say on this subject." He went back to his reading, waving me away. I stood and bowed slightly, though he did not notice.

Timothy followed me out of the room. "Wait, Onesimus."

I took a deep breath to calm myself, so I wouldn't say something I would regret.

"Yes, Master Timothy," I said trying to stay calm.

"You do understand, don't you?"

"Of course, Master."

"You are a valuable slave. If you were to marry, you would be distracted by a wife and family."

I stayed calm, knowing what he did to the last woman I had an interest in. I didn't want him involved. I didn't want Zoe harmed.

"He is doing this for your own good. Trust me."

"Yes, Master Timothy." I left as quickly as possible.

How I hated Timothy! I hated Philemon and every freeborn person in this house. I was not a brother, as he delighted in saying. I was a piece of property, nothing more. He would never see me as a brother.

I began to plan how I might escape.

CHAPTER 8
PAUL

Paul entered the synagogue and spoke boldly there... arguing persuasively about the Kingdom of God. Acts 19:8

A year later, I was with Philemon at the dock. We were saying goodbye to Apollos. It did not take a year for him to learn what Aquila taught him, and for that matter what I was able to teach him. Our house was the repository of wisdom for the Christian community of Ephesus and Apollos took advantage of it.

I became one of his greatest teachers. He would write lengthy sermons and ask me for references. He had a lot of knowledge, but he didn't know where it was from. One or two afternoons a week, he and I would spend a few hours in the library. He would read me what he had written and I would go to the shelf and take out the scroll he was trying to reference. Often, he was surprised where it was found, thinking it was Isaiah and discovering it was King David. But he learned.

Before the year was finished, he rarely misrepresented an author. That is when he felt it was time to go. Aquila wrote a letter of recommendation to the church in Corinth. Priscilla gave him a list of friends who might give him a room. Now we stood on the dock to say goodbye.

"I hope I see you again, Philemon." He shook my master's hand vigorously. Since I was a slave, he ignored me.

"That is my hope too, Apollos."

"I know you've thought about going to Rome to care for your family's investments. I hope you do."

"We'll see about that," Philemon said with a laugh.

"When you do, please visit me in Corinth."

"If ever I make it to Greece, I will most definitely do that."

Minutes later we were walking back to the villa.

"Are you again considering moving to Rome?"

"It is a wild dream."

"Let's go, Philemon."

He laughed. "Why would I want to go to Rome?"

In my mind I said, "To get away from this place that I hate so much," but I was more diplomatic with him. "It has always been your dream to see Rome. You talked about it when we were youths."

"Things are different now." He seemed content.

"But imagine what we could do there. You've always wanted to improve those investments and see the great city too."

"I've been thinking of selling my properties in Italy. My father agrees with me."

"But why?"

"This is my home," he indicated Ephesus with his arm outstretched. "I want to be with my wife and have children. I want to help the church here. I am among family and friends."

Dejectedly I walked beside him. I wanted to get out, but increasingly I saw nothing but this dreary life ahead of me.

It was not a week later that Paul arrived, with Timothy. To my relief, he insisted on renting a house near the market. Timothy would be living with him. That was even more of a relief.

The day I met Paul, was on the Sabbath. He met us at the door, as we were going to the synagogue. Nobody noticed that Paul inclined his head to me, yet he did not say a word to remind me of our last meeting.

Paul was expected in the synagogue. News of his arrival spread quickly among the Jewish community. Since his last visit, Aquila, Apollos, and Philemon had been speaking a lot about the person of Jesus. It was a common topic of discussion in Ephesus. In the market, one would ask another what he thought about Jesus. Another would tell what he had heard about Jesus and would ask another if he thought it were true.

Paul was already known to be a leader among the followers of Jesus. Stories about him were about as wild as any about Jesus. They said he had healed the sick. They said he raised someone from the dead. They said he had escaped prison in the middle of the night, only to be found seated at the gate of the prison waiting for the return of the guards the next morning. No matter what stories were told about Paul, all agreed he knew more about Jesus than any man in the province. Anxiously, the citizens of Ephesus waited for answers from Paul, including the leaders of the synagogue.

When we entered with Paul, I found a place behind a pillar to stand quietly, hoping I would not be noticed. I was known in the synagogue. I was a slave of the wealthiest Jew in Ephesus. None dared refuse me entrance, but none allowed me to sit either.

Sceva, the leader of the synagogue, stood when Paul entered. "We were just beginning, Paul." He motioned for Paul to join him at the front. "We are desirous to hear more about Jesus, whom you have taught across the Empire."

Paul stood and opened the scroll of Isaiah which was in front of him. He knew where he was going. He glanced at me and there was a flicker of a smile.

He cleared his voice and proclaimed loudly, "The Spirit of the Sovereign Lord is on me, because the Lord has anointed me to preach the good news to the poor. He has sent me to bind up the brokenhearted, to proclaim freedom for the captives," he looked at me again, smiled and continued. "And release from darkness for the prisoners, to proclaim the year of the Lord's favor."

He placed his hand on the scroll at the place he was reading. "I am here today to proclaim to you that Jesus, himself, uttered these words in the city where he was raised, Nazareth. When he was finished saying these words, he told the crowd, 'Today this scripture is fulfilled in your hearing.' This same Jesus I share with you today."

He stepped out into the assembly and continued, "One day, not so many years ago, I heard a man preach to the Sanhedrin about Jesus. He reminded our religious leaders about the history of our people. Abraham heard the voice of God, telling him, 'Leave your country and your people and go to a land I will show you.' In faith, Abraham left the land of the Chaldeans and wandered until God said, 'I will give you this land.'"

I heard someone near me whisper, "Is he going to give us a history lesson, or tell us about Jesus?"

"'Your descendants will be strangers in a land not their own,' God told Abraham. And it came to pass. For four hundred years, they served as slaves in the land of Egypt. But God did not leave them there. He sent a descendant of Abraham, Moses, to take his people out of Egypt, with miracles and signs from heaven. Moses led God's people to the Jordan River and Joshua brought them across, to defeat their enemies. Mighty judges ruled the land and defeated Israel's enemies, until God provided Israel with kings who ruled the land for many years. It was never intended for Israel to be ruled by kings, but man is ever sinful. One king, Solomon, built a mighty temple as tribute to God Almighty."

There were many voices grunting their approval when talking about the Temple. Some were nodding their heads in agreement. Some, though, seemed confused at the direction Paul was headed.

"Again, in Isaiah it says, 'Heaven is my throne, and the earth is my footstool. Where is the house you will build for me? Where will my resting place be? Has not my hand made all these things, and so they came into being?' This is what the Lord declared to Isaiah. Stephen declared to the Sanhedrin, 'You stiff-necked people, with uncircumcised hearts and ears! You are just like your fathers: You always resist the Holy Spirit! Was there ever a prophet your fathers did not persecute and kill?'"

The mood of the crowd changed. Many sat with a shocked look on their faces, while some had become angry.

"This is not what God wants from you and never has. He is not interested in your sacrifices and feast days."

"Then what does he want from us, Paul?" An elderly man asked.

Paul walked close to him and said softly. "He wants you. He wants your body as a living sacrifice. This is what is holy and pleasing to God." Paul turned to speak to the rest of the assembly. "This is your spiritual act of worship. Do not conform any longer to the pattern of this world, but be transformed by the renewing of your mind. Then you will be able to test and approve what God's will is – his good, pleasing, and perfect will."

I slipped out and stood in the morning sunshine. A cool breeze was blowing from the north. It was not winter yet, but there was a promise of it in the air.

Paul's words moved me. I did not know why. They made sense, more sense than I had ever heard spoken before. But I could not reconcile those words to me, a slave. I had to transform my life into the life desired by my master. I could not renew my mind into a servant of Christ. I was the slave of Philemon. The words sounded good, but they were not for me.

A week passed and again we were in the synagogue. The room was hushed when Paul stood to speak. He seemed like he was waiting for something. In front of him was the scroll of Jonah. I recognized it, because I had been asked to copy it once for Archippus. But Paul did not open it.

Suddenly a man near me stood. "Paul," he said. "Tell the people here how you happened to hear what that man said."

"The man was named Stephen, a devoted follower of Jesus."

"I have heard a rumor that you were there, so you heard what he said in person."

"I was. I was a student of Gamaliel. He was a member of the Sanhedrin. I was there in the room, carrying his things."

"You did not tell us what happened to that man."

"The Sanhedrin had him put to death." Paul suddenly looked tired and old to me.

"It is said, Paul, that you participated in this act. You are one of the ones who had Stephen killed. What was the method of his death?"

"Stoning." Gasps came from many. One man rose and left. Several others stood as if to leave.

"You tell us how to relate to God," a different man shouted at Paul, "yet you are one of this man's executioners. You made him sound like a great man."

"Stephen was a very great man."

"And yet, you killed him?"

"I was zealous in keeping all the laws of the Temple. I thought his beliefs were contrary to our traditions."

About a quarter of the men there left.

"It was a moment that is forever engraved in my heart and mind. Stephen had what I thought was a vision of God as he was dying. That was what I thought at the time, but now I know he saw Heaven open for him and to receive him. Do you want to know the rest of the story?" Paul shouted the last, so those at the door would hear. A few stopped and turned.

"I persecuted Christians, the same people I am now a part of." I could see the pain on Paul's face. His voice cracked. "I hunted Christians throughout the city of Jerusalem. I brought them before the Sanhedrin and accused them publicly. Some were executed. Many were imprisoned and whipped. Some died in the prison of despair. Yet, I grew bolder. One day I begged the leaders to allow me to go to Damascus, where I heard some of the leaders of the Christians were hiding. They granted me permission, gave me papers allowing me to arrest those I suspected, and even gave me a contingent of temple soldiers to protect me and do the arresting."

"How could you do that to your fellow Jews?" one man said weeping.

"We were a short distance from Damascus. We could see it in the distance. Suddenly the day went black. We stopped, terrified. A light from heaven flashed around me. It was like a fire, only brighter. It was not hot. It made me feel at peace, as if I had been wrapped in my mother's arms. A voice came out of the light and said, 'Saul, Saul, why do you persecute me?'

"I felt a deep sadness coming from the voice. The comfort I had felt only a moment before vanished. 'Who are you, Lord?' I asked falling on the ground. Within the light, I saw a face. He was sad, but at the same moment, I felt more love directed toward me than I ever thought possible. Not even a mother could love her child like that. I began to weep.

"'I am Jesus, whom you are persecuting,' the voice replied. 'Now get up. Go into the city and you will be told what you must do.' The light vanished and I realized I was blind.

"'Did you see that?' I asked groping in the darkness.

"'We saw a light surrounding us and it seemed there was a voice,' one of the soldiers answered me. They did not hear the words.

"The soldiers guided me to the synagogue, where I was given a room. I did not know what to do. I was frightened, but at the same moment, I had more peace than I can explain. It seemed right. I could not explain it at the time. Remembering the words that the voice had said, I waited, knowing I would be told what I must do. For three days, I was like that. I did not eat. I could not sleep. I did not know what day it was. I stayed on my knees and begged God to reveal what he wanted me to do.

"After three days, a man arrived. 'I am Ananias,' he told me. His voice quivered. I could tell he was afraid of me. 'God gave me a vision,' he continued. 'He told me where you were staying and told me to seek Saul of Tarsus. I know who you are. You are the one who has done so much damage in Jerusalem to the saints.'

"'I am he.' The shame of what I had done flooded over me and I began to cry. 'This man, Jesus, came to me on the road. He spoke to me and blinded me. He told me to wait until he told me what I must do.'

"Ananias came close to me and laid his hands on me. I felt them burning into my head. 'Brother Saul, the Lord – Jesus, who appeared to you on the road as you were coming here – has sent me so that you may see again and be filled with the Holy Spirit.' The heat in his hands seemed to turn into oil, like fine oil being poured over my head. It washed my eyes and the scales began to fall away. In moments, my sight was restored.

"'Saul, the Lord also told me that you are his chosen instrument to carry his name before the Gentiles and their kings and before the people of Israel. He will show you how much you will suffer.'

"Gentiles!" a man said horrified.

"That day, Ananias introduced me to the Christians of Damascus. They were terrified, but as they listened to my story, some came to believe. Before the day was over, Ananias baptized me. His wife fed me and I regained my strength. In the next weeks, I began to see the connection between the scriptures that I was taught by Gamaliel and the Jesus I met on the road. I saw Jesus in the prophets repeatedly.

"I know what I have done to Christians in the past, but I cannot deny what Jesus has done in my life since I met him on the road to Damascus. Now I come to you, my fellow Israelites, living far from your home, like me. I come to you and ask you, what will you do with Jesus, now that you know He has risen from the dead and has sent me to teach you?"

He did not wait for an answer, but strode out of the synagogue. I was by his side, long before Timothy and Philemon could catch up.

"Paul?"

"Yes, Onesimus."

"Is that true?"

"Every word and more."

"Did you kill Christians?"

"I never cast a stone, but I accused them to the Sanhedrin. So as much as any who cast a stone at them," he looked at me, "I killed Christians."

I was stunned. Who was this man before me? He seemed so gentle and filled with love, yet, he freely admitted to being the cause of many Christians' deaths.

"How..." I could not form the question I wanted to ask.

"You want to know how I can live with the guilt?"

"Yes." He stopped in the middle of the road. Timothy and Philemon were approaching.

"I know God has forgiven me and I know that if God is for me, who can be against me? Who will bring any charge against those whom God has chosen? Who is he that condemns? Christ Jesus who died – more than that, who was raised to life – is at the right hand of God and is also interceding for me. Nothing can separate me from the love He has given to me. He chose me, Onesimus. That is the one thing I know. Nothing else matters."

"You once told me that God has a plan for me?"

"Yes, Onesimus."

"Why me?"

"Because he loves you."

Timothy and Philemon caught up and our conversation was over.

News of Paul's speech before the synagogue spread rapidly. By the next morning, everyone in Ephesus was talking about him.

"Was this man a persecutor of Jews?"

"No, but of those who practice the Christian sect of Judaism."

"Isn't he a leader of that sect?"

"Yes."

"Then why did he kill them?"

"I don't know the answer."

I heard conversations like this every time I stepped out of the villa.

Another week passed and Paul again headed for the synagogue. This time there was a crowd standing on the steps, some with their arms crossed over their chests. They looked angry and defiant.

"You are not invited to enter, Paul," Sceva, the leader of the synagogue announced.

Paul stopped where he was.

"You are not welcome in Ephesus," a second man shouted from behind the synagogue leader. A dozen others shouted their agreement.

"You are teaching things contrary to what we have been taught," a third man said. Paul looked at him, causing the man to flinch.

"If you are going to stay in our city and teach in our synagogue," the synagogue leader continued, "we demand that you teach what is acceptable."

"Judge for yourselves whether it is right in God's sight to obey you rather than God."

"We don't care if what you say is right," the man shouted as he moved back into the crowd.

"I cannot help speaking what I have seen and heard. I will preach what Jesus taught. I will teach why Jesus was crucified. I will teach about Jesus' resurrection." Several grumbled and one made the sign of the evil eye.

"Then you are not welcome in this place."

"Onesimus, help me." Paul sat on the edge of a fountain where the Jews washed their hands before entering the synagogue. He began to untie his sandals. I assumed that is what he wanted, so I bent down and helped him take off the sandals. When his sandals were off, he took water and began to wash his feet. I looked at him strangely, not knowing how to respond.

"I will only teach Jesus," Paul said standing. I took his sandals and held them, waiting and wondering. "From this day forth, I will no longer teach in your synagogue. I wash your very dust from my feet."

The Jews on the steps gasped.

"Your blood is no longer my concern. It is upon your heads."

Paul left that place with me following with his sandals. Timothy and Philemon could not speak, nor did I. But I could see the sorrow in Paul's face.

Paul was quiet the next day, even when the family and Philemon's friends gathered in the courtyard, like they did every week. There were fewer in attendance. Archippus saw it and began to cry. Paul stood by him and gently caressed his head.

"Give us a message, Paul," Aquila begged.

But before he could respond, there was a commotion at the door as Tyrannus, the teacher, entered. He rushed in and fell at Paul's feet, crying.

"No, no, no!" Paul shouted. "You must not worship me."

Tyrannus did not rise, but looked up at Paul. "You prayed for my daughter. When you left, she became quiet. I supposed she had died."

Abigail began to cry. Apphia put her arm about her, as she cried too.

"Your daughter?" Paul asked.

"She lives!" Tyrannus wept. "When she became so still, I thought you had failed. I began to weep and asked God why she had not been spared. But then I remembered the words you said. 'She *will* be healed,' you said. I heard a deep sigh. I looked at my daughter as she sat up and stretched. The fever had left her. She smiled at me and kissed me."

"Praise God," Paul said.

"You healed my daughter, Paul."

"No, Tyrannus," Paul said taking him by the shoulders and forcing him to rise. "I did not do this. God used my hands to touch her.

God used my voice to speak to you. But your daughter was healed by the power of Christ's resurrection."

Tyrannus began to weep on Paul's shoulder.

"I heard that the Jews have rejected your word and ordered you to leave."

"They have rejected me, yes."

"And then you washed your feet and rejected them?"

"I did."

"I beg you not to reject Ephesus. We need you. I am not a Jew, but I want to know more about this Jesus. I believe in him, Paul."

"I have nowhere to teach."

"I have the largest school in Asia. There are others who want to learn about Jesus. We are not Jews and we do not reject you or his teachings. My school has a meeting room that can seat a hundred or more. If necessary, many more could stand. It is open to your use, as long as you are here in Ephesus, be that one more week or twenty years. I shall completely empty the school for you on the Day of the Sun." That was the Roman name for the first day of the week. "There are classrooms that you can use on other days, if you need to meet with smaller groups."

"I do not just teach the educated, like you see here. I also teach the illiterate men of the streets, the ones who clean the sewers, the men who work at the docks, the farmers, merchants, and poor. I teach the dirty, as well as the clean."

"My hall is open for anyone and everyone who wishes to learn from you. If they come in the name of Jesus or Paul, they will be admitted."

"Take me to see your school."

Paul accompanied him to his school. Philemon proudly went with them, as did I. There were many good memories of when Philemon and I were here, learning the wisdom of the Empire.

The Hall of Tyrannus, as his school was called, was a two-story building, next door to the Temple of Apollo, the Greek god of learning. When one entered from the Sacred Way, he would pass through a wrought-iron gate, with intricate designs of the Trojan War. There were three marble steps that led into the interior.

The first room was a two-story auditorium with slit windows near the ceiling. These windows lighted the room with shafts that bathed the room in warm afternoon light. There was a stage at the far end, where Tyrannus often had guest speakers. There were, as Tyrannus said, benches that could seat at least one hundred.

Paul went to the stage and stood looking out at us. One of the windows emitted a shaft of light on Paul. The man looked to me like he belonged to another world.

"And you see, Paul," Tyrannus began to show him the rest of the school. "Here to the side are classrooms. We use most of them during the day, but we can always free one for your use, if necessary."

Paul stepped down from the stage and followed Tyrannus looking into room after room.

"And here," Tyrannus indicated, "is the garden." The garden was in the shade of the building and part of the wall. There was not a lot of green, only a few pots filled with herbs and one tree. "On a beautiful day, you can meet here and teach." It was difficult not to laugh at Tyrannus' excitement.

"This is a beautiful place, Tyrannus."

"Then will you teach here?"

"As I walked through your school, I felt a reassurance from God. I will stay here for a while, as long as God allows it."

Thus, began Paul's stay in Ephesus.

Timothy did not stay. After only a few weeks, Paul asked him to journey to Macedonia, where there was a thriving church, started by Paul. It had been many years since Timothy had done anything to me or insulted me, but I could never forgive him for what he had done. I was glad to see him go.

I spent more time with Paul than I expected. It seemed he had need of my abilities more than once a week. Soon Philemon simply assigned me to be in his service whenever Paul wished it. I brought him scrolls. I looked up passages. I wrote ideas Paul had for sermons. I copied scrolls for Paul's later use. To me, it seemed that Paul simply wanted my company.

"If you have no other use for me," I would say when I accomplished Paul's requests for the day. "Then I will go."

"Sit and talk with me, Onesimus," Paul would always ask.

"Paul, you always forget I am just a slave."

"I never married, therefore, I have no children."

"What does that have to do with me?"

Paul rolled the scroll he had been reading before he looked at me. "I imagine that if God had given me a son, he would be like you."

"Paul, sometimes you say the most ridiculous things." Paul laughed. I studied him. This was what he saw in me, but I didn't understand. "I am just a slave, Paul."

"You are a man, Onesimus." He stood up and looked me in the eye. "An exceptional man, Onesimus."

This disturbed me. Nobody looked at me as anything more than a slave. Paul saw me differently. He did not see my lot. I was destined to serve Philemon or some member of his household as long as I was useful. After I lost my usefulness, I had no idea what would become of me.

"Why do you talk to me this way?"

"I want you to understand how wide and long and high and deep is the love of Christ."

"Paul," I said exasperated.

"To know Christ's love that surpasses all knowledge."

"You have no understanding of the life of a slave. What you speak of is what free men can imagine. Not a slave."

We had this conversation, or one nearly like it every week. I managed to leave before he could say much more.

I saw many extraordinary things done by Paul, or as he would say, through him. Women came to him begging him to heal their children. I saw, incredibly, children who looked on the verge of death, miraculously healed. He was never afraid to touch them no matter what disease afflicted them or how filthy they were. Paul would place his hands on them, shut his eyes, and say, "In the name of Jesus of Nazareth, be healed." The child would invariably look into Paul's face, sit up, and smile, the disease gone.

One day, a woman came to Paul and begged to see him at the school. She was dirty and smelled of years of being unwashed. Paul did not hesitate, but stood in front of her, close enough to place his hands on her shoulders.

"What can I do for you, woman?"

"My child is sick. The doctors won't visit her. I cannot afford medicine."

"You wish me to come to your house and pray for her?"

"No." She held up a dirty cloth. "If this God of yours has powers to heal, then pray for this cloth. I will place it on her head."

Paul took the cloth in his hands, "In the name of Jesus of Nazareth," he prayed. "May this child be healed the moment this cloth touches her head."

He gave the cloth back to the woman and she disappeared. The next day, she appeared at the gate of school with the child. The mother was crying for joy.

"I want everyone to know about this man, Paul," she said to everyone who passed. "He prayed for this cloth and I laid it on my daughter's head. Now she is healed."

Others did the same thing after that. A man came from Pergamum who wanted his wife healed of a disease that had wasted her body for years. Paul prayed for a cloth and she was restored. A man fell at the dock and was unconscious for days. A friend had Paul pray over a cloth. When it touched the man, he was restored, as good as new.

Paul also prayed for people possessed with evil spirits. I didn't even know that these existed, until Paul came to Ephesus.

One day, walking in the market, he came upon a boy who laughed uncontrollably all the time. I had seen that boy many times and assumed he was just a rude youth. Paul saw him and shouted, "In the name of Jesus, come out!"

The boy shook violently and fell to the ground. I thought he had died, because he became so still. Suddenly he came to his feet and began to weep, "Thank you!" he said through his tears.

Every time I saw him after that, he was a smiling helpful young man. He knew me as a companion of Paul, so always smiled and inclined his head to me.

There were many more like that. A man with uncontrollable anger. A woman who would shriek at people for no reason. A girl who would fall shaking. A boy who could not talk, nor look someone in the eyes. The man became calm, as did the woman. The girl no longer fell. The boy suddenly could look a person in the eye and tell them about Jesus. All of this and more.

What was I to think?

One day I learned something that surprised me. It was not just using the name of Jesus. That was not what caused the miracles. There was a power behind that name; what Paul called the Holy Spirit.

The head of the synagogue, Sceva, had seven sons who were training to be priests, like their father. They, like all of Ephesus, had seen Paul praying for people, using the name of Jesus. They saw the sick healed and those possessed by demons freed. They wanted to prove that Paul was a charlatan, so they brought a man with an evil spirit to the square in front of the synagogue, and called people to listen.

"We want you to know the power of our god," the eldest said. "This man has an evil spirit. You all know him. At times, he falls into the fire when he shakes, and has even fallen into the harbor, only to be rescued again and again."

"In the name of Jesus, whom Paul preaches," the second son proclaimed. "I command you to come out of this man."

The crowd watched the man's face changed into a horrible and grotesque visage.

"Jesus I know," the man growled with hatred. "And I know about Paul. But who are you?"

He screamed. He was being held by two of the brothers, but he overpowered them, ripping their clothes from their bodies. As the other brothers came to their rescue, he beat all of them and tore their clothes, leaving them exposed before the horrified crowd. The brothers fled crying and nursing their wounds. The crowd dispersed in fear of the demon possessed man.

I told Paul what I had seen and he insisted on finding the man. After an hour-long search, we found him, sitting two blocks from the synagogue, in a dark alley. I was too afraid to enter with Paul, so he went in alone. The man saw Paul and cowered, howling in a corner like a wild animal. I shook in terror of the sight I saw.

"In the name of Jesus, whom I serve," Paul said in a calm voice, "Leave this man and never return."

The man shook and fell to the ground weeping. Paul waited patiently. A massive seizure took the man. He rocked side to side, kicking and frothing at the mouth. I thought he would die, but he did not. When the seizure ended, the man, panting, looked up at Paul.

"Thank you," he cried falling prostrate.

"Stand up," Paul commanded. Less fearful, I came to his side. "You are a man. Jesus has healed you. Now it is your responsibility to stop sinning and serve God. You will start coming to the school regularly, so I can teach you."

"Thank you, Paul."

"Do not thank me. Thank God who was merciful on you."

We left there with Paul tired and me speechless. We did not talk all the way to the villa. I knew something troubled him, but I did not want to pry.

"Archippus is sick," he finally said as we entered the street of the villa.

"He has been for a few years."

"That makes me sad."

"You can pray for him."

"God does not always choose to heal." I did not know how to respond. "Archippus will live a long time, but he will never regain his health."

"How do you know this?"

"I don't know. There are things which God shows me. Sometimes he tells me why he shows me these things. Other times I just have to wonder."

It was one of those days that Archippus did not rise from his bed. Often, he stayed in bed most of the day, his stomach in great pain. Other slaves said his stool was always loose and at times he had accidents in bed.

"My fellow soldier in Christ," Paul greeted as he entered. The room smelled of sickness.

"Paul," Archippus said accepting a hug.

"Sit up, my friend."

"Onesimus," he said. "Pour me some water." I gave him a cup of water and helped him drink.

"How has your day been, Archippus?"

"I am weak."

"You have a lot of work to do, Soldier."

"I am growing old. My time is done." Archippus looked at Paul with pleading.

"What do you want to ask me?"

He began to weep. I knelt by the bed and began to wipe his tears. Paul remained calm.

"What do you want to ask me?" Paul repeated.

"Why does God not heal me? I remain sick and useless."

"You are not useless. God has a plan for you, just like we discussed." What plan did God have for his life, I wondered? "It is just for you to begin."

"How can I do anything laying here in bed day after day?"

"Then it is time to rise and begin, even if you are sick."

"Am I not going to be healed, Paul?"

"I do not have the answer to that. I just know that God wants you to do what He commanded. You are not exempt from sharing His word."

Archippus did not answer.

"Tell me this," Paul continued. "You have always been rich. You have gold, silver, houses, lands, and slaves. You have never been without. If God keeps this pain in you, will you still serve him?"

"Yes, of course."

"Tomorrow I want you to leave the house and look at the world around you. Not here on the wealthy streets. Go to the market. Go to the docks. Look at the faces of the people there. See the children in rags and the ones who never bathe. Look at the filth and imagine yourself being one of them."

"Paul?"

"God wants you to understand the world around you, so you have more compassion. Maybe one day God will heal you, or maybe he will use this to teach you humility."

"I am nothing but dry old bones. I can do nothing for God."

"Even dry sticks can help to build a fire." Paul sat on the bed next to him. "Jesus said that it is almost impossible for a rich man to enter the Kingdom of Heaven. He said is easier for a camel to go through the eye of a needle, than for a man such as yourself to enter the Kingdom."

"But I believe in Jesus."

"And Jesus has provided that miracle of a rich man entering Heaven. You will one day see the face of God, but today is not that day."

"I will do the things you ask of me."

"You will go to the market tomorrow?"

"Even if I am sicker than today."

I never learned what Paul had commanded him to do, but Archippus was out of bed more. The pain did not leave him and there were days he could not rise, but when he did, he often visited the market. He always returned smiling. I never learned what he did there.

CHAPTER 9

ARTEMIS THE GREAT

They were furious and began shouting, "Great is Artemis of the Ephesians!" Acts 19:28

"What can we do to inherit the Kingdom of God?" A group of booksellers asked Paul.

"Stop promoting the books you print," Paul said simply. A crowd was there and listening to the conversation. A crowd was always around Paul.

"What do you mean? We publish the classics of Greek and Roman literature. We even print copies of Hebrew poetry."

"You also publish books of sorcery that tourists buy when they visit Ephesus. This city is known for the sorcery books you publish."

"They are nothing but innocent fabrications for the tourists."

"Some people use them to summon demons and curse others. Why do you think this city is so filled with sickness that can only be attributed to demons?" The men's mouths were agape at the accusation.

"You also publish pornography that you sell not only in Ephesus, but around the Empire."

"Paul, don't you understand that these are harmless works meant for a laugh among the upper classes?"

"You might call it that, but these books of yours destroy families. Husbands who should be caring for their wives and children spend hours a day in these sick books of yours. When their wives no longer fulfill them, they turn to prostitutes, usually little girls who have been sold into slavery because of their beauty. These girls are abused and mistreated. Some die in the bed of a rich man."

Another man asked, "What can we do?"

"I said you can stop publishing these and you can do more. Burn any of these books you have in your possession."

That night, hundreds in Ephesus gathered in the street outside of the Temple of Artemis and burned thousands of books. Paul preached a sermon on the very steps of the Artemesium. The priestesses were afraid that he would ask the people to burn the temple.

"I have not come here to destroy this temple," he said to the terrified priestesses. "I have come to teach the people of Ephesus of the one true God." His face was lit by the fire of the burning books.

He turned to the crowd, but continued to address the priestesses. "Tell Artemis to go into the streets of her city and heal her people," he commanded. "She is nothing but a statue of stone. There is no life in her. She cannot heal your children."

The high priestess gathered her flock within and locked the door of the temple behind her.

"Paul, you are damaging business here in Ephesus," Demetrius, the head of the silversmith guild said.

"I see business thriving."

"Yet my business is weakened by your preaching."

"How is that? Explain it to me."

Demetrius held up a small silver statue of the goddess. "People will not buy the work of the silversmiths any longer."

"Then I advise you to stop making idols of demons like Artemis."

"She is sacred to the people of Ephesus and the entire province of Asia."

"She is nothing more than a demon, Demetrius," Paul said as he walked away.

The next morning, Demetrius called together the silversmiths and goldsmiths, and others who made images of the goddess to sell to tourists.

"Men, I have called you here to speak about Paul." They grumbled. "You know our income is dependent on the goddess. We receive a good income from making idols for the tourists and pilgrims."

"Not lately," complained a goldsmith. "I haven't sold anything in days. I might have to close my shop."

"You see how this fellow, Paul, has convinced and led astray large numbers of people here and in practically the whole province of Asia?"

"He says that manmade gods are no gods at all," another smith added shaking his head. He held a tiny statue of the goddess in his hand. It could easily be concealed in his closed fist. Often, he made ones like this that one could connect to a chain and be worn around the neck.

"What are we going to do about it?" the goldsmith asked.

"There is danger not only that our trade will lose its good name, but also that the temple of the great goddess Artemis will be discredited, and the goddess herself, who is worshipped throughout the province of Asia and the world, will be robbed of her divine majesty."

"Artemis the great must not be demeaned by a mere man. He must be stopped!"

"Great is Artemis of the Ephesians!" One man shouted.

"What are we going to do?" another asked.

"We will let the entire city know what Paul is doing to the goddess," Demetrius answered.

"Great is Artemis of the Ephesians!" the goldsmith shouted.

The others quickly echoed his words as they poured into the street shouting, "Great is Artemis of the Ephesians!"

One man carried a golden statue of the goddess high above his head. They continued to shout and a crowd quickly grew around them. Their numbers swelled as they approached the temple precinct, where temple slaves were cleaning the remnants of the fire. These servants dropped their brooms and followed the smiths. A hundred more passersby, excited for something to do, followed them through the streets, shouting, "Great is Artemis of the Ephesians." Many who followed did not know what was happening, but they liked the excitement of a demonstration.

The crowd moved as one to the theater. Someone brought a key and unlocked the gate. The crowd, which now numbered over a thousand filled the theater, as Demetrius stood on the stage and encouraged the cheers. Somewhere along the way, two Christians had been grabbed and dragged into the theater. One moment the shouts were lauding Artemis, the next they were saying to kill the two Christians.

I saw most of the spectacle in the street and followed them to the theater. I knew Alexander and Aristarchus, as men who frequented Philemon's on the first day of the week. I could see that neither were being beaten, but the crowd would not let them speak either.

One near the gate yelled to his neighbors, "We should drag that man who preaches against the goddess here to answer these charges."

"And then we should execute him before the goddess for his crimes of impiety."

I ran back to the Hall of Tyrannus, because I knew Paul was there.

"I will go speak to this crowd," Paul was insisting, as Tyrannus and Aquila held him back.

"No, you will go to Philemon's immediately." Aquila insisted.

"They are out for blood." I said panting.

"What did you hear?" Paul asked.

"One moment, they are crying, 'Great is Artemis,' and the next they are saying. 'kill the Christians.' Alexander and Aristarchus were forced into the theater by the crowd."

"Are they safe?" Tyrannus asked looking down the street.

"They don't seem harmed yet."

"I am going to the city clerk," Tyrannus said as he started down the road. He turned back, "Get Paul to safety and lock my school."

"Come with me, Paul," I said as I tugged him away from the school.

"No, I should be at the theater."

"Great is Artemis of the Ephesians!" The roar echoed through the city. I could feel the sound in my bones and feared for the life of Paul.

"In this, Paul, I will insist." I used my strength to pull him away and finally he relented.

Philemon's household was terrified. The roars of the crowd could be heard even there and occasionally what sounded like cheers from a gladiator fight.

"What is happening, Onesimus?" Philemon asked. Apphia gripped his arm in terror. She was crying.

"The silversmiths stirred up a crowd, I think because of what happened last night. They have gathered in the theater."

"How many are there?"

"The theater is full, so over a thousand, I would guess."

"Why did you bring Paul here?"

"They have taken two Christians, Alexander and Aristarchus. They are yelling that all Christians should be killed. Paul wanted to go in there, but they would have killed him, so I brought him here."

"You did right."

"He must get out of Ephesus," Apphia said.

"You are leaving, Paul," Philemon commanded.

"You do not order me to leave, Philemon."

"Yesterday you told me that you felt God had instructed you to leave Ephesus. You said your work here was complete. What greater sign of that being true do you need than this?"

Paul pursed his lips. I had never seen him angry, but he was now angry. "Do not use my words against me at a time like this."

Apphia said, "You are too valuable, Paul. You are needed. Not only here, but to the other churches you have started. You must finish your writings and you must finish what you began with the churches."

"Apphia, please."

She hurried out of the room.

"She is right," Archippus interjected. "You have plans to go to Jerusalem to speak to the apostles and you said you planned to go to Rome. Now is the time to go."

Aquila arrived with Priscilla. They had a small satchel and a cloak.

"What is this?" Paul asked.

"For your journey," Priscilla answered.

Apphia returned with a small bundle. "Here is food for your journey."

"Onesimus, take him to the gate," Philemon ordered. "Under no circumstances are you to allow him to go in the direction of the theater. Do you understand?"

"Yes, Master."

"At least let us take a moment for prayer before my journey," Paul said in tears. The family, and Aquila and Priscilla, gathered around him, placing their hands on his shoulders and head. I heard a whispered prayer.

"Now go," Aquila said with tears. "Hurry."

They pushed us out of the villa's gate.

"There is no reason for my head to be covered," Paul said resisting the cloak.

"It is cold enough," I said putting the hood over his head. "Besides, they won't recognize you.

"Great is Artemis of the Ephesians!" The city still shook with the cry.

Paul turned and looked in the direction of the sound. "I shouldn't be leaving."

"Paul if you go back, I will be beaten for not doing as instructed. Is that what you want?"

Paul turned and looked at me, "No, Onesimus."

"Then come on," I said, pulling him down the street.

I walked with him a hundred steps outside of the gate. I checked his satchel and found room for the parcel of food Apphia gave him. I started making sure that his cloak was on correctly.

"You've done enough, my friend." He took my hands to stop my fussing over the cloak.

"I believe you, Paul." He looked questioningly at me. "It's not what you think."

"Then tell me."

"I believe you really do consider me a friend. I don't understand why, but I know you do."

"Because I believe God has chosen you for great things."

"I have no intention of ever becoming one of these Christians."

"Because of your slavery."

"I am a nobody to them. I do my service. That is all they want."

"I don't think I will ever return to Ephesus. I can feel it inside."

"I know," I said beginning to tear up. "I feel that too."

"But I will see you again," Paul said laughing.

"That will never happen."

"God has barely begun with you, Onesimus."

"Go Paul!" I pushed him down the road, and turned toward the gate.

"Goodbye, my son," he shouted back at me.

I turned and saw him walking away. I missed him already. My stomach hurt thinking of him being gone. I did not understand this strange man who befriended a slave and called him *son*.

CHAPTER 10
COLOSSAE

In him all things were created: things in heaven and on earth, visible and invisible. Colossians 1:16

The following winter, when Philemon developed a cough that would not go away and Apphia suffered a miscarriage, it was decided the family would move to Colossae. The air was cleaner and the noise of the city was less. Both Philemon's doctor and Apphia's midwife encouraged the move. They both needed the fresh air of the mountains and not the humid air of the crowded filthy port. Soon everyone agreed.

Colossae was a small town with no paved roads. Most of the houses were small, painted in cheerful blues, yellows, and greens, but they were old and the colors faded. There was not much of a wall around the city. If it had not been safely placed in the center of the Roman Empire, it would have been vulnerable. But here, no one feared invaders.

Fields of wheat stretched out for miles beyond the city walls. Boys left each morning with their small herds of goats to wander in the hills. Women swept the dusty streets. Dogs roamed freely. I don't think any of them had an owner. The market was small and quiet.

It was not easy moving Archippus and Abigail. Both had suffered a year of bad health and they seemed to age rapidly. The carpentum could only hold three people, though not comfortably. Apphia refused to be locked inside it, giving Philemon's parents more room. Besides the carpentum, there were half a dozen wagons with far too many possessions. Apphia and Alyx spent the days sitting on the back of a wagon talking, though the last day, Apphia was too ill to be anywhere but in the crowded carpentum.

Arrangements in Colossae were very different from those in Ephesus. None of the rooms of the family had adjoining cubicles for slaves. Personal slaves, were relegated to a cot outside the door. I was no exception. The freedom I had for a year with my own room was now gone.

Zoe did not join us. Most of the slaves in Ephesus stayed behind. Junia already had a house full of slaves and the extras from Ephesus were not welcomed. Abigail would not leave Agata. Alyx would not leave Selene. Both Archippus and Philemon agreed I was too valuable to leave behind. From the moment, I walked in the door of the Colossian villa and saw my new situation, I hated Colossae more than Ephesus.

The house was much smaller. There was one bathroom for the family and it was small. In the slave quarters, there was not a bath, but there was water. I would be unable to stay clean like I had in Ephesus. The food for the slaves was meager. We were given bread and gruel. Only occasionally was there something left over from the table. Since I no longer served at the table and the cook, who eyed me suspiciously as one of the Ephesian slaves, did not give me any of the leftovers.

Philemon made close friends with two men in Ephesus who were members of the growing Christian community. Demas had been appointed by Paul, when he was in Lystra, to guide the community. He was Greek, originally from Paphos in Cyprus. He traveled with

Paul for some months, before staying behind in Colossae. He talked often about visiting Gaul or Spain. Aristarchus was a Macedonian. He had lived in Ephesus while Paul was there. He was one of the men grabbed by the mob and beaten in the theater. Philemon encouraged him to join him in Colossae. He came, but longed to go to Rome. Both Demas and Aristarchus, encouraged by Philemon, soon took a journey to Rome.

My life changed drastically. My living conditions were worse, but I saw an opportunity for freedom that I had not imagined in Ephesus. The transgressions of my youth were completely forgotten, and now, at least once a month, I was asked to journey back to Ephesus to deliver money, contracts, letters, and packages from one place to the other. Increasingly they trusted me with more money and with things of value.

I remember the first day I was given money to deliver in Ephesus. I walked calmly out of the town, until I was at a bend in the road. I hid behind some bushes and looked through the packet. Philemon had given me enough money to stay at three inns going to Ephesus and the same for the return. It was not a lot, because slaves were sent to the stables in the inns. The money in the packet was not a lot either.

I took a deep breath and put the money back in the packet. I would have to wait.

Philemon trusted me implicitly, and was always eager to make that fact known.

"You give Onesimus very important errands," Apphia commented one day as Philemon was handing me a contract authorizing the sale of a rental property near Rome. I said nothing.

"I trust him, Apphia."

"Why?" she asked. I don't think she was implying I was

untrustworthy. I think she wanted to understand. I liked her and could not imagine anyone kinder, not even Abigail.

"He has been with me since we were both children. He slept at the foot of my bed. He went to school with me. He learned better than me. Isn't that so, Onesimus?"

"I can memorize better." Philemon laughed. I knew I was more intelligent, but I would never admit it.

"He is a valuable slave," Apphia added. I inclined my head to her to say thank you, as was expected of me.

"He is more than that, my dear. Onesimus is like a brother to me."

Apphia laughed.

"I grew up in a house full of sisters. He was my first companion as a boy and has remained close to me ever since. Yes, I would call him my brother."

"Thank you, Master," I replied, ignoring his sentimentality. "I will have these papers delivered and bring back the things you requested from the villa."

I did my duty, but I still looked for a way out.

On my second trip, I discovered a small temple a short distance past the first inn. It was unused and very old. It was not the typical Hellenistic style adopted throughout the province. It looked much older, maybe as far back as the Persians or even the Ionians before them. There was no longer a door on the temple. Inside was just a square room, empty, except for litter that had blown in from the door. The roof had caved in on the southern side. The rest seemed about to crash to the floor.

I looked around for signs of life. There were none other than small rodents, and some birds who nested in the rafters. Nearby were a few collapsed walls of other buildings, possibly houses where the priests had lived. Brambles and weeds covered them. I looked more closely inside the temple. I don't know what I was looking for, but I was struck with an idea. There was a niche in the back wall about the size of my hand. It was easily covered by a few well-placed rocks. I laughed because I now had my idea.

A year after we had arrived, Archippus' health had improved, but not Abigail's. On one of my trips to Ephesus I was asked to bring Aquila and Priscilla home with me. The walk with them took a day longer, mostly because we stayed too long at the inns.

When we arrived, we learned that Abigail was in bed and could not rise.

I entered the room with them and stayed unobtrusively at the back. There was a smell I did not recognize. I wondered if that is what some meant when they said it smelled of death.

"Aquila, you must do something," Archippus pleaded.

"I am not a doctor. There is nothing else I can do." Priscilla wiped Abigail's head with a cool, wet cloth.

"I have seen you pray for others and they were healed. Some were healed in an instant."

I remembered the conversation Paul had with Archippus. He said God had a reason for him to be ill. Archippus, in his illness, had frequented the markets and became acquainted with many. I eventually learned that he gave money to those in need, quietly, so nobody would know. He had paid to have houses repaired. He gave money to widows. He had financed businesses of several of the poor, including a lady that baked bread on the Sacred way. I always stopped at her bakery when in Ephesus.

Now in Colossae, he did much the same. It was a smaller place and word got out that he gave money to those in need, which sometimes meant beggars came to the door of the villa. They were rarely turned away.

I had come to think this was what Paul was referring to. He wanted Archippus to use his money for the good of others.

Archippus was never fully recovered. There were many days, even as much as a week, that he was in bed coughing. But when he could, Archippus would be found wandering the streets of Colossae getting to know the poorest people in the city.

The poor did not know his title, but they knew he had been a soldier. "It's Archippus, the soldier," they would say in greeting. It was only a few years before that he would have been indignant being greeted as just a soldier and would have introduced them to his wrath. Now he smiled at the title.

Demas was often with him, before he left for Rome, talking to the people about Jesus. Some of those people would visit Demas to learn more about Jesus. A few became Christians, followers of the Way.

"I have prayed for her, Archippus, but sometimes God has a different plan." Aquila said. Abigail gripped his hand. Her strength was gone.

"There must be something you can do." His bottom lip started to quiver and a tear slid down his cheek.

"Archippus." Abigail let go of Aquila's hand and held out her hand to her husband. Aquila moved out of the way as Archippus sat beside her on the bed and softly caressed her hand.

"He has answered my prayer, my love," she said reassuringly.

"You are dying, Abigail," he whispered through his tears.

"I know. I have been ill for a very long time. Something has been growing inside me for years."

Archippus cried, as he placed his head on her breast. She brushed his thinning hair with her shriveled hands.

"Years ago, when I saw you seeking God, I began to pray. I knew you were looking for answers. I prayed that if God were real, He would show himself to you and to me. He did. Oh, the glory of the last few years, knowing that God is real." Archippus sobbed. "I know I will die soon, but I go to be with him. And I know that you will join me soon, as will our children."

"I can't live without you."

"You will find strength in the Lord, like Paul told you. You will share Christ before you die and many will know Him because of you." He sobbed loudly. "Be brave my soldier."

She closed her eyes as he continued to cry. The minutes were long, but her breathing finally ceased. Priscilla saw it and began to cry. Alyx hid her face in Priscilla's shoulder.

"A fine woman of God has gone to be with the Savior," Aquila said putting his hand on Archippus' shoulder.

I did not think it would move me. She was the first who reminded me that I was nothing more than a slave. Yet she had always been kind to me. I began to cry like the others.

It became quiet as the Lady Abigail's spirit left that room.

"I am too old to marry, Philemon."

"You are still beautiful and you are from a good family."

"I am too old to marry," Alyx repeated. Her hands were folded neatly in her lap. Her face was businesslike, not pleading or submissive.

"I have found you a suitable husband," Philemon leaned back in his chair and crossed his legs. He often did this in business discussions in an attempt to appear relaxed.

"I have a different plan. I told these to mother and she agreed."

"Alyx, it is my responsibility as head of the household to find you a husband."

"Eliezer is almost as old as father. We will never have children. When he dies, I will be sent back to you as a widow."

"There is a possibility of children." Philemon said. Archippus laughed, but did not join the conversation. "Well, there is, Father."

"There is another thing about him, that you have forgotten."

"What is that?"

"He does not follow the Way of Jesus and has told you that more than once. You are asking me to marry a man who is not a Christian like you or father." This made Philemon quiet. "Are you asking me, Brother, to forsake the religion I learned in your house, to live with this man? He does not even go to the synagogue on the holy days. How could I expect him to allow me to continue following Christ?"

"What will you do with yourself if you do not marry?" He asked with a desperation in his voice.

"I have thought about this for a long time." She took a deep breath, leaned forward, and continued confidently, "I will dedicate myself to the service of Jesus."

"What does that mean?"

"I will care for the sick and elderly. I will visit the poor. I will feed the hungry." She took a scroll she held in her hand. "Father gave me this deed to two houses in Ephesus. I earn money each year, which is mine. I can use this money or I can sell the property and use that. I am not a poor woman with this. I do not have to depend on your generosity."

"You will always have a place in this house," Philemon comforted. "I would never throw you into the streets."

"Then allow me to use my time and resources to further the Kingdom of God. Didn't Jesus say to the rich man, 'Sell your possessions and give to the poor and you will have treasure in heaven?'"

"Yes."

"And didn't Solomon teach us that those who are kind to the poor are lending to the Lord?"

"Yes."

"I never knew I raised such a daughter," Archippus said with a laugh.

"I read and I listen, Father."

Philemon leaned forward. "Is this really what you want?"

"Yes, Brother."

"You will never have a husband or children."

"I am satisfied the way I am now. Though I have done some investigation. If I sell the properties in Ephesus and place them in your bank, I will gain more than enough interest to live off of and be generous."

Archippus began roaring with laughter.

Two days later, I was again headed for Ephesus to give the deeds to Alyx's properties to Philemon's real estate broker. I did not stay at the inn. It was too expensive and the barn was filthy. I took the money for the cost of the inn to my little temple. I was there early enough in the evening to see that my niche was still empty, except for some rat droppings. I carefully added the two coins that I would have spent at the inn and covered the niche.

I sat back thinking. Was this what I wanted to do? There had to be more to life than running errands and fulfilling the wishes of the ungrateful masters I had been allotted. The coins were given to me. I was being careful. They would serve me one day.

Sitting on the step of the temple I watched the night appear and the stars grow brighter. It wasn't long before clouds covered the sky. A wind began to blow and drops began to fall. I crawled into the temple and slept, dreaming of a windswept hill covered in trees.

A few days later, I was in Ephesus. Because I did not sleep in the last inn either, I was early enough that no one would expect me. I wandered about the streets looking for a shop I had remembered.

There was a woman who made clothing. Philemon had said he wanted a new robe made from bleached white cotton. I found the shop not far from the gate.

"Hello," I said in greeting to the lady in charge.

I vaguely remember seeing her before and hoped she didn't know me.

"What can I do for you?" There was no recognition in her face.

"My master is looking for a bleached white robe. May I see what you have?"

She pulled out three from a shelf and let me examine them. They were all nice. While she was looking for a few others, I examined her shelves. There were some fine robes, but not so fine as to draw attention to them.

She gave me the cost of those I examined and I promised her, after I spoke with my master, that I would be back with the purchase price. I laughed knowing that Philemon would like these.

I took the papers to the broker, along with Philemon's instructions, and was finished before noon. Instead of staying at the villa, I hurried back to Colossae. My promptness would impress Philemon.

I only saw Zoe once in those years. I came to Ephesus to bring back the scrolls of Malachi, Zechariah, Hosea, Joel, and one book of the Psalms. In visiting the villa, I could not avoid her.

I never told her that I had asked to marry her. I don't think she knew either, because I doubt Philemon remembered a day later. She was not my Rhoda, but she was as close as I would ever get. I did not understand love, but assumed I could grow to love her.

"It is good to see you, Onesimus." She and I were sitting in the courtyard, next to the pool. She had brought me some bread and cheese to eat. We never would have had a meal here in the past, but there were none of our masters were here now.

"How are things here?" I asked.

"Thestius thinks he is the master. He works us harder than Philemon ever did."

"What do you do now?"

"Much like I did before. I keep the rooms clean. I am not stopped in my duties to run an errand like I would be if the Mistress were here." She paused and looked sad. "She was a good lady. Much better than Diana."

"What about your dreams?"

She laughed. "You remember that?" She turned her face to look at me. There was a sad smile on her lips, but she laughed anyway.

"Of course, I do. Why wouldn't I?" She kissed me on the cheek.

"You always seemed more absorbed in yourself than anyone else." I must have frowned, because she laughed and caressed my forehead. "I don't mean it in a bad way. You've always been thinking of books and learning. You are not an ordinary slave. I am surprised you have never been sold as a teacher."

Teacher? That was something I had never considered. I could use that.

Zoe laughed. "Again, you are thinking. I am here, Onesimus. Speak to me."

I had never thought of myself as self-centered, but maybe I was. I had one thought and that was freedom. I could do my duty, but always looked for a way out. Zoe needed her freedom too.

"What are you thinking about, Onesimus?"

"You didn't answer my question." I squirmed a bit. I wasn't sure if my concern was for me or for her, but I thought it could work.

"Yes, I still dream." She looked at the floor and fidgeted with her collar. I lifted her face to look at me and saw tears in her eyes. "But that is just a dream. I understand reality. My reality is the life I am living now, so I will find joy in the little moments, like a visit from my friend from Colossae."

Another year passed and I overheard news from Ephesus. I was busy, ordering what was becoming a new library. It did not have the wealth of volumes as the villa in Ephesus, but had many Hebrew and Greek versions of the prophets.

Apphia was sitting in the courtyard when Philemon entered.

"Do you remember the slave I told you about?" he said angrily.

"The Egyptian that you bought because he was big?"

"Yes. He is supposed to be a deterrent for someone who might try to break into the villa in Ephesus. His duty is to guard the gate, but it seems he does more than that."

She had been embroidering a shawl, but put it away to listen. "What is happening?"

"He has gotten one of the other slaves pregnant. Thestius questioned her and she confessed it was the Egyptian."

I stopped, fearful of what I would hear next. I know Zoe wanted a child, but would she resort to this?

"What are you going to do?"

"I am going to have both beaten and then sold." I turned to listen.

"Philemon, take a moment and relax."

"Relax? When this is going on in my own house." He was so angry he started pacing. I dusted off a shelf, pretending that I could not hear them.

"I remember Paul teaching that a master must provide for his slaves what is right and fair."

"They have embarrassed my home. They must be punished."

"And if it were your sister?" I saw Philemon's expression. He did not answer. "Well?"

"My sister would never do that."

"But if she did, would you have her beaten?"

"Of course not."

"Then do the right thing for your slaves too."

I waited, continuing to pretend I had not heard anything. Philemon sat and stared in front of him, thinking.

"I am going to ask the slaves to set our lunch out." She kissed him on the forehead.

I waited until she was gone.

"Master Philemon," I asked boldly. "Was the slave Zoe?"

"Who?"

"Your mother's slave, Zoe."

"I know who Zoe is, but I don't know what you are talking about." Philemon looked at me for a long moment, then realization came to him. "No, the slave was not Zoe," he said quietly. He said no more, but he was clearly still upset.

The next day, I was sent to Ephesus with a message. The girl was not to be beaten, but Thestius was ordered to give her as a gift to a weaver in the city that told Philemon he was understaffed. Instructions were that she was to work for him and allowed to keep her baby.

The male slave was not to be beaten either, but was sold.

I gave the instructions, but did not stay to see if they were carried out. I was ready for the next stage of my plan.

CHAPTER 11
ESCAPE

Where can I go from your Spirit? Where can I flee from your presence?
Psalm 139:7

It was so easy to do. I kept expecting something to go wrong, but I was able to do it without problems. I had a satchel containing the money, papers explaining the transaction to the banker on the Sacred Way in Ephesus, bread and cheese for the journey, and papers that gave me, a slave, permission to travel alone. I walked out of the villa in Colossae with no one noticing my departure.

A week before, Philemon read me the letter I would be delivering to his broker in Ephesus and informing me I would make the journey. Inside I could barely contain my excitement realizing how much money I would be carrying. There was enough to live comfortably for months, maybe even a year or more if I was frugal. I barely slept the nights waiting.

"Does it have to be me?" I asked the evening before I was to leave, feigning frustration. "Your father wanted me to finish copying the scroll Aquila sent him."

"There is time for that. It can wait." Philemon was busy writing a second letter he wanted me to deliver.

"But…" I intentionally hesitated.

"What is the problem Onesimus?"

"It is just such a long journey." I pretended that my frustration was growing. "I just wish there was someone else who could do this, instead of me. I go so often. I was thinking it might be time for someone else to do it."

Philemon's look confused me. Was he angry? He had never raised his voice to me, but I had never questioned his orders either. I was beginning to think I had gone too far.

"Onesimus, listen to me," he said softly. He signed a paper and folded it. "There is no one I trust, as much as I do you." I took the bowl of hot wax and placed a small amount on the fold in the letter. He pressed his seal into the wax. "If you ask not to go, I will find another. But please reconsider. There is no one else who I trust as much as I do you."

"That is a lot of money, Master." I calculated the cost of a ship across the Aegean to Athens or Thessalonica, food for the journey, new clothes, and inns along the way. How long could I survive on this until I found a job as a scribe or teacher? Six months? A year? If I was frugal, I thought close to a year. "Sometimes the roads aren't very safe. What if something happens to the money?"

"That is why I'm asking you. There is no one I trust more. I have always thought of you as my brother."

Again, with the brother nonsense? If I am your brother, give me a piece of land and a woman of my own. I hated this man, but I cautiously did not show this hatred. I bowed my head, in pretended submission.

Philemon put the letter in the satchel. "It has to be you. Go to the kitchen. Take bread and cheese for the journey. Leave at daybreak." I didn't argue anymore. I did as he requested, glad my ruse worked.

My heart was racing as I opened the gate early the next morning. The house was quiet. A few slaves had risen, but the family was asleep. The sky was turning from purple to blue, with clouds in varying shades of orange, pink, and gray. A thrush sang in a nearby tree. I closed the gate behind me and the sleepy porter locked it.

I passed a lady sweeping her stoop. She eyed me suspiciously. At least that is what it looked like to me. Maybe it was my guilt. She smiled as I passed. It was only my imagination.

I crossed in front of the synagogue. A young rabbi was unlocking the door. I knew him, but did not know his name. He inclined his head to me and smiled. He suspected nothing.

As I entered the market, there was a lady and her daughter taking fresh bread out of the oven. Neither noted me. A farmer was setting up a stall of fresh vegetables and another of peaches and pears. The only noise came from a farmer unloading a cart of chickens in neat cages. He also had baskets of eggs to sell.

The town was slowly waking as I walked out of the city gate. I had done it. No one questioned me. I wanted to run in my excitement, but that would look suspicious, so I walked at a steady pace.

Normally, the walk from Colossae to Ephesus would take most of four days, three days for someone who didn't stop too often. That included stops at a few select places along the route for a midday break and stopping at an inn for the night. Philemon had given me extra coins to stay at the inns, as always. As I walked, I calculated that if I did not stop at midday, I could be at the inn long before sunset. If I kept walking, I could find my ramshackle temple along the road where I could sleep and save the money. If I did this each day, I could be in Ephesus a day early. There was so much to do in Ephesus. I was known there. I had to be careful.

As darkness settled in on the first night, I found my small unused temple. It was quiet. I ate a small loaf of bread and a little cheese. I had eaten very little all day. I was tired and frightened.

I had gone this far without being caught or robbed. I was nervous about fulfilling my plan. For several years, I had worked on the little details. The money hidden in the temple. Clothes and food. Passage out of Asia. And I needed to speak with one person in Ephesus. Now was the opportune time. I could almost taste freedom. But I was frightened that I would fail.

As the darkness conquered the day and sleep was beginning to sweep over me, I dreamed, though I was partly awake. I remembered a man, many years ago, who said that there was a plan for my life.

"A plan," I scoffed as I awoke in the darkness. "A plan for me to be a slave."

I could see the man's face, as clearly as if I had seen it yesterday. I remembered the fear I had sitting in that cage, just a boy having freshly lost my mother. I remembered loving Rhoda and losing her so quickly. I remembered the pain Timothy had inflicted on me, both physically and emotionally.

"Was that the plan?" I asked. I only heard the crickets chirruping. But I could still see the gentle face of the man who had given me bread.

"If you are real," I asked cautiously, "and not a dream I have conjured all these years, make me successful in getting away from here." There was only silence.

I stepped out of the temple and saw the sky painted with stars. The night was so bright I could see the outline of the trees very clearly. But there was no moon, only millions of tiny shimmering jewels set in the sky.

Sleep overcame me.

When I awoke, I heard voices nearby. Stealthily, I left the temple and saw a stream I failed to notice before about a hundred paces away. Two women were washing clothes. I walked near. They eyed me with suspicion. I ignored them. I washed my face in the stream and took a long drink of water. I walked away, barely acknowledging their existence.

I walked back to the temple and gathered my things. I went to the niche and moved the rocks. Coins I had collected on successive journeys to Ephesus were all there. By themselves they did not amount to much. But added to the packet Philemon gave me, they would add significantly to my escape. I added them to the coins in my satchel. I breathed deeply, feeling free for the first time in many years.

The second day was a repetition of the first. I ate very little and rested little. Early in the morning I passed the inn that was half-way to Ephesus. I was elated at how fast I was making the journey. So again, I did not stop to rest midday. I was tired from walking, but I was happy. Once I caught myself singing at the top of my lungs. A shepherd on the side of a hill looked at me strangely. I was so happy I waved at him. He smiled and waved back.

That night, the smell of roasted meat made me decide to stay at the inn that was half a day from Ephesus. I showed my papers to the innkeeper and he offered me a place to sleep in the stable. I asked for some food and he offered a bowl of cold soup.

"I would like some of that roast, if I may."

"That is not for slaves."

"But I am paying you."

"Do you want me to tell the magistrate that you are causing trouble?" I took the soup. I had to end this life as a slave quickly.

I woke when a rooster crowed. I looked outside and it was dark, but there was a thin line of gold along the eastern horizon. It was time to leave. From this inn, Ephesus was within a half day's journey. If I hurried, I could be there before noon. I wanted gone from this place and this life.

Suddenly she was before me, Ephesus, the dazzling city of Artemis. The white temple with its golden roof shone brilliantly in the late morning sunlight, the blue sea beyond it. Her city was not to be my home. I thought through my plan carefully. There were two stops I had to make before I would go to the dock. Inside the gate, two blocks along the Sacred Way, was the shop of a lady who made fine clothing. She was my first stop.

"Good afternoon," I inclined my head as I greeted her. I knew she could not read, so I boldly put my plan into action. I took out the papers that indicated I was a slave and showed them to the lady. "My master wanted me to stop at your shop before I return to Colossae."

"I can't read this," she said returning the paper to me.

"My apologies." I looked at the paper, pretending to read. "He wants me to buy two robes for daily use. Nothing too elaborate, but nothing shabby either."

"What is his size?" she asked.

"We are the same size."

She looked through some stacks and found a green robe that had intricate designs along the hem. The color was nice and the fabric soft.

"Try this one on," she said as she handed it to me.

"I can't do that. What would he think if I wore his clothes?"

Instead she held it up against my chest. "It should fit him, if he is the same size."

She found another that was white with a dark blue hem. I was about to take just those two when I saw a third one, it was dark blue, almost purple.

"I like that one too." When she quoted the price, I cringed. Dressing like this would eat through my money too quickly. "Just the green one and the white one. He didn't give me enough for that one."

She carefully bundled them for me and I hurried down the street.

Not far was the street of Philemon's villa. I had to be careful here. This could be dangerous if I did not play my part well. I didn't have to yell inside because Thestius was at the gate instead of the big Egyptian brute.

"Onesimus," he said with a broad smile.

"Good morning, Thestius."

"Why are you here in Ephesus?" Thestius looked down the empty street. "Is the master coming?"

"No, I am on a journey for him." I indicated the clothes in the bundle and my satchel. "He is in such a hurry for me to return, that he ordered me not to stay the night. I am to complete my errands and be at the inn by nightfall. I think I am running behind."

"Well come in and get something to eat."

"One of my errands involves Zoe. The mistress, Apphia, asked me to speak with her privately."

"I will get her." Thestius hurried away.

I entered and stood by the library. I made a quick decision and grabbed two scrolls that I knew were valuable. I could sell them one day. One was a dissertation on Socrates by a Syrian scholar. The other was a play by Aristophanes. I was about to choose a third when Zoe entered the library.

"Onesimus," she smiled pleased to see me.

"We have to do this quickly," I said standing close to her, whispering so no one would hear us.

"Onesimus?"

"You and I will get on a ship today and sail for Greece." At least a year ago, I had decided that I wanted someone with me when I found my place as a free man. I wanted a wife. Zoe was not Rhoda. I was not fool enough to think that. She was plain whereas Rhoda was beautiful. Yet, Zoe was my one friend in life. She cared for me. I had long ago decided that she loved me. If she didn't love me, at least she would be happy being free with me.

"What?" She looked around, suddenly afraid.

"Stay quiet and do as I tell you."

"I'm not going anywhere."

"Yes, you and I can finally be together. It will work, but you have to do what I tell you."

"You don't love me, Onesimus. You love Rhoda. I am not her."

I stared at her, wondering why she wasn't cooperating. Surely, she hated being a slave as much as me.

"That doesn't matter. We can escape being slaves."

"I've been my whole life in this house. I don't want to go anywhere."

I stared at her in disbelief. "This is our chance, Zoe."

She shook her head slowly. Her face was sad. "No, it is your chance, Onesimus. I won't be a part of this."

She started to walk away. My disbelief was quickly turning into fear. I had known she would join me. This was unexpected. Now I could imagine Thestius taking me and reporting my escape to Philemon. I was a dead man.

I grabbed her arm. "If you tell them, they will have me put to death."

"I won't tell anyone." She eased her arm free, "but I won't help you either. If you are going to escape, then do it before questions are asked."

"Zoe, come with me please."

"No, Onesimus." I could not believe she was telling me no. I was shocked. I wanted her to escape with me, but I could see I would be alone. I was angry. I was hurt. I was frightened.

"Goodbye, Zoe."

Quickly I left the villa and hurried down the street. I couldn't take the Sacred Way because I was too well-known, so I hurried down a crowded secondary street. A few blocks from the docks, I slipped into an alley. A little boy was playing with a ball. I ignored him as I stripped out of my clothes, a dull unbleached robe, and put on the green robe I had just bought. The boy looked at me curiously, so I threw him the old robe. He laughed.

There were about ten ships at the dock and half were unloading cargo, meaning they had just arrived. I saw one ship that was loading cargo, crates and urns. It would be leaving soon.

"Where is the captain of this ship?"

A dirty middle-aged man looked over the side. "That would be me." He studied me, looking over my clothes.

"I am needing to sail west. Where is this ship heading?"

"Delos for a day, then Athens and Corinth before returning here."

Athens! A city a scholar would dream of. I could live in a place like that.

"How long will that take?" I was excited and hoped I was not giving away my excitement.

"If the winds continue the way they are now, and this time of year they should, we will be in Delos in three days. We will stop at Delos for a day and then one more day to Piraeus, the port of Athens."

"I would like to buy passage."

"I won't feed you." I thought of what remained in my satchel. There was bread for one more day. I would have to buy something, furthering my chances of being seen.

"When do you leave?"

"We are almost finished loading. If you are not here when we set sail, then look for another ship."

I hurried along the dock. I bought a few loaves of bread, a small jar of wine, and more cheese. When I turned to look at the ship, I could see they were preparing the sails to leave.

"Onesimus?" A woman's voice called to me. I turned to see Priscilla. "What are you doing here? On some errand of Philemon?" She was smiling, as if encountering an old friend.

Fear gripped me. I was discovered. I did not answer. Slowly I backed away.

"Onesimus, what's wrong?" She asked coming close to me. She reached out to calm me, but I flinched from her touch. "Onesimus?"

"You won't understand." I looked at the ship.

"What is the matter?" I could sense the concern and the confusion.

"Good bye, Priscilla." I turned and ran to the ship, with her calling after me. I jumped onto the ship, just as it was pushing off from the dock. The sailors laughed at my antics, but I ignored them.

In the distance, I could see Priscilla looking at me with confusion. The look on her face changed as she realized what I was doing. Her hands instinctively covered her mouth. She stood on the dock as the ship sailed out of view. I lost sight of her as the city of white and gold vanished over the horizon.

This journey was different from my last sea journey. I didn't have a lot of privacy, but was given a place to sleep in the captain's meager cabin. The crew left me alone. A few times the captain spoke to me, but he never inquired about my history or who I was. The clothes worked. I appeared to be a man of means. I played my part well, keeping to myself, reading a scroll when I sat on deck, and speaking to no one.

"That island in the distance is Delos," he said one morning. He pointed to a low gray isle in the distance. "We will stay the night, if you wish to stay at an inn. I will have one of the crew tell you when we are leaving the next morning." The gruffness had left him and he had become more subservient.

"Thank you, captain."

"I have not been rude and asked what a man like you is doing taking a freighter across the Aegean."

"What do you mean?" I was nervous that I was about to be questioned.

"Usually the likes of you would take a passenger ship."

"The likes of me? Explain what you mean?"

"It is easy to see that you are a man of education and wealth. I don't understand why you would take a ship like mine."

I smiled because he was believing my story. "There was supposed to be another ship, but I was delayed on my journey from Pergamum." The story came to my head as I spoke. I was a runaway slave. I would have to live a life of lies. "I was robbed and my slave was killed just a day out of Ephesus. I was supposed to be on that ship. My father is expecting me in Athens. I should be there today, but you understand the delay."

"Of course, young master." I smiled at the title he gifted me.

"My father will hear about your generosity." I placed my hand on his shoulder in a gesture of gratitude. "I know you will be rewarded."

He smiled, for the first time revealing the missing teeth in his mouth. He no longer seemed like a gruff sea captain, but like a kindly old fisherman.

As I watched Delos approach, I knew I had succeeded. Maybe the prayer I prayed at the temple was effective.

As we came close to the docks, there was a group of boys, no older than I had been when I was first taken into slavery, who were repeatedly jumping into the water to retrieve shells one of the others would throw in. They lined up in a row, and one boy would throw the shell as far as he could. At the count of three, they would all dive into the water, their arms pointing in front of them like an arrow and their bodies very straight.

I had never seen people swimming before, even at the dock of Ephesus. I never had the leisure to watch things like that before. It seemed interesting to me how they would propel themselves in the water with their arms and legs. They would disappear into the clear turquoise waters and rise with one arm in front. They pulled that arm back, like the oar of a ship. As that arm reached back, the other would go above the water, past the head, and out front like the other arm had been. They repeated that process over and over, all the while kicking with their feet. It propelled them through the water.

It was early afternoon when we arrived at Delos. The island was barren. Few trees adorned the naked hills. But signs of life were everywhere. We disembarked to a crowded port. The captain directed me to the hill in the distance, where I could look upon the temples, eat a good meal, and find an inn to sleep for the night.

The stench of the port made me desirous to get away, so I walked up the hill. The crowded port gave way to beautiful inns and gardens and soon the religious center of the town. Delos was reputed to be so sacred that no one was allowed to die there or to be born there. They said that Apollo and his sister, Artemis, were the last to be born here. Yet history tells a different story. The Athenians, wanting to create a sacred island, had all the dead dug up and moved to another nearby island. Now someone who was ill or badly injured was removed from the island, just in case death was near. A woman who was pregnant was not allowed to step foot on the island. If one was discovered to be pregnant, she was forced to leave.

It wasn't long before I was above the town, looking down on the crowded smelly port. I saw a lot of activity in one area, that I decided I would investigate, but first I wanted to see the famed holy sites.

The Sacred Way was lined with a dozen snarling white marble lions of enormous size. That avenue led to the Temple of the Delians, sacred to Apollo and Artemis. I looked for a while on a statue of Artemis. Here she was depicted as a youthful maiden of incredible beauty. I could not reconcile how the goddess with the dozen breasts could be the same as this one, yet the Greeks said she was. In this, I began to think Paul was correct. Maybe these Greeks did not really know what they worshipped.

The sun was beginning to set, so I looked for a place to stay. When I reached the port, I came upon the building I had seen from the hill. Horror hit me. There were hundreds of naked men, women, and children in chains. Some were dark like the Egyptians, or even darker Ethiopians, but some looked like me. I stared at a man with hair and eyes like mine. His eyes showed the terror of where he was.

Delos, I came to find out, was the center of the Roman slave trade. Hundreds poured in here weekly, were bought, sold, and traded. I watched as mothers had their daughters ripped from their sides screaming. I watched boys whipped and herded like cattle onto boats. Men prodded and poked girls as young as Rhoda had been. I wanted to hit everyone I saw. I wanted to scream. I wanted to vomit from the stench. How could they treat people like this?

"What does the young master seek here?" An oily man said to me in a broken Greek accent.

"Nothing," I answered. "I want nothing here."

"There are fine women to keep you comforted at night," he pushed me toward one girl, who couldn't have been more than ten years of age. She was terrified at the sight of me.

"No," I said, pushing away from him. "I told you I don't want anything."

As I walked away from him, he shouted back at me. "We have boys too."

I walked until I found the ship. I did not want to be on this island any longer.

"You are back so soon?" the captain asked.

"I don't want to miss leaving in the morning. May I sleep here?"

"Of course. The cabin is all yours."

I was shaking when I entered the cabin. I was hungry. But I was also frightened at the sight of so many mistreated people. My head was spinning as if I was drunk or drugged. As darkness washed over the land, I fell asleep.

I dreamed of a vast green field. It seemed to me to be as vast as the Sea. Around me were flowers of bright yellow and white. Trees were heavy with fruit. I saw no people, but somehow, I knew I was not alone.

Light seemed to surround me, but I could not find the source of it. As I searched, I noticed that there were no shadows. Curiously I looked at a tree. There was no shade under the tree. The limbs were bright on top and bottom. One leaf did not shade the next. On the right, the tree did not cast a shadow, nor on the left. It was as if it were enveloped in light.

I searched for the light as I walked along a river, bluer than the sky, but crystal clear. In the distance, I saw the source of the light. I could not make out what it was. A city? A mountain? A person? Something was so bright I could not make it out.

I woke to the sound of the crowded dock. Walking out onto the deck, still wrapped in my blanket. I saw the sun topping the hill, with Apollo's sanctuary glistening in the morning light. It looked dull compared to my dream.

CHAPTER 12

ATHENS

All the Athenians and foreigners who lived there spent their time doing nothing but talking about and listening to the latest ideas. Acts 17:21

"The wind is with us, young master," the old captain greeted me when I came on deck.

"Good," I said wrapping the blanket tighter. It was cold out on the sea. "How long will it take to get to Piraeus?" I could see land in every direction.

"We are approaching the island of Aegina, so we will be there before sunset."

"Will I be able to make it to Athens before dark?"

"Likely not. It is a bit of a walk." I knew I could walk it, even if it were dark. Athens was my freedom. "There are many good inns in Piraeus. I will introduce you to one run by a friend. Tomorrow morning you should be able to make it to Athens easily in an hour or two."

I went back into the cabin and slept a few more hours. I wanted to be rested for my walk.

It was dark, just like the captain said, when we arrived in Piraeus. It was a city teeming with life. Warehouses, taverns, and inns crowded next to each other along the docks. They were lit with torches and fires. Ships were everywhere. Some were off shore, unable to dock. I feared this would be my fate, but there was a place for our ship.

I was the first to step off the ship, when we docked.

"Give me a few moments, young master," the ship captain told me. "I will speak with the port master and then help you find a suitable inn for the night."

"Thank you," I said as he was leaving. "There is no hurry."

I looked around and nobody on the ship was paying me any heed. This was my chance. I had paid the captain half of my passage upon entering his ship. Now I was cheating him out of the final payment. Quietly I started walking down the pier, pretending to be looking around. I headed toward several buildings that appeared to be storehouses. I slipped between two and kept walking until I found a road that headed north.

Along the road were storehouses, tenements, inns, and taverns. When I bothered to look up, I noticed in the far distance was a hill with white buildings on it, lit up by the glow of a city. The road was straight in that direction. The storehouses quickly disappeared, as did the inns. There were many houses along the road, but after a few minutes they became sparser.

I worried that there might be thieves along the road, but I quickly felt at ease. There were many other people walking either toward Piraeus, or toward what I assumed was Athens. There were also guards patrolling the road. A few wagons passed. Those going to Athens were filled with barrels, crates, and things under tarps that I could not make out in the dark.

When one approached, I decided to ask for a ride.

"Excuse me, sir," I said walking beside the ox-driven cart.

"I don't take no riders."

"I can pay you."

"You can walk faster than these old oxen. If you are in such a hurry to get to Athens, then walk."

"It is a long walk. I'd rather ride."

He scoffed, but did not add further to the conversation. When I looked ahead I realized why. We were approaching the outskirts of the city. Buildings were again closer together. Houses were lit, even though it was dark I could see my surroundings. Many people were sitting on their stoops chatting with neighbors. The smell of food was making me hungry and I was sorry I did not stay in one of the inns at Piraeus.

Soon there were paved roads that crossed the highway. There were people everywhere. I heard music as I passed some houses. I could smell meat roasting. I heard the laughter of children. There were villas larger than Philemon's in Ephesus, but many more humble houses. Soon the gate and wall of the city were in front of me.

Not far from the city gate, I came upon an inn that was open on one side of the ground floor, so patrons could eat outside. I could smell something roasting and I was hungry.

"Can I get something to eat?" I asked a girl who was serving.

"Sit down wherever you like." The place was crowded. There were a dozen tables with benches on either side. I sat down at a table near me that was already crowded. Nobody said a word as I sat beside half a dozen men. They were too busy eating and drinking.

In a few minutes, the girl came by and placed a plate of cucumbers, onions, and olives drenched in vinegar, oil, and salt in front of me.

"Beer or wine?" she asked.

"Take the beer," the man next to me said. "The wine is as sour as vinegar."

"Beer then," I said.

"Will you have roast or soup?"

"I want the roast."

"Can you afford it?"

"Yes. And I want a room too."

"I'll ask my mother if there is a room available."

The beer was good, but the vegetables were even better. I was so hungry that they vanished before the girl had left the table.

"Can I have some more?" I asked returning the empty plate to her.

"I'll bring some more when I bring the roast," she laughed as she placed a basket of fresh bread, hot from the oven, on the table. Several men reached for the bread. I did too, because it smelled so good it was making my mouth water.

"This boy is hungry," the man next to me said.

"Are you from around here?" I asked drinking the cool beer.

"Yes and no."

"What do you mean?"

"I have a place to stay when in Athens, and a place to stay when I am in Piraeus. Like most I live on the sea."

"I just arrived. My ship docked at sunset."

"Where are you from?"

"Ephesus." The girl brought me a plate filled with steaming roast lamb and another of the oil drenched vegetables. I greedily began to devour the roast.

"By the looks of your clothes, you are not a worker."

I worked, I thought, but that was the old me. I was trained for my new work and I would be the best.

"I am a teacher. I will be looking for a position here in Athens."

Others at the table laughed.

"There are hundreds of men, just like you, seeking that line of work in Athens. Before long we'll see you at the docks, like everyone else."

Before I could even think, a lie formed on my lips. "That might be true of most, but I have been offered a position. My father is one of the most renowned teachers in Asia, Tyrannus of Ephesus. He has arranged for my apprenticeship with one of the best in Athens."

"Who might that be?"

I continued eating while I thought. What was the name I had heard before? Demetrius? Alexander?

"Mnesarchus?" one man asked at the far end of the table.

"Yes, Mnesarchus," I responded with my mouth full of food.

There were nods at the table, so I guessed right.

"Those of us who are unlettered don't know about such things," one man said. The others laughed.

"I don't know where his school is, so I will have to search tomorrow."

"He is on the other side of the Stoa of Attalos."

"Thank you," I smiled. I had arrived.

I had a comfortable room, with a window that looked out on the street. I could see the skyline of the Acropolis in the distance. I laughed that I had succeeded. I was in Athens, the center of learning for the entire world. Nobody knew me. Everyone accepted my story. By tomorrow I would be employed as a teacher in the greatest school in the city. My eyes were heavy. I laid down on the bed and was asleep in moments.

I set out early the next morning, not even bothering to take some bread for breakfast. I wanted to explore this great city before I settled into the school.

No matter where I turned, the Acropolis was in front of me, gleaming white in the morning sun. The Temple of Athena, the Parthenon, was not as large as the Artemesium, but more stunning. It was located on a rocky, fortified hill with the city surrounding it. A dozen temples were in the enclosure, including ones to Apollo, Pan, Roma, and Augustus. A magnificent entrance, called the Propylaea, guarded the temples beyond. I could see marble statues lining the steps of the Propylaea and an even larger bronze statue of Athena towered above the buildings.

At the foot of the Acropolis was the Agora, with the Temple of Hephaestus at its entrance. It was like a miniature replica of the Parthenon, surrounded by poplar and linden trees. At this time of year, the lindens had just begun to bloom, filling the air with their sweet fragrance. An ancient olive tree was in front of the temple, with a marble plaque at its base that read, "A gift to Athens from her patroness, Athena." It was said that Athena created the olive tree, and it was olive oil that had originally made Athens so wealthy.

Everything one could imagine was in the Agora. There were shops displaying homespun wool for blankets, draperies, and rugs, and others with finer linens and silks for clothing. Other shops displayed embroidery, brocades, and finely detailed lace. It was the beginning of summer and the shops selling linen were more popular. There were a dozen cobbler shops selling boots, sandals, and shoes. One shop had fine shoes made of linen, intended to be worn in the houses of the wealthy. Another had boots of dyed leather, some of which sported gold or silver buckles. Pottery abounded. There were pots for everyday use: cookware, plates, and serving dishes. There were more elaborate pots painted red or black for religious purposes or decoration. Ladies selling flowers walked through the Agora, tempting you with their sweet blossoms. Spice sellers waved away the flies from their oregano, saffron, mint, thyme, coriander, cinnamon, and marjoram. There were urns of many sizes selling many flavors and colors of wine. Some were strong, but others sweet. The olive oils were just as varied. Some were intended for cooking or flavoring foods, while others were for the lighting of homes.

In the midst of all the items for sell, were food vendors. Lamb and pork marinated in oil and spices were skewered on sticks and roasted on open fires. I bought one to eat as I wandered through the Agora. There were also fresh breads of barley and wheat, hot from the oven. Other breads were covered in honey and sesame, and some stuffed with creamy goat cheese. There were booths selling a dozen varieties of beans and lentils. Onions, garlic, dried fruits, figs, grapes, and apples abounded. There were butchers with freshly slaughtered goats, sheep, and pigs. A few stalls sold the more expensive beef or chicken, and a variety of birds. The fish seller had fresh fish brought up from Piraeus in the night, but he ran out of fish about the time I arrived.

There were temples, fountains, and government buildings facing the Agora. Men in fine robes stood outside of a bank. A line of peasants waited at the door of a building that advertised the greatest lawyer in all of Achaea. Women chatted noisily at a fountain, as they filled their pitchers with water. Not far from the fountain was an altar, inscribed with the phrase "To the Unknown God." A man stood by it, talking to all who passed by. As I came nearer, I could hear him pleading with a youth who had stopped to listen.

"The time is here to leave youthful pleasures. God is in our midst. You must repent of your sins and turn to Jesus."

"I have never sinned, old man." The youth laughed and walked on.

Was this man a follower of Christ? He did not preach like Paul. He was more like Apollos when I first met him. If he was a follower of Christ, then this little Jewish sect of my masters was everywhere.

He looked at me and started to say something. His mouth was open, but then he closed it and turned from me, not looking back. I walked on, because he made me uncomfortable.

I was directed to find the School of Mnesarchus beyond the Stoa of Attalos, a two-story white marble building with a red tiled roof on the far side of the Agora market. The stoa housed finer shops of gold and silver smiths, sellers of gems, and scribes on the first floor. The second floor had offices of merchants and lawyers. On the steps to the stoa was a group of men listening to one man who passionately tried to engage the crowd.

"Man must seek pleasure," he intoned. "Wasting our lives in the pursuit of good goes against the teachings of Epicurus. The gods, themselves, spend eternity enjoying blissful pleasure."

I stood behind a very fat man who was sweating, though the morning was cool. His robe was white, but was stained yellow about the neck because of his constant sweating. I could see that there were yellow stains near his armpits. But he was not poor. He wore a golden ring on his left hand with a red stone. A slave stood behind him fanning him.

"The gods want us to pursue a life of pleasure so we can be more like them. The responsibility and duties society wishes to force upon us is alien to them. Pleasure, is all that they desire."

I had read Epicurus and knew this was not what he taught. I was feeling emboldened by my new-found freedom, so I spoke up. "Epicurus said that pleasure was not meant to be unbroken nights of sensual pleasure, as some understand it to be through ignorance, prejudice, or willful misrepresentation." I had gained the attention of those surrounding me.

"Then what did he mean?" Asked the sweaty fat man.

I turned to him and continued, though loud enough that the others could hear. "By pleasure we mean the absence of pain in the body and of trouble in the soul." I then turned to the speaker, who was angry that I had interrupted him. "It is not an unbroken succession of drinking bouts and revelry, not by sexual lust, nor the enjoyment of fish and other delicacies of a luxurious table, which produces a pleasant life; it is sober reasoning, searching out the grounds of every choice and avoidance, and banishing those beliefs through which the great tumults take possession of the soul."[3] They were quiet listening to me. "Epicurus in his letter to Menoeceus."

The fat man began to roar with laughter. The crowd broke up when the speaker stormed away.

"Everyone in Athens, the locals and foreigners, spends their entire lives doing nothing but talking about and listening to the latest ideas." He held out his hand. "Gaius Junius Sabinus, Senator."

"Senator of Rome?"

"Yes, I have had enough of the politics in Rome and have come to Athens for a change." He guided me to walk with him in the shade of the stoa. "In Rome, all they do is argue politics. This man will restore the glory of the Republic, some say. Others want to give more powers to the Emperor. Others talk about how giving a free daily ration of bread to the poor in the city will make them vote in favor of this senator or another. Or they ask if Nero will be another Claudius or even if he will be like Augustus. And yet, it all stays the same."

"What is your political persuasion?"

"Me?" He laughed. "Nothing has changed since I first entered the Senate when Tiberius was Emperor. He was corrupt but so was Caligula. Claudius was not a bad emperor, but the people surrounding him were more corrupt than those in the days of Tiberius. I don't doubt Nero is as corrupt as those." He stopped looking out on the busy agora. "I don't see any change and don't see how I, as a senator, did anything meaningful in life. So, I am retired to Athens to write and listen to philosophers."

He studied me for a moment. "I've never seen you here before. Athens is a large city, but those who are educated are actually few in number. I thought I knew everyone."

"I only just arrived from Ephesus yesterday." I could feel a story growing in my mind to explain why I was here.

"Ephesus? I have business contacts there. What is your name?"

If he had business contacts in Ephesus, he would know the names of Archippus and Philemon. I had to tread carefully. "My name is Stephanos, originally from Laodicea, near Ephesus. My father worked as an accountant for the Tribune Archippus."

"Ah Archippus! I met him years ago in Spain and have stayed in contact with him through letters. His son is a tough businessman."

"That he is! When my father died, I was left with enough money to travel. I was educated by Tyrannus, the same as Archippus' son, Philemon. I was hoping I could find employment at a school in Athens. Have you heard of Mnesarchus?"

"He is not far from here. I will introduce you."

"Thank you, Sir."

As we walked, he continued the conversation. "Tell me, how is old Archippus?"

"His wife died recently, and because of his health, he moved to Colossae in the interior."

"I never understood why a good Roman soldier would marry a Jewess. He could have married a daughter of a senator and entered Roman politics. He was a bright youth and would have gone far."

"Abigail, his wife, was a beautiful woman." I could still remember her caressing my cheek on the day I became a slave in her house. Her amber eyes were warm and inviting. I no longer could picture what my mother looked like. I saw Abigail when I thought of my mother.

"A man of means marries for wealth or power. He can obtain a beautiful woman to take care of other things."

We arrived at the school that was not much different from Tyrannus' school in Ephesus. The gate was barred and a bored slave stood guard.

"Tell Mnesarchus that I am here to speak to him."

"He is in class, Senator," the slaved responded wearily. "I don't think he wishes to be bothered."

"How dare you speak to me that way, slave?" the senator shouted. "You are a slave and do not refuse my request. Go and deliver my message at once."

I could feel my neck and cheeks go red with anger. I hated to see a man treated like that, be he slave or free. Somehow, I would have to enter the world that treated slaves like this, but I did not know how I could. I could never see myself treating another human with such contempt.

"Slaves think they are equal to free men these days. They become puffed up thinking they can oppose a free man." His anger was causing him to sweat more, but his slave had stopped fanning him. I caught the eye of his slave and pointed at his neck. The slave noticed his master sweating and began to fan him.

Mnesarchus came to the gate to greet the senator. He was a tall thin man, of about fifty years. His hair was thinning, and though he brushed over a lock to cover the bald spot, it was still obvious. It was also obvious that he did not like being dictated to by a Roman. The senator ignored his look of consternation.

"Mnesarchus, this young man is from Ephesus, a student of Tyrannus." Mnesarchus held out his hand for me to shake it. "I've already heard him speak. He is looking for work as a teacher."

"As is half of Athens," he responded coolly.

"He is an intelligent young man. I can vouch for him." He placed his hand on my back. I had a strange feeling about this man, but did not know how to respond to him. He was friendly, but why would he do this for me, a stranger?

"I will speak with him, Senator."

"Stephanos, please come to my villa. I would like to dine with you and learn more about you."

"I need to look for a place to live. I stayed in an inn last night."

"Then stay at my villa. Tomorrow I will have a slave help you search for a suitable place to live." He smiled at me and left.

Mnesarchus did not seem pleased by my friendship with the Senator. He looked me over. "I have too many teachers. I have been considering letting a few go. What would I do with another?"

"I am well-read. There is not a classical author you can mention that I can't quote his work. Test me," I begged.

"What does it prove if you can quote a few authors?"

"I beg you to try me out. A trial of a few days or weeks. I will work hard, doing whatever task you wish. I have money and can stay in an inn until then."

"I would recommend that you leave Athens." His look was almost one of disgust. "Unless you intend to pursue your friendship with Senator Sabinus."

I cocked my head, not understanding what he was implying.

"I just met the senator moments ago. He was kind enough to show me your school."

"He said he heard you speak."

"There was a man at the Stoa misquoting Epicurus. I corrected him and the senator made acquaintance with me because of that. Nothing more. Please, Sir, I need to work."

"There is a colleague of mine that has a fine school in Corinth. His name is Demetrius. Tell him I sent you. If you can survive a year or two with him, then I will consider hiring you."

He turned to enter the school. "Yes Sir," I responded. Despair was sweeping over me.

"And stay away from senators," he counseled as he disappeared inside.

I sat down in the shade of a pine on the backside of the stoa, not sure how I would continue. I assumed getting work as a teacher would be easy. I would have assumed the help of a senator would assure me a position, but it seemed Mnesarchus looked at it as hindrance.

I heard a laugh and caught a glimpse of red hair. Thoughts of Rhoda swept over me as I looked in the direction of the red hair. There was a woman, younger than me, laughing with a group of women wearing bright colored clothes. Her back was turned to me. From this distance, she looked like Rhoda. My heart stopped and I couldn't catch my breath. I had dreamed of this girl for a decade. Could she be here?

I slowly walked to where she was, studying her closely. The body was the same, though she was a bit fuller. That would be expected as a girl grew into a woman. The hair was the same. I could see her shoulders sprinkled with freckles just like Rhoda. She wore a green dress and was bare footed.

Her friends noticed I was staring at her. They giggled, but she didn't turn around.

"Your laughter, ah, that seduces my heart. When I turn to look at you, I feel I am going completely speechless."[2] I repeated the line from Sappho I had quoted to Rhoda so many years ago. If she were Rhoda, she would remember me.

Her friends laughed and slowly she turned around. This woman was beautiful, but she was not Rhoda.

She smiled at me, "Welcome to my home, young master." She pointed to the house.

"He is a beautiful," one of her friends cooed.

"And he is young," a second one said.

"Then I am lucky today," the red head said.

"I'm sorry," I said turning red with embarrassment. "You looked like someone I knew once."

"I can become her," she came close to me and caressed my cheek. She wore perfume that smelled like roses. She took me by both hands. "Come with me." Her white teeth smiled at me.

I entered her house, confused and wondering why I was invited in. Then she began to undress and I understood. I looked at the door, wanting to flee.

"Is it your first time with a woman?" She slid her nearly naked body next to mine.

"Yes," I answered nervously. She took my satchel and set in on a chair next to the bed, then began to undress me.

"Fifty denarii," she said casually as she sat on the bed. I stood there naked, wondering what she wanted me to do, then decided she wanted me to sit next to her. I leaned in to kiss her. When I did that, she put her hand on my chest and repeated, "Fifty denarii."

"Oh," I said understanding that she wanted me to pay her. I reached in my bag and pulled out the purse with my coins. Her eyes lit up seeing the money. I handed her five coins each worth ten denarii. After she placed them on a side table, she introduced me to the joys of her bed.

I woke up, not realizing how long I had slept. It was beginning to get dark. The woman, whose name I had never learned was sitting dressed, looking out the window.

"Finally, you wake up."

I dressed, now embarrassed about my nakedness.

"May I come back one day?" I asked. My satchel had been moved, but I didn't think anything of it at the time. I put my satchel over my shoulder.

"My door is always open for a man willing to pay." She didn't look away from the window.

Smiling, I bent to kiss her. She stopped me. "If you want romance, that will cost you a lot more." It felt like a dagger.

I left confused. I wanted to stay in Athens to visit her bed again. But as I walked, I began to calculate how much she cost. I could not afford to do this often or I would soon run out of money. Though maybe if I had a good job, it was a possibility.

What if she agreed to marry me? I'd need a good house to live in, and money for food and clothes. She could leave her life of prostitution and be happy with me. Then I remembered. I did not have a job in Athens. I needed to go elsewhere to find work. Probably I would never see her again.

I turned and looked back at the house. She was standing outside, on the step of her door, laughing at a man as old as Archippus. My heart sank. As quickly as I had had dreams of a life with a woman who reminded me of Rhoda, they were washed away in embarrassment and shame at what I had done.

I had a picture of the prostitute in my mind as I walked the streets of Athens, looking for the Senator's villa. That picture was soon erased by the image of Rhoda, clean, pure, and kind. The prostitute was not Rhoda. She had red hair, but beyond that, they were complete opposites. The joy began to turn into guilt. Not only had I wasted money, but I had been untrue to the woman I loved.

The Senator's villa was luxurious. All the furnishings and murals were the most expensive that money could buy. As I waited to be introduced to the Senator, I noticed that the brightly colored scenes on the walls of the room where I waited were of naked men and women, engaged in acts of drunken revelry and debauchery. Abigail would never have allowed a scene of nakedness on her walls. If there were people in the paintings, they were dressed and engaged in quiet pursuits of the home. These paintings were of a bacchanalia.

A boy, clad only in a loin cloth guided me to a banquet that was already underway. Another took my satchel to a nearby room, where he said I would be staying.

"Welcome, Stephanos," the senator smiled when I entered. "I am so glad you are finally here." He patted the seat next to him on the dining couch. Cautiously I sat on the edge of the couch, examining the room.

The senator was dressed in a flowing robe of purple silk, golden brocade about the sleeves and collar. His fingers were covered in golden rings and bracelets. On his head was a crown of gold fashioned in the shape of grape leaves. His skin had been oiled and doused in tiny flakes of gold and silver, meant to make him sparkle in the candlelight. He smelled of wine mixed with jasmine.

There were five other dining couches, all filled, so there was no other place to sit. As I sat next to him, not yet reclining, I noticed that each of the other couches had one older man and one boy or youth sitting next to him. My stomach twisted as I began to realize what might be expected of me.

Was this why Mnesarchus was so disgusted with me? Could he think that I was a plaything of this old man?

I nervously took a few bites of food and studied the room. There were no girls serving the food, only boys, who wore very thin loincloths that hid very little. Though some of the men were carrying on a heated conversation, a few were fondling the boys next to them.

The senator put his oily hand on my arm. "Here, Stephanos. Drink some wine," he insisted. I took a sip of the wine and noticed the other men watched me as I drank. It was bitter, not sweet like table wine should have been. I saw one boy laying across the couch. Except for his heavy breathing, he could have been dead, because he did not move. The man at his side, was caressing his near lifeless body, much as the prostitute had caressed mine. I knew the wine was drugged. I had to think fast or I would be in the bed of this old pervert within the hour.

"Senator," I said. Lately I discovered I could create stories rapidly in my mind. Maybe it was from years of reading so many authors or maybe it was because of necessity, but lies could flow easily. "I discovered a book today in the Agora. A beautiful old copy of an Epicurean manual on dining."

"Sounds interesting." Though he didn't sound as if it interested him in the least.

"Very. I thought of you when I bought it."

"You will have to show me sometime." He started to place his hand on my shoulder, but I stood.

"Let me get it for you. I bought it as a gift for you."

He called a slave. "Show Master Stephanos to his room, so he can bring me this book." He turned back to the table and took hold of a roast fowl, tearing the leg from the body. It dripped grease over his purple robe.

The slave led me to the room. I could tell it was not a room for a guest, but the senator's own bed room. The walls were painted with pictures of naked boys, centaurs, and satyrs doing abominable things. The bed was draped with purple satin sheets and pillows of elaborate brocades of gold, purple, and red. There were two golden statues on either side of the bed, one of a drunken Dionysus, the god of wine, and the other of Eros, the son of the goddess of love.

I saw my satchel on a table by the bed. Nervously I went to retrieve it. The slave paid little attention to me. Out of the corner of my eye, I examined him. Either he was drunk because he swayed back and forth, trying to maintain his balance, or he was drugged too. Either way, I knew he was no match for me.

I grabbed my satchel, swung it at the slave, knocking him over, and ran. I was at the gate before the slave realized what I was doing. I fumbled at the latch, but before I heard the shouts from within, I was out in the dark street.

CHAPTER 13

CORINTH

The righteous hate what is false, but the wicked make themselves a stench and bring shame on themselves. Proverbs 13:5

I slept outside the Hephaisteon, the Temple of Hephaestus, under the cool shadows of its Doric columns. I noticed when the sun rose above the horizon. I sat up and cautiously looked around. There were a few people in the Agora, but none yet at the temple. The events of yesterday were a blur. I think what little I had of the wine caused me to sleep deeper than I expected.

I opened my satchel and looked through my things. Everything was there, but I noticed my purse was open. A few coins were loose. After I had given the prostitute her money, I had securely tied it. I counted my money. Several hundred denarii were gone, almost half of my money. I groaned, realizing that the prostitute had stolen from me.

I could report her to the authorities, but that could get complicated. What if the senator reported me. I hadn't stolen anything from him, but I am sure I hurt his pride. If I went to report being robbed, I might discover that the senator had reported me. I could then be discovered as a runaway slave. I couldn't afford to report the woman. I needed to leave Athens as quickly as possible.

My two scrolls were still with me and safe. My intent with the scrolls was to sell them to help finance my escape. I pondered my situation. I could live off what remained in my purse for a few months, but I needed to find work, and I needed to be frugal.

I groaned as I stood and considered the situation. Athens had not been the paradise of the educated, a place where I could enjoy the fruits of my education, but a hell of debauchery. I had to get out. But first I would sell the books.

I was cautious that morning, as I waited for the book seller to open his shop. I wanted to be inconspicuous and I wanted to stay far from the Stoa of Attalos, in case the senator returned. The problem was that the book seller was in one of the shops of the stoa.

I stood in the shadow of the temple of Hera. From there I was inconspicuous and could easily see the shops as they opened, one by one. There was no one on the steps debating philosophers. There was no senator that morning. The streets were quiet. I waited what seemed an eternity as shop after shop opened. Finally, the last to open was the bookseller's shop.

"Excuse me, sir," I said entering. I realized I did not look as good as I had just the day before. I had been in these same clothes since I stepped off the boat in Piraeus. My clothes needed washing and I needed a bath. That made me nervous. I did not want to be thought of as a beggar or a thief. Yet here I was selling stolen property. "I was told I could sell some books to you for a good price."

He eyed me suspiciously and indicated that I should hand over the books for his inspection. I reached in my satchel and brought them out. I had made sure to care for them, keeping them dry and wrapped in cloth. That was one thing I learned in Ephesus. Books to me were as priceless as gems or works of art. Maybe because to a reader like me, they were works of art.

"This one is from the Syrian critic, Diosthenes. It is from Antioch and one of the best critiques of Socrates I have ever read."

He looked at me, doubting I could read. He opened it and examined it carefully. "It looks genuine. Where did you get it?"

"It was my father's. He worked for the merchant Philemon of Ephesus and only recently died. It was one of several books my father had. I have no money, so I am forced to sell them."

"And the other one?"

I handed him the other, a comedy called *The Birds*, by Aristophanes. It was a beautiful book, filled with skilled illustrations of birds and scenes from the play. Archippus was proud of it when he first bought it about ten years ago. Before he became a Christian, it was a book he always showed a newcomer to his library.

"Have you read this one?" He looked at me questioningly.

"Hear us, you who are no more than leaves always falling, you mortals benighted by nature, you enfeebled and powerless creatures of the earth always haunting a world of shadows, entities without wings, insubstantial as dreams, you ephemeral things, you human beings: turn your minds to our words, our ethereal words, for the words of the birds last forever!"[4]

Of course, I had read it. I knew every single word. I had even read two different commentaries on Aristophanes and could quote what the critics thought of this play. I was as educated as any man in Athens, but they would not get the benefit of my education.

He stared at me, but I could not read his thoughts. He returned his gaze to the play, slowly unrolling it and examining the drawings.

"It is a beautiful work. I can give you two hundred denarii for it. I have no use for the other."

"They are both valuable. The Syrian scroll cost over one hundred and *The Birds* is worth two or three times what you offered. It is from one of the finest illustrators in Alexandria. The calligraphy is impeccable. It is much more valuable than just two hundred."

"When it was new. Now it is used. As for the other, there are hundreds of dissertations on Socrates here in Athens. Few will consider a Syrian critic of any merit compared to an Athenian. They might consider an Alexandrian critic, but, as you said, he is Syrian. I will give you two hundred and fifty for both, but only because of the quality of the Aristophanes."

"I need more than that. I am journeying to Corinth and have to find a way to provide for myself."

"If you can read and write as well as you can memorize Aristophanes, you should have no problem finding work as a scribe."

"Three hundred?" I bargained desperately.

"Two hundred and fifty is as high as I will go." He sat back in his chair, crossing his arms over his chest. He would not bargain with me any further. "You will find no one in Corinth that will offer even one hundred, if you aren't robbed on the highway. That is my final offer."

I had no recourse but to accept. I took the money and hurried out of Athens.

I stayed the next night at an inn in Eleusis. I could not afford to be extravagant any longer, so I agreed to a shared room. I kept my satchel under my head when the others were in the room. I slept uncomfortably.

I awoke to others stirring in the room. I looked out the window to a fabulous view of the sun sparkling on the sea and the beautiful island of Salamis. I had a long walk to Corinth.

I bought a warm loaf of bread stuffed with lamb, olives, and onions. It warmed me and I quickly forgot the problems of yesterday. Soon I would be comfortable in a school in Corinth. Maybe I would do well in this other school and he would recommend me to Athens in a year. Or maybe from Corinth there were other options. It was an important port, so I would have to explore the possibilities.

While eating, I looked at the architecture of Eleusis. It was originally a fort on the border of Attica, but that political division ceased to exist following the conquest of Alexander's father Phillip. It still was an important city because of the mysteries of Demeter. A beautiful temple, the Telesterion, was dedicated to Demeter and her daughter, Persephone. It was several stories high, with white Doric columns on its first and second level, each double the height of a man. Statues of gods and important Athenians lined the stairs up to the temple. The temple was closed this time of year. At the end of autumn, Demeter's daughter was hidden in her husband's abode, so the goddess would hide herself from her devotees.

Someday, maybe, I could explore this place, but I wanted to be in Corinth, and it was more than a day's walk. The morning grew hot, but by early afternoon I made it to Megara, once a prosperous city state. Today, it was little more than a market along the road from Athens to Corinth. I bought a bread stuffed with cheese at the market, but kept walking. I was told there was an inn at the village of Kineta, several miles down the road. I arrived there at dusk only to discover that Kineta was nothing more than an inn with several houses around it, but the inn was nice and the roast goat I was served was enough to make me sleep peacefully in a room above the stable shared by all the lodgers.

I arrived at Corinth late the next afternoon. I washed my white robe in a fountain in the market near the entrance to the city. It was hot and a breeze blew from the west. It dried quickly in the afternoon sun. Ignoring the stares of others, I washed my body as well as possible. I wanted to be clean when I met the school master the next morning.

I looked around at the market of the crowded city. All the buildings had a new appearance. I remembered from my history that the Romans destroyed the city and it was only recently rebuilt by Julius Caesar, and later Augustus Caesar. It was a thriving metropolis, now the capital of Achaea. The greatest importance of the city was that it straddled the Isthmus of Corinth, a very thin piece of land between two gulfs. Ships could unload on the Saronic Gulf, transport their goods across the city, place them on ships in the Corinthian Gulf, and save weeks of travel avoiding the Peloponnesus.

The market by the docks on the Saronic side were filled with every imaginable item the East. Cathayan silk and Egyptian cotton. Grains from Scythia and Libya. Wine and pottery from the Aegean. Olive oil from Attica and Asia. Gold and silver from Thrace. Timber from the lands of the Black Sea. Iron and tin from Asia. Copper from Syria. Papyrus, cotton, and glassware from Egypt. Spices, and gems from the realms beyond. And of course, slaves from every corner of the Empire. If there was something you wanted, you could find it in this market.

I walked quickly by the auction houses. The roar of the crowds around them sounded like thunder. I shuddered, fearing the immensity of Roman slavery. I could not even begin to estimate the number of slaves in the Empire. I was familiar with the personal and domestic slaves of the elite, people like Philemon's family. These were the slaves of a particular look, slaves who would look pleasant in the house of a rich person, because nobody wanted an ugly person waiting on them. But there were slaves who were destined to work in mines and quarries, or rowing on the ships that crisscrossed the Mediterranean. They were strong, but the hard work rarely allowed them to live more than a few decades. A slave of thirty years, who worked in the mines of Attica, would be considered an old man. The latifundia in Rome, and the ranches and plantations throughout the Empire, were worked by a different class of slaves. They lived their lives on the land, but they had the freedom to marry and bear children, who would one day work the land like their parents. Yet they could not travel freely to even the next town. If their master so decided, they could be sold, like any other slave.

There were some slaves who had been born free, but sold themselves so they could survive. Beautiful girls became concubines of the wealthy or prostitutes in every city of the Empire. To a family in poverty a beautiful girl was a curse. A young man with the ability to read and write, someone like me, might sell himself to a nobleman's home to be a tutor for his sons or to a school as a teacher. Those with too many debts might sell themselves or one of their children to pay off the debt. In any of these cases it was risky. Once a person became a slave, all their rights disappeared. Their new master might decide to sell them for some slight offense. So, a teacher might end up in the mines or rowing on a ship, and a girl who lost her beauty had no hope.

The only way a slave could change his status was to buy his freedom. Few could ever do this because a master would add to the debt each year with things like the cost of food and shelter. My choice, to run away, was dangerous. If caught, the authorities were obligated to return the slave to his master. Though often the authorities would profit from the runaway by selling him. If he was sent back to his master, there was the possibility of the mines or worse. A master could offer his slave to be killed in one of the gladiator arenas.

My chances of being discovered were slim, but if caught, my life would be over.

I located the School of Demetrius, near the western docks. It was a school for the Roman community of Corinth. As the capital of Achaea, Corinth had a large Roman population, and they wanted their sons educated. The boys who attended this school would be like Philemon had been. They would be expected to excel in the Latin of their homeland and the Greek of the classically learned man.

It was already dark when I found the school, so I found an inn nearby. I only ate a little that evening, because I was nervous about the next day. The inn had a place where I could hang my robe to finish drying in the heavy wind blowing off the Corinthian Gulf. The inn also had a place to bathe. The fountain had provided little to really clean myself. I needed to be presentable and clean for my next meeting. After weeks of travel, even I could smell that I was filthy. Until now, I never appreciated how clean I was living as a domestic slave. I longed to be back in the world of clean clothes, good food, a regular bath, and the books of a fine library. The bath at the inn felt good, but it was not the same as the bath provided for the slaves at Archippus' villa in Ephesus.

The next morning, I arrived at the school early. Nervously, I approached the gate to the school and was stopped by a burly slave.

"What do you want?" His strong arm across my chest forbade my entrance.

"I was sent by Mnesarchus of Athens."

"For what purpose?" He sneered at me, then pushed me back away from the gate.

"He suggested that I come here to speak with Master Demetrius about being a teacher."

"The likes of you?" he laughed waving me away. "Go away, boy."

"I have had difficulty on the road, including the loss of my slave," I tried to sound condescending like a free man would be, but I found it difficult. "I am a free man of Asia. I demand that you allow me to speak with Master Demetrius."

"Look behind you," the slave indicated with his chin.

I turned to see an old man, wearing pure white. His head was as bald as an egg. I quickly assumed this was Demetrius and bowed to him. "Master Demetrius, it is an honor to meet you," I said in Latin.

"And who are you, boy?" he asked in perfect Athenian Greek. I could tell nothing about him from the way he looked at me. Mnesarchus had shown immediate contempt. This man showed mere disinterest.

"I am Stephanos, a free man of Ephesus," I answered in Greek.

"Well?" He was impatient to be done with this interview.

"I was educated in the School of Tyrannus of Ephesus. When my father died, Tyrannus suggested that I seek employment as a teacher, because of my skills in both Latin and Greek. I can speak the language of the Hebrews, as well."

"I have sufficient teachers, actually too many. Maybe you should try my colleague in Athens, Mnesarchus." He waved me away as if he had no more use for me.

"Please, sir," I asked with pleading. "Tyrannus sent me to Mnesarchus with a letter of recommendation. My first night in Athens I was robbed of money, several precious scrolls, and my letter of recommendation. Mnesarchus had no use for me, saying he was letting several teachers go, and sent me to you. I beg you to see what I am able to do and if you are pleased, you can hire me."

"Mnesarchus had no use for you?" He laughed.

"No, Sir."

"Mnesarchus is my nephew. He hates me. If he sent you to me, then he either knew you would rob me or embarrass me. I do not wish to be robbed and I will not be embarrassed by my nephew. I have no use for you. Begone."

He spoke to the guard at the gate. "If he tries to enter again, contact the authorities to have him arrested. I can't believe I wasted my time on this man."

The slave took a step forward, forcing me to back up. He then laughed and closed the door in my face.

I stared at the wooden door in disbelief. I had failed. I had nowhere to turn. It should have been so simple to find work as a teacher, yet I was not wanted. Could I go from city to city looking for work as a teacher? Should I start looking for work as a scribe for half the money? I thought about what was left in my satchel. How long would that last me?

Now where was I to go? Should I travel north through Thessaly and Macedonia or south into the Peloponnesus? Do I stay here and look for work as a scribe? I had money, but not enough for long. I would stop eating meat, which was too costly. I could stick to bread for a while. But I didn't have a home of my own and inns were too expensive. What was my next move?

Through the din of the city, I heard singing. It was a familiar song. As I listened, I started humming the tune. Then the memory of the words became clear and my despair seemed to wash away as I listened.

"The Lord is my shepherd," I could hear the voice of a young woman above the others. Paul always called Jesus the good shepherd.

"I shall lack nothing." Her voice was clear, like a bell on a crisp winter morning. Paul always said that God will provide for his people.

"He leads me beside quiet waters, he refreshes my soul." Nothing around me was quiet. The peace I ran away to find was not what I was experiencing. What would Paul advise me to do at a time like this?

"Even though I walk through the darkest valley, I will fear no evil, for you are with me; your rod and your staff, they comfort me." I was afraid. How could I stop living a life of fear? These singers were followers of the Way of Christ, Christians. I stood, because I knew they would help me.

"You prepare a table before me in the presence of my enemies." I was hungry. It did not matter who these people were, I needed to eat.

"Surely your goodness and love will follow me all the days of my life." I turned a corner and the singing became clearer. "And I will dwell in the house of the Lord forever."

I stood in front of a modest house, with the gate wide open. Christians were inside, singing a psalm. My mind raced, knowing how Archippus and Abigail were taught to care for those in need by Aquila and Priscilla. I did not know how long my money would last, but for a few days, Christians could help me. I knew the words to say, because I had spent years around Christians. Maybe they could help me find a job as a teacher or scribe.

A girl of about eighteen stood just outside the door listening, like me. Her face was lit up with joy. Quietly I stood behind her. She hummed the tune, with her eyes closed.

"I love the music," she said. I did not know she had seen me. I sighed with relief.

"It is lovely," I confirmed. "I've heard this tune before. A psalm of David."

"You are not from here," she said looking at me for the first time. Her look was curious, not judgmental.

"No, I've been travelling, looking for work." The service inside was beginning to break up and a few people came out the door to enjoy the sunshine.

"Do you follow the Way of Jesus?" the girl asked.

I needed help. These Christians could help me. A little lie wouldn't hurt anyone, but I was telling so many that I was beginning to get confused. "I am from Ephesus," I said, not answering her question.

A man was coming out the door and stopped next to me when he heard me. He was well-dressed, middle-aged. "Ephesus?" he asked.

"Yes, Sir," I answered. He looked like an important man, probably an important member of the church. The girl was just a girl. A man of means was more likely to help me, so I directed my attention to him. "Have you heard of Tyrannus of Ephesus?"

"The teacher? Of course," he answered with a broad smile. "He has been most beneficial to those of our faith. Paul wrote to us about him."

"I studied with him since I was a boy. He gave me a letter of introduction to Mnesarchus of Athens to work there as a teacher. He didn't need me, but suggested I look for work in Corinth. I was robbed on the road of my money and my letter. Demetrius did not believe me and refused to even interview me. I am desperate now. I don't know where to go or what to do. Maybe I should return to Ephesus, but I fear I will run out of money."

"I am Erastus, city treasurer here in Corinth." He guided me into the house. "You are a Christian?" He asked.

There were maybe two dozen people inside, about half near the door at the back. There were more out the front and back doors. Several women were preparing a table of food. I could smell the delicious baked breads and a meat that had been roasted to perfection. My mouth began to water. I was hungry.

"I am, Sir," I said as I followed him into the house. I decided a little lie would hurt no one. I would get some food, a place to sleep, and maybe someone could help me find a job. Nobody would be hurt. Nobody would discover my lies. "I have been taught the Way by a man named Aquila, and his wife Priscilla. When Paul was in Ephesus, I studied with him also."

"How is Priscilla?" a woman asked with a smile. She overheard our conversation. "She is my dearest friend."

"She is well," I answered with a smile. "She was the last person I saw leaving Ephesus." The last part, at least, was true.

"Paul is a great teacher," another man said at her side. "He spent a great deal of time with us before he went to Ephesus."

"If you have studied under these friends of ours, then you are most welcome here." Erastus pointed to several women preparing a table with food. "On the first day of the week, we typically share a meal together after our worship time. It helps us to grow closer together and become more like family. Will you join us for a meal?"

"I have no money to pay you for your hospitality. It would be better for me to look for a place to stay and find work first."

"Nonsense. Our church is open to you, a friend of our friends."

The familiar Christian smiles surrounded me. I was not one of them, but they were easy to spot. They were happy. They did not seem concerned that some were rich and some were poor. There were both Greeks and Romans here, and probably a few Jews. But how would they react to me, a runaway slave, if they discovered the truth?

"What is your name, young man?" the woman asked, handing me a small loaf of warm bread.

"I am Philemon of Ephesus." I don't know why I said his name. I could have continued being Stephanos. But the name fell out of my mouth before I could control it.

"Come," the man said taking me by the arm. "Let me introduce you to our teacher." I smiled at people as we crossed the room. He led me to a man with his back turned to me. His hair was black with a sprinkling of white hairs. His form looked familiar. "Apollos, this is Philemon of Ephesus."

Apollos turned and looked me in the face. He started to speak, but then he recognized me and stood looking at me with his mouth agape. Fear swept over me. I felt my neck grow dark and heard ringing in my ears. I felt nausea wash over me. I thought I would vomit. Then Apollos spoke to me.

"Onesimus?"

"I can explain."

"You are mistaken, Erastus," Apollos said. His smile was curious. "This is Onesimus, the slave of Philemon of Ephesus."

"What?" he asked. He stared at me with disbelief. "He said is name is Philemon. He did not say he was a slave."

"I received a letter just the other day from Aquila, saying that Philemon's slave had run away after robbing his master."

"Apollos, I can explain."

I looked around at the faces that had moments before accepted me as a member of their community. Now I saw confusion and anger. I would never be accepted as an equal to any of them. I would always be a slave, and now a runaway and thief. I would be turned in to the authorities and sent back to Philemon in chains. Even here I could not find the peace and freedom I sought.

"Please do, Onesimus." That name sounded distasteful in my ears.

How do I explain this? What could I say or do to get free from this? I had walked into a trap.

I could see a clear path to the door, so I ran. I knocked a boy over and almost knocked down an elderly woman. There were a few screams and there were shouts.

"Onesimus, wait!" I heard Apollos shout. No, I screamed inside. I would not wait to be bound and turned over to the authorities and returned to Philemon in shame.

"No!" I shouted.

The girl at the door looked confused. Friends, like her, I could never have. I wanted to explain, but all I could say was, "I'm sorry." I ran out the gate.

Again, I found myself running through an unknown city, bumping into people and making them angry. I could feel the tears streaming down my face as angry shouts surrounded me. I would never be truly free.

As I approached the western port, I turned and saw nobody pursuing me, but that did not mean I was safe. In moments, they could report me to the authorities, who would search for me. I would be caught. There was a ship that had finished loading and looked as if it were about to leave.

"Let me speak to your captain," I shouted at one of the sailors.

"I am the captain of this ship." A big man with a broad chest looked at me from the dock. He scowled, as if he could see I was not important.

"Where is this ship going?" I asked. I looked back to see if I was being followed, expecting to see Apollos approaching.

"Patras and from there to Brindisium," the captain said as I turned back to look at him. He had a look on his face that I could not interpret. There was a smile on his face, as if he had been told a joke, but was holding back his laughter.

"I wish to buy passage."

"Come aboard," he laughed and giving me a hand to help me aboard. He stepped into the ship immediately after me. I realized it was leaving.

As I watched Corinth slowly fading from sight, I wondered if I would ever escape. The Christian community was so small and they all knew each other because of teachers like Paul. How could I be so stupid as to forget that not only did Paul teach in Corinth, but that it was the home of Aquila and Priscilla for many years? Now Apollos, a man I had helped learn the Jewish scriptures, was there. How could I escape?

I looked at the mountains rising in the north of the gulf. I longed to scale those mountains and hear their voices. It had been more than twenty years since the voices of my forest had greeted me. Would they recognize me as a kindred spirit or see me as an alien?

The captain made a joke with several of his crew, in the pidgin Latin of these seas. I looked at them and realized they were talking about me. I was determined I would get off the boat at Patras. How far away was it? I did not remember.

I found a quiet corner in the prow and wrapped a blanket around me, to ward off the cool, salty spray. I was exhausted and fell asleep instantly.

CHAPTER 14

ITALY

You will seek me and find me when you seek me with all your heart.
Jeremiah 29:13

I awoke to a busy port, with as many ships as were at Corinth. I stood, dropping the blanket and looked around me.

"Where are we?" I asked the captain, standing next to him.

"Patras."

I hugged myself, a little cold from the morning air.

"I'll go ashore to buy me some provisions for the journey to Italy."

"You're not going anywhere," the captain laughed.

"What?" I looked at his face filled with an evil mirth.

"You're a runaway."

"I am Philemon of Ephesus," I said defiantly. "I will go ashore if I please."

"I've never heard the name before," he said with a shrug. "By the looks of your rumpled clothes and distraught face, you ran away. I could see the confusion on your face in Corinth. Were you about to be caught?" He laughed.

"No, I…"

"Now you don't know where to go. Do you?"

"I have money. I can pay you."

"Probably stolen. It will just make me a bit richer." I started to move away from him, but he grabbed my arm. He was strong. "Take him," he ordered his sailors. "Bind him." Two sailors grabbed me, while a third bound my feet. My clothes were torn off me. I stood naked while my arms were bound tightly behind my back.

"Help!" I yelled. The sailor on my left struck me across the face. My vision blurred and I tasted blood. He then stuffed a dirty rag in my mouth. I was pushed to the deck, hitting my head roughly. I felt the warm blood dripping from my forehead.

One of the men took my satchel and handed it to the captain.

"Well, what have we here?" the captain asked as he bellowed in laughter.

"A thief, by the looks of him," one of his sailors said.

"It seems I will profit from selling you," the captain said shaking my purse so the coins jingled. "And you have provided me with a gift in addition to that."

The crew laughed with their captain.

The journey was a blur. I am not sure how many days we were at sea. I felt the roll and splash of the waves. The nights were cold, but the days were unbearably hot and the sun burned my naked body. I cried. I slept. I moaned. I dreamed the ship was taking me to the blackness of hell. I thought of the words the old man who sat by the well said about the sea. I now hoped the sea would end it all and swallow me. I no longer wanted to exist.

I was startled awake as one of the men forced me into a sitting position and took the gag out of my mouth.

"Here," he said putting a piece of bread in my face. "Eat."

"I can't. My arms are tied." My throat was parched from days of the rag being stuffed in my mouth. I was thirsty.

"Captain?"

"Untie his hands so he can eat. Give him water too."

"Where are we?" I asked the sailor as he untied my hands.

"We will be in Brindisium in the hour."

"Italy?"

"Yes."

I ate the bread, but was too weak to eat quickly. My fatigue and sorrow was such that I didn't care. The water slid down my throat. It was rancid, but strengthened me.

Nobody was watching me, so I untied my feet. Slowly I devised a plan. As we came nearer to the shore, I would jump in the water. I recalled the boys in Delos and how they swam so successfully. Either I would die from drowning and this nightmare would be over, or I'd swim to safety. I doubted the latter. My body was burned by the sun. I ached and felt feverish.

I could hear the waves and the gulls as they circled overhead. I knew we were close. The captain saw me as I stood, but he was so assured of my captivity that he ignored me. I looked at the shore, realizing I had made it all the way from Asia to Italy. Either I would die today, or escape. Either way, I would be free.

To the right, the docks were lined with row upon row of ships, some anchored offshore because the docks were so crowded. To the left, where we headed, there were just a few ships, and further away a rocky shore. I decided quickly and dived into the water, like I had seen the boys do.

A green haze surrounded me. Sparkles of light broke over my head. My hands touched a muddy bottom. I turned my body around and pushed my feet into the mud as hard as I could. I came out of the water gasping for air. I looked and saw I was farther from the ship than I anticipated.

I heard the laughter of the sailors as I went back in the water, taking a gulp of water instead of air. I came back up coughing. I turned in the direction of the shore, remembering how the boys had swam. I pushed my right arm out in front of me and pulled it back through the water like an oar. I repeated that motion with my left arm. I was moving. It took a few stokes to get the rhythm of one arm then the other. I then realized my feet were trailing behind me, not helping my speed. I started kicking them and it made me move forward. I quickly grew better. I would not drown. I would make it.

The minutes passed before I felt the rocks under my feet. I stood and pushed through the waves. When I finally looked at the shore, I saw some men waiting for me, including the captain. I stopped, realizing I had failed.

Two men came into the water and took me by the arms. I didn't struggle. It was useless to try to escape.

"Thanks for voluntarily giving yourself a bath," the captain laughed.

I was led to an auction house. The captain shook hands with a greasy man. He wore only a skirt. His fat, bare chest was covered in hair. He laughed with the captain then came to me, looking me over. He lifted my chin to look in my eyes.

"I am Philemon of Ephesus," I said in Greek.

"What?" the slave dealer asked in Latin.

"I am Philemon of Ephesus," I repeated in Latin. "This man has abducted me and robbed me. As a citizen of Ephesus, I demand my freedom."

“I don’t care who you say you are,” he said as he paid the captain.

“Say hello to my sister, your wife,” the captain said pocketing the money. They were brothers-in-law. I could expect no mercy.

I was given a robe to wear, and a small loaf of bread. My stomach churned with fear and despair. Why had I left my comfortable home in Colossae? It wasn’t long before I was forced up by a strong slave and led out of the auction house. I looked for a way to escape, but the streets were crowded. The slave held my arm tightly. When I tried to wrench free, he gripped me tighter.

In pidgin Latin, he said, “No try run.” He kept a firm hold of my arm as we followed the slave dealer through the streets.

We arrived at a nice villa on the edge of town. An elderly woman in colorful robes of yellow and purple, answered the door. Her hair, which was died a bright red, was tied above her head with a band of silver. Several curls fell over the band. She had a necklace of yellow glass beads round her neck, and more bracelets of the same beads around her wrists. Several fingers had rings with yellow or purple stones.

The slave dealer spoke to her quietly, all the while she looked me over. Finally, she signaled for me to come to her.

“Why is your skin so red?” she asked touching my shoulder. I had forgotten my sunburn, after everything that had happened. She touched my chest and I felt the sting of the burn.

“The ship captain captured and robbed me. I was stripped of my clothes, my possessions, and my money. I was left on the deck of the ship to burn in the sun.”

“He says you are a runaway slave.”

“I am Philemon of Ephesus. I was en route to Rome to take care of my father’s business interests. My father is the Tribune Archippus, one of the most important men in the Province of Asia.”

"Why would a rich boy, like you, travel alone so far?"

"My slave grew sick in Athens, where we were staying at the School of Mnesarchus." In desperation, I kept the lies coming. "He died after a week there. I am expected in Rome, so I came on my own. Now please, take me to the proper authorities, so I can have these men arrested and my money returned. You will be rewarded."

"I'll take him," she said to the dealer. She ignored my protests. "Go around to my banker. You will have your money."

The strong slave pushed me inside. "Be gentle with him," the lady ordered. "He will make me a lot of money."

The gate was locked securely behind me and was guarded. Inside, the villa did not compare to the villa in Ephesus. It had the appearance of lavishness, but was gaudy. At the front, were several comfortable rooms that belonged to the mistress of the house. The patio sported tables and dining couches. Pots and urns were filled with fragrant flowers. Statues of naked youths and maidens were between the columns. More than a dozen rooms were on either side of the patio.

The mistress' wrists jingled as she signaled for a girl to come. The girl was young, maybe only twelve or thirteen. She had black hair and eyes, and creamy white skin.

"Take him to the room at the far end. Get him some ointment for his burn, and some food. Bring him a clean robe too. I want him in good condition for tonight." She left me in the girl's care.

The girl walked me to the far end of the patio and opened a door for me.

"Where am I?" I whispered. She did not answer. I looked at her eyes and saw they were glazed over as if she had drunk too much. Her face was expressionless. I wondered if she were drugged.

"Why don't you answer me?" I grabbed her wrist, but she gently pulled away. She indicated I should go into the room. I stepped in and the door closed behind me. I heard it latched from the outside.

I looked around at the room. The walls were painted a turquoise-blue, like the sea around Delos. There was a bed with clean linens, which somehow surprised me. There was a table, a chair, and a small chest. I looked in the chest and discovered it was empty. There was a small window near the ceiling that lighted the room. I stood on the chair to see if I could get out, but the opening was too small. There was another, smaller window on the door. I looked out and saw nobody.

I sat on the edge of the bed, but within a few minutes, exhausted, I fell asleep.

I don't know how long I slept, maybe only a few minutes. I was startled by the sound of the latch and then the door opened. The same girl entered carrying clean clothes and a tray with bowl of soup, a small loaf of bread, and a small jar of watered wine. There was also a jar of ointment. She sat them all on the table and opened the jar, indicating that she was going to put the ointment on me.

"Speak to me," I demanded.

She shook her head no.

"Are you not allowed?

She didn't answer.

"Are you unable to speak?"

She nodded her head in the affirmative.

"I'm sorry."

She shrugged her shoulders and indicated for me to remove my robe. Reluctantly, I did. She made no reaction to seeing me naked. Her face was expressionless. I turned so she could rub the ointment on my back. It was both cool when it first touched the skin, but quickly warmed under her massage.

"Can you leave it here, so I can put it on the rest of me?"

She nodded her head, wiped her hands on a towel at her waist, and stood to leave.

"Thank you," I said. She looked at me. For a moment, I thought she would smile, but she did not as she turned away.

The soup was made from barley, with a lamb bone with barely a bite of meat. It also had onion, garlic, and a root vegetable I didn't recognize. It was delicious and satisfying. The bread was still warm and drizzled with honey. The wine was good and sweet, and not too watered down. It was a meal to make a man regain his strength.

What was this place? As a slave, I had never had a room this nice. I felt the robe that was left on the table. It was unbleached linen, very soft. The bed was comfortable. The food was good.

As the sun was setting, the mistress came to my room.

"How is the burn?" she asked lifting the robe off my shoulder.

"Better. Thank you."

"Good. I will require you to entertain a special guest tonight. I sent him a message about you."

"Will you contact the authorities for me?"

"You can buy back the price I paid from tips from customers."

"Tips from customers?" I was confused. "What is this place? What are you requiring of me?"

"You will do whatever he asks." She left the room and I noted that the door was not latched this time. I waited a moment, then quietly opened the door to see slaves lighting torches and others setting trays of delicacies and jars of wine on the tables.

"You aren't supposed to leave your room, the mistress said." A slave, not much older than me, stood in front of me, not allowing me to leave.

"I'll go back in. Just don't latch the door, please."

"Go in," he whispered looking over his shoulder. "I don't think anyone noticed."

I went in and he shut the door, but did not latch it.

"What is this place?" I asked.

He looked through the window. "Hell."

I sat back on the bed and waited. The mute girl returned and took the tray of food, but brought in a pitcher of wine and clean cups. She shook her head to indicate that I shouldn't drink it, and then she left.

I waited again.

The house slowly filled up. I looked out the window and saw men lounging on the couches. Slaves waited on them. The men freely groped and fondled the slave girls. I quickly assumed I was in a brothel. It was confirmed when one of the girls led a man to a room.

I stepped away from the door and leaned hard against the wall. Why was I here? I looked out the window again. Memories of the senator in Athens filled my mind with dread. I began pacing the room, wondering what I would do.

There was music playing and girls laughing, but I began to realize, like the other slave said, it had the sound of hell.

"There is a purpose for your life," I heard the voice of the man from two decades ago.

"God has a plan for you," I heard Paul saying.

I stopped my pacing and stared at the door.

"God, if you are real and you really did say those things to me, then let me get out of here tonight."

I heard the voice of the mistress approaching. "I have a new one, especially bought for you, Praetor."

The door opened and a man that could be the brother of the senator stood in front of me. He had a forest green robe, trimmed in gold. A fat gold necklace was around his neck. Every finger had rings of gold and precious stones. The smell of sweat and perfume filled the room.

"Very good, Claudia," he said with a lecherous grin. "Very good, indeed."

I gasped for air. I could hear my heart pounding in my chest.

"I will leave you two to get acquainted." She caressed his shoulder intimately and looked at me. Her look seemed to remind me to do whatever he asked. She closed the door behind her, but I did not hear the latch.

"Pour me some wine," he commanded, as he sat on the bed.

I didn't move.

"Come now," he said sweetly. "Let's start with a little wine. So, pour me a cup."

Nervously, I poured the wine, spilling some on the tray. I looked at the door and noticed that it was slightly ajar. I could see torchlight coming inside. I knew I could escape if the moment was right.

I handed him the wine and he drank it all in one gulp. "Sit beside me," he patted the mattress.

I shook my head no.

He reached out and took my arm, pulling me closer. He was a big man, but he wasn't strong. Clumsily, he began to fondle my chest and arms. I kept the desire to vomit under control. Quickly I devised a plan.

"Let me get you some more wine," I said moving away from him. I rattled the cup as I tried to fill it.

"Pour a cup for yourself while you are at it." I could tell he was studying me, even though my back was turned. "What is your name, boy?"

"Onesimus." It was the first time in weeks I had used my name. If my plan worked, it really didn't matter.

"Haha. I hope you will be useful to me."

I took a deep breath. "No, sir. You will be useful to me." He looked at me with confusion.

I threw the wine in his face. As he started to scream, I slammed the pitcher across the side of his face. I didn't have time to take a ring or look in his purse, or even in what condition I left him.

I pushed the door open, startling a girl who screamed. I walked quickly down the portico, knocking over another girl carrying a tray. Nobody understood what was happening yet. Some of the customers were even laughing at me. I reached the entrance to the villa when the call went out to stop me. At the gate were two men, much older than me, but no guard. I pushed my way through them, making one lose his balance.

In the morning, I had seen that the villa was outside the city gate, so I did not run in the direction of city lights. I ran toward the darkness. I heard shouts behind me, but I kept running. My feet were bare and I felt the cuts of sharp rocks. My robe was torn by branches and brambles I could not see.

I must have run for an hour or more. When I finally stopped, I fell to the ground, looking at the expanse of the sky above me. The stars seemed to swirl around me, twisting and turning. I was too dizzy to stand.

"He heals the brokenhearted and binds up their wounds. He determines the number of stars and calls them each by name. Great is our Lord and mighty in power."

I remembered the prayer I had made, the day I escaped. I was cold. I was bruised. I felt a heavy weight on my chest. I understood what it meant to be brokenhearted.

"God!" I called out through my tears. "If you are real, save me."

The night swirled dizzily around me. I gripped the rocks at my side so I would not fall. I slept and dreamed of being in my forest, tired from running.

I awoke to the sound of a running stream. I bent over the cold water and drank deeply. I was refreshed, the fatigue falling away. The sun warmed my shoulders, even as the cool mountain breeze left me feeling chilled. I loved these autumn mornings.

I looked in the water and saw a boy with dirty yellow hair. I could not make out the color of his eyes, but I somehow knew they were blue. He was smart and strong, but smaller than the other boys his age. He frowned back at me, because he was always alone and didn't know how to speak to others. He thought he was better than the other boys, so no one played with him. But he was the descendant of Rubobostes, a warrior-prince of the Singidava Getae, who had defeated the Romans when they invaded his land. What need did he have of the friendship of other boys?

I heard a call from the distance and looked up, the water dripping from my chin. Could I possibly hear my mother from so far away?

"Prince!" she called. Yes, it was her. This was the day, so I must return home quickly. I wiped the water on my robe as I stood, taking my last breath of the clean forest air.

"Son!" she called again.

So, I ran.

It was autumn. The leaves were falling around me, daring me to catch them, as they fell. The forest was more visible now, than in the summer, because the leaves were no longer blocking the sun. I could always run faster in the autumn. The cold mornings invigorated me. I was born in autumn, so this was my season.

The forest was mostly oak, but also locust and pine, in the deep recesses where only I ran. It smelled so old here. I arrived before the mist departed. Now I was leaving before the sun broke through the clouds completely.

"Prince, my son!" I heard my mother calling again, so I ran to her.

I quickly reached the edge of the forest, where the fir and beech and alder trees were. To me they looked like dancing maidens. The old man who sat by the well, used to say that some believed they were inhabited by maiden spirits. If they were, then I wanted their favor. I waved my farewell to them as I reached the fields of wheat and oats.

A rabbit ran near my feet and I followed laughing as he disappeared into the brush. I always told the man who sat by the well that I was faster than the wolf. One chased me once, but I outran him. The old man thought it might be just a dog, but I know it was a wolf.

No one could run as fast as I could and no one could catch me.

"Prince!" My mother called again. I stop on the edge of the field and waved to her. I could not see her clearly, but I knew she was smiling. She always smiled when she saw me.

My village was only a few dozen huts, simple wooden structures with thatch roofs. Smoke was making little gray lines out of the middle of most. The smell of bread, beans, and meat filled my nose. It was the smell of good food. It was the smell of home.

"Come in and wash," my mother said, as I approached. She was not old, maybe only twenty. Her skin was clean, because she washed every day. Her hair was yellow, touched with just a hint of red. It looked like gold in the sun. Her braids were loose today and fell below her waist. Her teeth were clean and white. They smiled at me with such love. She was fat, but not from eating too much. A second baby was due in a few weeks. She had lost two after I was born, but this one was moving in her belly.

"The trees were calling me," I said as she gently pushed me into our hut.

"They always call you, my little prince," she said as she removed my soiled robe. "You will be a man soon," she said, sternly crossing her arms over her breasts. I felt the tears coming, at the joy of seeing my mother. "Wipe those tears away." Then she whispered, "They will name you today, my little prince."

"What will my name be?" I asked.

She took a rag and washed my face. She was rough, but I could feel the ferocity of her love for me. "I do not know. Wash the rest of yourself, my prince." She handed me the rag and I washed thoroughly, enjoying feeling clean.

My father came into the hut, just as I was putting on a clean robe. He watched me as I tied my sandals.

I looked at him, admiring the man he was. He was tall, much taller than my mother. Her head barely came to his chin, and I was just a little taller than his belly button. His hair was dark, almost black, with braids that fell to the middle of his back. There was a scar across his bare, smooth chest. It was from a war with the Thracian tribes across the Great River, he said. A dark blue tattoo of intertwining spirals covered the left side of his chest. He wore a silver torc around his neck, whose two ends came together like two eagle claws, almost touching. He smiled, showing a tooth that was missing, from the same battle he received the scar.

"Are you ready, my son?"

"I don't know."

"You will be a man one day. You must think for yourself. Look at yourself." He waited while I examined my hands and feet to see if I was clean enough. "Are you ready?"

"I am ready, Father."

Mother kissed me on the forehead as Father guided me out of our hut. Only the men would be at the naming ceremony.

We went to the hut of the man who sat by the well. He was the oldest man in the village, claiming to have survived more than one hundred winters. He was blind. Rarely did he venture beyond his hut or the well, just outside.

"What do we have here?" the old man asked.

"A runner," my father answered.

The old man laughed.

"I am a prince of the Singidava Getae, a descendant of Rubobostes," I ventured to add.

The men surrounding me quietly laughed. They liked my boldness. They knew I would be useful to the tribe one day.

"Something great is in store for you, my child," the old man said gently caressing my cheek.

"Will I be a prince or a runner?" I had always wanted to know.

"Neither," he said in a whisper. He cocked his head, seeming to study me out of his blind eye. "But both."

"What do you mean?" My father asked.

"You will run far from your home. You have always been a seeker, one who discovers what is hidden. But you must return to us."

Smoke from his hearth began to fill the tiny hut. The men who came with Father vanished behind the gray veil. Father turned his head, as if seeking someone outside the tent. They were leaving me.

"What is my name, Old Man?"

"You know your name." The smoke began to envelop him too.

"No, I don't know my name."

"You are Onesimus and you will be useful to us."

The scene around me became shrouded in mist. I felt the urge to run. I brushed the mist away from my face and the sunshine revealed I was on a vast plain, with grass growing up to my waist. I began to run, enjoying the freedom.

I sensed I was not alone, but when looking around I saw nothing.

"A good runner does not look back," I reminded myself. I kept running, but I distinctly heard the pad of an animal. I was closely being followed. I ran faster, now feeling a warm, wet breath on my neck.

I wanted to look, but was afraid. The animal was steady behind me. I felt he could pounce, but he chose instead to run with me.

I swerved slightly, so I could give him space. From the corner of my eye, I saw a lion, bigger than I imagined a lion to be. Now he moved to run beside me. He kept a steady pace beside me.

"There is a plan for your life."

Did it come from the lion? The plain grew dark.

"Keep running and you will find me."

I awoke. The stars were no longer spinning overhead. The moon was gone. I closed my eyes and concentrated on the faces of my mother and father. They were so clear to me now. I had forgotten, but now I remembered.

I shivered in the cold, no longer able to sleep that night.

CHAPTER 15
REUNION

Bear with each other and forgive one another … forgive as the Lord forgave you. Colossians 3:13

"The Holy Spirit spoke the truth to your forefathers when he said through the Isaiah, the prophet:

> 'Go to this people and say,
>
> You will be ever hearing but never understanding;
>
> You will be ever seeing, but never perceiving.'
>
> 'For this people's heart had become calloused;
>
> They hardly hear with their ears,
>
> And have closed their eyes,
>
> Otherwise they might see with their eyes,
>
> Hear with their ears,
>
> Understand with their hearts
>
> And turn, and I would heal them."'

It was Paul. He looked old and tired. His head was almost bald. Yet when he spoke he still had his fire. Nothing seemed to quench it. He saw me, as he finished, and smiled. The sparkle in his eyes had not lessened. He accepted my presence as if he expected me.

I had entered the city of Rome a few hours before. It truly was the center of the world. It was said there were more than a million people in this city, more than the entire province of Asia. Streets flowed like rivers of people. You couldn't move against the flow. I heard Latin spoken, but also Greek, and languages I did not know. There were people who looked Italian or Greek, but many more who were dark, like the people of the southern shore of the Mediterranean Sea. Some were as dark as night. There were people whose skin was whiter than mine, with red hair, green eyes, and covered in freckles. There were Germans too. I had seen a few that served as slaves. There were tall with blonde hair and ghostly blue eyes.

Every god that was worshipped in every corner of the Empire had a temple here. Most temples were very Roman, with steps leading up to pillared porches only in the front, though others showed a Greek influence, surrounded by columns. There were temples whose origin I had no idea, with statues of monsters with half-human bodies in front. All the temples had one thing in common. There were supplicants offering sacrifices all day long. The smoke from sacrifices rose to the heavens, mixing the stench of burning animals with the disgusting odors of the sewers and the masses of people.

I did not know where to begin, or where to go. In all my years of being a slave, I had not dressed as poorly as I was dressed today. I stole a wool robe that I found hanging to dry my second day out of Brindisium, because the one I had been given at the brothel was torn during my run. A day later I found some old sandals lying in a rubbish heap. I was chased away by dogs and sticks from farm after farm when I begged for food. A few people gave me a little, but most nothing more than a curse.

On my walk north, I kept my mind occupied by reciting the plays of the Greeks, the poetry of the Aegean Isles, and the histories of the Romans. Mostly the words of Isaiah came to my mind. Even when I tried to recite Homer, I heard the psalms of David.

> "You, God, are my God, earnestly I seek you;
>
> I thirst for you, my whole being longs for you,
>
> In a dry and parched land where there is no water."

Over and over that psalm of David filled my mind, but I felt no comfort in his words. I only felt the loss of my life.

One morning I stood on the edge of a cliff, overlooking a desolate valley. I wanted to jump to my death, to end this suffering. How easy it would be to fall. I was free, but where was I to go? My feet were bloodied and bruised from walking bare-footed in the rocky lands of southern Italy. What school would hire a man who looked like me? Not even a scribe would hire someone who was as filthy as me. I took a step forward, knocking rocks into the gully below. Their crash echoed across the valley.

But I did not jump, or allow myself to fall. I went around the valley until I found an easy place to cross. Something drove me ever northward.

When I arrived in Rome, I did not even know where to look for work. I considered selling myself back into slavery, just so I could eat. Or I could report myself to the authorities, in hopes they would send me back to Philemon. By chance, I found an office of a scribe. I stood in front of the door, thinking how I could convince the owner that I was someone of value, not the beggar I appeared to be.

That was when I heard Paul. He was standing just a few yards from me when I turned abruptly upon hearing the words of Isaiah. Though those words were meant as a chastisement, to me they were a comfort, because they were spoken by Paul.

"We will not help you or listen to you, because you share our holy words with Gentiles." The man, standing on the step of the synagogue spat the word. He wore the shawl of a rabbi, and the hair and beard were cut in the orthodox fashion, so prevalent among the Pharisees.

Paul turned his attention back to the man. "'Therefore, I will praise you among the Gentiles; I will sing hymns to your name,' as the psalmist said. And again, he said, 'Rejoice, O Gentiles, with his people.' And the prophet, Isaiah further said, "The Root of Jesse will spring up, one who will arise to rule over the nations; the Gentiles will hope in him."

The man standing on the steps covered his ears as if Paul's words were hurting him. Another man on the steps began beating his chest, as if in agony. One man spat in Paul's direction.

"Onesimus," Paul called to me. "Come and help me." People turned to stare at me, wondering how I, a man in rags, was involved with Paul. He held out his hand to me and I pushed through the crowd. Most moved quickly away, aghast at my filth. He turned back to the men on the steps of the synagogue and said in a loud voice, "Judge for yourselves whether it is right in God's sight to obey you rather than God."

"We reject your words!" shouted the man beating his chest.

"I cannot help speaking what I have seen and heard. I will preach what Jesus taught. I will teach why Jesus was crucified. I will teach Jesus' resurrection." Several grumbled and one made the sign of the evil eye. "I will teach Jesus to the Gentiles."

"Then you are not welcome in this place."

"Onesimus help me." Paul sat on the edge of a fountain where the Jews washed their hands before entering the synagogue. He began to untie his sandals. I knew exactly what he wanted, so I bent down and helped him take off the sandals. A hefty Roman soldier stepped next to Paul to stop me.

"Not now, Liberius," Paul said, waving him away.

I continued to unlace his sandals. Paul gently touched my head, as if I were his long-lost son. When his sandals were off, he took water and began to wash his feet. I felt the emotions rise in me. The road had been long and rough, but here I was. I had not been in the city an hour before I happened upon this scene. The tears flowed down my dirty cheeks.

"I will only teach Jesus," Paul said standing. I took his sandals and held them, waiting. "From this day forth, I will no longer teach in your synagogue or in any synagogue. I wash your very dust from my feet."

The Jews on the steps gasped.

"Your blood is no longer my concern. It is upon your heads."

Paul left that place with me at his side, carrying his sandals.

"Paul," the soldier commanded. "Put your shoes on."

"I will not, Liberius." The man was big and muscular. I supposed he was about forty. He looked well-fed and strong. I wondered why a Roman soldier was escorting Paul.

"This is Liberius, my guard," he said as if he knew my question. "I am waiting trial before Caesar Nero."

"You are free to walk the streets?"

"He is," Liberius answered, "but the fool won't stop talking, making everybody angry."

"Why Paul?"

"The Jews accuse me of blasphemy. The Romans say I encourage the people to abandon the gods."

"It sounds like Ephesus all over again."

"There are even witnesses from Ephesus that have come to accuse me."

"But you seem happy."

"These chains are my testimony to Jesus. You know nothing will stop me from sharing Jesus."

"You are not in chains."

"But I am a prisoner of Caesar." He pointed to Liberius who grunted.

It was like a dream walking beside Paul.

"Have you eaten?" Paul asked. I didn't answer right away.

"Yes," but it had been three days.

"Have you eaten recently?" Paul asked again smiling.

"Not for a few days."

"Who is this man?" Liberius asked studying me.

"His name is Onesimus," Paul put his arm around my shoulder, ignoring how badly I must have smelled. "He is a dear friend of mine from Ephesus. He is like a son to me."

I choked up, wanting to cry.

"He looks terrible and he smells. He looks more like a gutter dog."

"He does a little," Paul added smiling.

"But a gutter dog looks better." Liberius laughed at his joke.

"I can explain."

"You can tell me later. For now, it is good to have my son back."

How far I had fallen! I was once a prince, then a slave, now a runaway. Yet still, without hesitation, Paul called me his son.

We turned a corner into the crowded Subura slums of Rome. A few blocks in was a house that Liberius opened with a key on his belt. Paul had a small house. A large room at the front looked like Paul used it for an office. It had a table, four chairs, and a bench across one wall. Two other rooms had beds inside and at the back was a kitchen.

"This is where I meet with guests," he was excited to welcome me in this humble home. "This is my room," he indicated to the room on his right. "This is Timothy's room."

I stopped. He must have sensed my fear of Timothy.

"He will do what I say, Onesimus."

"He will turn me in."

"He will do what I say. For now, you will be my guest."

"Do you know what I have done?"

"Yes, I know what happened. I have been praying about you for weeks." He took a clean, white robe off a shelf and handed it to me, then led me to a small room off the kitchen. "This is all I have for you now. My apologies that it is so small. I will get us something to eat while you bathe." He indicated a basin filled with water and a cloth. As he was closing the door behind him, he added, "Be here when I return."

He left with Liberius. I was alone in the house. It was the nicest place I had been since Athens. I wanted to run, but I was also tired. I could not explain how I came upon him like this, but I wanted to stay with Paul. I could flee or I could rest. I splashed cold water over my face and bare chest, feeling good to be clean again. I would stay for a while.

I heard the door open. Assuming it was Paul, I went to greet him, a towel in my hand. Timothy stood before me. He stood as still as a statue, staring at me. His right hand lightly touched the door. His left hand held a scroll to his side. His mouth was slightly agape. Only his eyes were not still. They searched me up and down, deciding if I was a ghost or not.

"Timothy," I said, breaking the silence. I did not call him master and I could sense he recognized that. I looked him in the eyes, with not a hint of submissiveness. I felt a lot of different emotions: fear, sorrow, anger, relief. I feared he would turn me in, but I was also relieved to see a familiar face. I don't know how to explain that. I hated him for what he had done to me, and to this day, still felt sorrow over the loss of Rhoda. But Timothy was a face from home. "It is good to see you."

"Onesimus. I can't believe you are here." He looked around the room. Did he think I had done something to Paul?

"I am here, Timothy."

"Paul said you would be." He closed the door and put the scroll on the table. "How he knew it, I will never know."

"I'm not surprised. His god thinks he is special."

"What do you mean?" He walked around the table, so we were on opposites sides of each other. For a moment, it looked as if he put it between us for protection.

I sat down, thinking how to phrase what I wanted to say. I felt calm, even though I was alone with the man I considered my enemy.

"Paul knows things. A normal man would not know the things Paul does. He has a relationship with his god that is special, unique. You knew him before me. You know what I am talking about."

"I do." Timothy cautiously sat down in a chair across from me. I could tell he wanted to say something, but I could not tell if he was angry or just curious. I was not going to encourage either his anger or his curiosity. I stared at him. In my fatigue, I could not look angry.

Finally, he asked, "How did you come to be here?"

"I saw Paul at the synagogue today. He was washing his feet of the Jews, much like he did in Ephesus."

"I told him to stay away from them, but he won't listen."

"He said he was now going to the Gentiles and ignoring the Jews."

"Good." Timothy looked around the house. "Did he invite you to stay here? You are here alone? Where is Paul?"

"Yes, he invited me to stay."

Timothy looked instinctively at his room, as if fearing he had just lost it.

"He put me in the room behind the kitchen. I'm not taking your room. If that is what you're thinking."

"Of course not." His gaze shot back in my direction. "Where is Paul?"

"He left with that big man who is his guard. He said he went to buy food."

"That big man is Liberius."

"He is very protective of Paul."

"Many of us who care about him are."

"I won't do him any harm."

The door opened again. Paul carried a basket filled with fresh, hot food. I could see bread on the top and could smell a roast bird of some kind. Timothy stood to help Paul.

"Timothy," Paul said. "We have a guest."

"I see that," he said with a sigh. He started emptying the food on the table. Without looking at me, he said, "We must report him as a runaway slave."

"Runaway?" Liberius asked surprised.

"Yes," I answered him looking at the floor. So, this is how it would end. I breathed a sigh of relief. I actually was glad it would soon be over.

"He is my cousin's slave. He stole money and costly scrolls from his master and ran away."

"Paul, Timothy is right. He should be reported. You don't need anything else to make you look bad."

"All will be taken care of, but not today." Paul ignored them both as he prepared the meal.

Liberius grunted.

"Sit," Paul ordered his guard. "Let's eat."

Liberius sat as if he was not Paul's guard, but a friend. I wondered about him. Paul was watching me as Liberius helped himself to bread and took a knife to cut some cheese.

"You are wondering about Liberius?" Paul asked. Liberius scowled at me.

"Maybe a little."

"Be afraid, little man," Liberius said pointing the knife at me. Timothy remained serious. Paul laughed.

"He is one of two guards appointed by the palace to watch me. If I were to escape, he would be put to death. Another will come at sunset. He watches the door at night and sees that no one enters or leaves."

"You are free to walk around the city?"

"You saw the answer to that today."

"But are they not afraid you'll try to escape?'

"I am a citizen of Rome. I cannot be held unless charges are proven against me. Until then, yes, I am free to walk the city. As long as the case is waiting for the Emperor to hear it, I may not leave the pomerium until the trial is complete."

"The pomerium?

"That is the sacred boundaries of Rome. Centuries ago it was within the walls of the city, but now the city has grown so much that most of the city is outside of the pomerium."

"So, you cannot leave the city?"

"Even to walk across the bridge over the Tiber for a picnic in the Gardens of Augustus would be tantamount to an escape."

"I would be obliged to put the sword to him," Liberius said through a greasy chicken leg.

"Why are you here, Paul?" I ate slowly, fearing I would become sick if I ate too quickly.

"I've always wanted to return to Rome."

"I heard the first time you were sent here by the Sanhedrin."

"Partially correct. I could have been set free, but I appealed to Caesar. As a Roman citizen, they had to respect my appeal." Paul spread some butter on a warm loaf of bread and then some honey. He then handed it to me. "Try this."

The bread was good and hot. The butter creamy and fresh. And the honey tasted like it had just been taken from the hive. Together they created a taste that comforted, as well as invigorated me.

"But why are you here this time?"

"When my case was dismissed, I was told I could say what I wanted about the Jewish god. Caesar's secretary didn't care. But he warned me not to call Jesus greater than Caesar. That was Caesar Claudius."

"He ignored what the secretary said, of course," Timothy added.

"I would not expect less," I said.

"I was in Crete and angered the local Jewish leaders. They reported me. As I was about to be released, because the governor could not care less about Jewish arguments, one Jewish leader reported that I said Jesus was greater than Caesar. The governor asked if I believed that. I had not said that, and told him so, but I will not deny my Christ before anyone, so I said, 'Christ is greater than even Caesar Nero.'"

"And they sent you back here?"

"Not at first. I think the governor felt it was something between me and the Jewish leaders. He was going to set me free, but some others came to him and accused me. What a coincidence that there were Jews from Corinth, Ephesus, and Jerusalem in Crete at that time. It was like they followed me there to accuse me. The judge ordered me taken to Rome and ordered that my accusers appear in Rome as witnesses in a year or be charged with perjury. They have been arriving over the last few weeks."

"Are you afraid?"

"You know me, Onesimus. What do you think?" I did know him well. He would not be afraid to stand trial for Jesus.

"No, you are not afraid?"

"And what about you, slave?" Liberius asked.

"Be kind to him please. He is my guest."

"My apologies, Paul. I don't want more problems for you. If he is a runaway and one of your accusers finds out, they will add this to the mountain of accusations."

"Onesimus has been more than a friend to me on more than one occasion. Remember when I told you about the crowd in Ephesus?"

"When they were going to sacrifice you to the goddess with many breasts?"

Paul laughed. "Yes, that one. Onesimus is the one who snuck me out of the city, even risking his life to do it."

"Tell him about yourself, Onesimus," Timothy said sitting back in his chair. Anger was rising in him. I could tell he wanted a confrontation.

"What should I tell him?"

"How you escaped from my cousin, Philemon. How you robbed him of his money and several precious books. How, after years of loving care, you broke his trust and broke his heart."

"Enough, Timothy."

"I was never in his loving care. You know nothing."

"Enough, Onesimus."

"Paul, you have a responsibility," Timothy said rising from the table. "He is a runaway slave. Reporting him will pay back Philemon and his family for all the good they have done for you. It is not right that you harbor his slave."

"He's right, Paul," Liberius said. "If you turn him in it will look good for your case before the emperor."

"Both of you are right." Paul looked at me with sadness. "But for now, we will say nothing."

"Why?" Timothy slammed his hand on the table.

"Because I said so," Paul said softly.

"The law is specific in cases like this."

"I know, Timothy. You and I have talked about this."

"You talked about me?" I asked.

"When he heard you had escaped, he believed you would come here." Timothy said. He shook his head as if in disbelief.

"I came here by accident. It was not my plan."

"Paul, you must do what is right."

"We will discuss this, but not today."

"But…"

"Do you respect me, Timothy? You have called me your father before."

"And you've called me your son. You know I respect you."

"I know that all will turn out well for Philemon, and for Onesimus. You know how I feel about this young man."

"You told me you thought of him as your son. But I thought I was your son."

"After all you and I have been through together, do you not believe that you are my son in the Spirit?"

Tears came to Timothy's eyes. He started to say something but became choked up and could not speak.

"I ask that you give me a little time. I intend to write a letter to Philemon. You can deliver it with the others. Until you leave, I just ask that you respect my wishes."

"Yes, Paul." Timothy left the house.

"I need some fresh air too." Liberius pushed himself away from the table.

"Don't wander too far," Paul said.

"I'm tied to you with a chain, old man." Both laughed.

I stood and began to take care of the dishes.

"Sit, Onesimus. We haven't spoken."

"I can at least be useful if I am here."

"You are not my slave. You will not wait on me."

I sat back down.

"Timothy won't report you. He will do as I ask."

"But he is so angry. No one can know how he will react."

"He has travelled with me for half of his life. When I first met him, he was arrogant and easily angered."

"That is the Timothy I know."

"But Christ has changed him. Give him a chance. You will see."

"What am I going to do, Paul?"

"Stay with me for a while and rest."

I put my face in my hands and began to weep. "Nothing worked out as I planned. It has been a disaster."

"Yet, you are here with me. So maybe you didn't know the end to the plans."

I slept fitfully that night. Timothy came in after dark. He and Paul spoke quietly for a few minutes. I heard my name but could not make out the words clearly. Before Timothy went into his room, I clearly heard him say, "I will do as you wish." Shortly after that the house became quiet.

When I awoke, there was a different guard on the cot, in front of the door. I looked around for a broom, but didn't find one. Maybe if I made myself useful, I would be allowed to stay until I found work. I saw a night water pot, just outside Paul's room and another just outside of Timothy's. Instinctively, I did what I had done most of my life. I went to dump the pots.

"What are you doing?" Paul said from inside the room.

"I'm going to dump the night water pot. I assume in the street?" I asked.

"You are not my slave. You will not do that for me." Paul came out of the room and took the pot from me.

"I have to be useful to you if I am to stay."

Paul put his arms around me. "You are not my slave. You are my son."

CHAPTER 16
ROME

God chose the lowly things of this world and the despised things – and the things that are not – to nullify the things that are, so that no one may boast before him. 1 Corinthians 1:28, 29

I stayed almost a month in Paul's house. He never allowed me to do the chores of a slave. There was a woman who came early each morning to empty the night water pots, wash the dishes, and sweep the house. She would take with her any clothes that needed washing and bring them back a few days later.

"Why do you let her do this, but not me?" I asked one day after she left.

"Her son was dying when I arrived in her house. He might have even been dead. I could not detect any breathing from him. Luke said he thought he was dead."

"Who is Luke?"

"You will meet him."

"So why does she clean for you?"

"I prayed for her son and he was restored to health. The next morning, she arrived and began sweeping the house. I told her to leave, but she said her service to me was the closest thing she could do to repay God for healing her son. She has been back every day since."

"I can do the duties she was doing."

"It would hurt her feelings, and besides, you have value to me in other ways."

I discovered my value later that day. Paul wanted me to copy letters for him. He had dozens of letters that he wrote to friends and to churches he had established or nurtured. He wanted copies for Timothy, who was leaving in a few weeks for Ephesus; for Luke, who I soon met; for the apostles in Jerusalem; and for some of his churches. He knew with my acute memory, that I would keep them accurate, which was important to him. He wanted everything to be word for word the same. Some of these were long and took me a day or two to complete. But most were short, so I could do several copies a day. This was a work that I enjoyed.

Paul's letters were filled with such fatherly love for the people he had worked with for so many years, that I felt a calm assurance as I read them. I began to see through his eyes. His love was for the people he had guided in this new religion. More than that, it was love for a god he believed in and loved more than life itself.

Becoming Paul's scribe helped me learn the neighborhood. I had to buy more parchment, ink, and quills. I wondered if after a few weeks with Paul I could find work with a scribe or as a teacher in a school. The hope I had lost was being restored. One of the verses I had heard repeatedly from Paul was beginning to seem like a reality to me.

"I know the plans I have for you," declares the Lord, "plans to prosper you and not harm you, plans to give you a hope and a future."

I did meet Luke on my third day with Paul. He was a Greek from a wealthy family in Corinth. He had studied at the prestigious School of Asclepius in Epidaurus. There was not a better medical school in the entire Roman world. He also studied history in Alexandria and philosophy in Athens. Before meeting Paul, he was the most renowned doctor and philosopher in Corinth.

"How are you feeling today, my friend?" Luke asked sitting next to him and examining a place on his neck.

"I could not be in better health." Paul responded, feigning frustration at being examined.

"The cough?"

"It is just the crowded city that does that to me. It has nothing to do with my health."

"I brought you some herbs." He opened a packet, showing the dried leaves to Paul. I smelled licorice and thyme. "Drink this as a tea, with honey. Let the water boil with the leaves, then let them sit until cooled. Add the honey while it is still hot. If you can get a lemon or bitter orange, squeeze the juice into the tea just as you are about to drink it."

"A good wine from Gaul will help me more than this." Paul coughed.

"Onesimus," Luke directed, handing me the packet of herbs. "Could you start steeping the tea for me? There are enough leaves here for about ten cups, so don't put too much in the water."

"Yes, sir."

"He's not my slave, Luke."

"You told me that. But if he is your friend, then he will do what is necessary to help you get better even if you won't."

From the kitchen, I listened to their conversation.

"How are you coming with your letters, Paul?"

"I have completed this one to Ephesus." Paul handed him a letter that he had shown me that morning. "It is, of course, a letter of encouragement to Aquila and the church of Ephesus, but I wanted to discuss how the Church is the Body of Christ, because if the church could understand that, they would lead more holy lives."

"I am eager to read it," Luke said examining the letter.

"I will have Onesimus make you a copy."

"Paul tells me that you could make an excellent scribe," Luke called to me.

"I can read and write," I said coming out of the kitchen.

"He says you can do more than that."

"You are among friends, Onesimus. Speak freely." Paul added.

I wiped the leaves off my hands on a towel as I reentered the room. "I can memorize things."

"I can too, but it takes a lot of effort." Luke was kind. I knew I could grow to like him. "How does that make you different?" I had the feeling Paul had already told him a lot about me, even my ability to memorize. His question was not meant to mock me or challenge me, but was like the method Paul used when asking me a question. He wanted me to examine myself and then verbalize it.

"If I see something written, it sticks in my head. In my mind, I see the words as if they were on the parchment." As I said this, I wondered why God had given me this gift. It would have been so much easier if I were ordinary. "It doesn't matter what I have read, I can still see it in my head as it was written, exactly as it was written, word for word. Even if someone misspelled a word, I see it that way. I can even remember the notes my first master wrote."

"Your first master?"

"A dyer of cloth in Byzantium. He spoke Greek."

"What languages do you speak? Greek and Latin?"

"Yes, and Hebrew."

"I have been trying to learn Hebrew for the last two decades. What a marvel to be able to read the words of the prophets in their own language."

"I also speak the language of my home, but I have never seen that written. I was a little child when I left, so much of what I know of the language is basic, like that of a child. My memory is foggy on that."

"You say you remember things that were written, yes?"

"Yes."

"Then maybe if you imagine those words written you would remember them too."

"I hadn't thought of that." My mind began racing. I could learn the language of my homeland. But first I'd have to find someone to speak it with.

"Paul told me you are a writer too."

"I am."

"What do you write?"

"I have two books I am writing, at the moment. The first is a collection of medical remedies I have encountered in my travels. Some are superstitions, which I ignore, but some of these remedies use the natural plants and minerals God has given us. I believe even the ugliest plant can have healing properties."

"Like madder?"

"It creates a beautiful color, from such a drab flower."

"I think colors make the world a more beautiful place." I thought about how the dyer had used the yellow flower to create a deep blood red.

"And it is beauty that gives us hope, which makes us healthier. So even the drab madder flower has a power behind it from the Creator."

"I never thought about it that way. I was always amazed that something yellow could turn things red."

"Tell him about your other book." Paul was enjoying watching his friends becoming friends.

"I am telling the history of Jesus and the creation of the Church."

"Oh? Tell me about it."

"There are many of us who want an orderly account of what happened in Jesus' life. Greeks think differently than the Jews, or Romans for that matter. Jews want to know how Jesus fulfilled prophecies."

"That's true," I said looking at Paul. "He is constantly quoting one of the prophets."

"Greeks want facts that are backed up with proof."

"So how are you writing your book?"

"I have been travelling throughout the Roman Empire interviewing those who were there. People who walked with Jesus. People who were healed. People who witnessed his crucifixion and his resurrection. I've interviewed many of Christ's disciples, his mother, and his brothers. I make it a point to corroborate my writing with at least two witnesses."

"Why is that?"

"It says in the Book of the Law, 'A matter must be established by the testimony of two or three witnesses.'"

"I'd like to read what you have written."

"Paul has a copy."

Paul had already stood and took a large scroll from a shelf. He placed it in front of me. I opened it and began to read.

"Who is Theophilus?"

"You are literate in Greek. Tell me who he is."

I thought for a moment. I could remember no one named Theophilus in all the books I had read. Maybe this was not a real person he was writing to. Who would want to read his book? The churches Paul and the other apostles had established. Therefore, it must be written to them. That made sense. Theo meant god and Philus was friend. "A man who is a friend of God."

He nodded his head.

"Do you see why Onesimus is valuable?" Paul said. Apparently, I had been the subject of their conversation. Maybe he told everyone I was coming. How did Paul see things like this?

"I think he is quite valuable, my friend."

Later that day, after I had read much of Luke's writing, I wanted to talk with Paul.

"Have you read Luke's writing?"

"Yes, I have. I know him well, we often travelled with each other." He was busy with a letter he was composing.

"And what do you think about it?"

"It is good and orderly, very Greek."

"You don't think it should be that orderly?"

Paul stopped his writing, put down his pen and gave me his full attention.

"Luke sees Christ differently than me. He is a doctor and sees the world through the mind of science. At first, I was not sure he was a believer. He wanted proof for everything I told him. If I told him something, he would say, 'that's not good enough.' He wanted something solid, not just my words."

"Is there something wrong with that?"

"No, but ultimately belief in Christ is a matter of faith. One can be presented with facts repeatedly, but can then choose not to believe."

"That makes sense. Does Luke believe in Christ now? Would you call him a believer?"

"I would most definitely. One day he told me he believed and he was baptized shortly after that."

"Does he still seek facts?"

"Yes, he wants people in the future to know that proof of Christ exists." He looked at the book in my hand. "How far are you along in his book?"

"Jesus has just arrived in Jerusalem to celebrate the Feast of Passover."

"Keep reading."

The next day a man named Glaubus arrived. He was very Roman, clean-shaven, bald head, haughty appearance. He wore a white toga, with part of the robe draped over his left arm. He looked like he had money and prestige. I quickly learned to like the man.

"I have spoken to Magistrate over Achaean matters. He has decided to take your case, rather than the Magistrate of Syria." He stood formally, while Paul sat.

"What of the ex-governor of Tarsus, where my family is from?"

"He has elected to stay out of it, since it did not occur within his territory. The Magistrate of Achaea is taking your case, because he has received a dozen letters from Athens and Corinth from friends of yours, including Apollos. All are telling about the good things you have done."

"When will I speak before Caesar?"

"His secretary is putting all the papers in order. The witnesses have all arrived and been interviewed. I have been allowed to read the transcripts of those interviews. There are a dozen different versions of the same story with so many mistakes I will have no trouble dissecting them. I think early next week you will be asked to defend yourself against the witnesses for the prosecution. I am not sure when you will be asked to stand before Caesar, but I think sometime this summer."

"Good," Paul smiled at the lawyer. "I am ready to give witness to

Christ in Caesar's household."

The lawyer was quiet, studying Paul.

"What is the problem, my friend?"

"The Emperor does not like anyone questioning his authority. I've heard rumors that you need to be aware of."

"What rumors?"

He sat at the table, weighing his words carefully. "He is looking for a way to eliminate the Christians in Rome and Italy. He doesn't like anyone who does not see him as a god."

"I can only speak the truth."

"I know, Paul." Glaubus had a sad smile on his face. "I wish there was a way to get you out of Rome. I fear for your life."

"If I leave, what will Caesar do to the Christians in the city?" Glaubus bowed his head.

Liberius who sat by the door, whittling on a piece of wood answered. "He'd kill every last one."

"So, you see, Glaubus, I have no recourse. I cannot ask that the lives of so many be placed ahead of my own."

"I will do what I can to have you set free."

"I want the chance to speak before Caesar. That is what I was meant to do."

Glaubus nodded in acquiescence to Paul's wishes.

"Send my love to your wife." Paul said shaking his hand. "How is she?"

"Since you laid hands upon her in prayer and Jesus healed her, she has had no further problems. She is as healthy as a maiden. She sings all the time."

That meant Glaubus was one of many who had experienced Jesus in their lives. No wonder these people were so devoted to Paul.

Every morning, shortly after Liberius arrived, Timothy went for a run. I did not know where he went, though a few times I was outside when he began his run. He arrived back an hour or two later, covered in sweat. He would come into the house, pick up a towel, and go to bathe in the public bathhouse down the road.

"Why does he run every day?" I asked a few days after I arrived.

"Why don't you ask him?"

"He and I are not very good friends." I cleared a place on the table so I could write.

"I don't think you are friends at all."

"No, we are not." I took a fresh sheet of parchment, brushed off the dust, so I could begin copying a letter Paul was sending to Thessalonica.

"He has a lot to think about. So, he runs."

"What does he have to think about? Timothy is just a man who reacts to situations for his own good."

"He has grown a lot since you two were youths. He is not the same person."

"I hope you are right."

"He has been studying with me about how to lead when I am gone.

I am sending him to Ephesus before the summer is over."

"I have heard you say that more than once. Why to Ephesus?"

"The church there has grown. There are many followers of the Way of Christ, about a dozen churches in the city and surrounding countryside. I need someone there who knows how I think. Aquila wrote me that he feels too old to continue the work, though I doubt he will stop until he dies. Timothy is young and knows what I think more than any man alive. Like you, I think of him as my son."

I did not like the idea of Timothy being my brother, but I would not say so in front of Paul.

"Why don't you go to Ephesus when this trial is over? It would be a good place for you to retire. I would go back to Asia with you."

"You'd go back with me?"

"I think you could help me make some arrangement with Philemon to pay off my debt."

"I don't believe I shall ever leave Rome."

"But your lawyer is working hard on your defense."

"I don't see a future beyond Rome." He was staring beyond me, as if looking for something over my shoulder. His pen was in his hand, but the ink was dry.

"What are you thinking about Paul?"

"For years, I saw many things. I was never afraid because I knew God had shown me these things. I saw the churches in Ephesus, Thessalonica, and Athens. I saw myself before the Sanhedrin and Caesar."

"You'll stand before Caesar and he will believe your defense."

"I don't think a Caesar will accept the teachings of Christ for many years to come. They all want to be gods."

"What about me?" I knew my freedom would be over the moment, Paul stopped protecting me.

"The day I met you, I knew God had a plan for your life." Paul said this in a whisper, almost as if it were a secret. "That is one of the things I saw."

"Paul, you don't know me."

"Why are you here, Onesimus?"

"You invited me."

"No, why are you here?"

"To serve you."

"You are not my slave. So why are you here? You can walk out that door and leave. So, I ask you again, why are you here?"

"I have nowhere else to go."

At that moment, Timothy walked in the door from his morning run. He was sweating and out of breath, but he heard enough of our conversation.

"You can go back to your master. That would be the right thing to do, Onesimus."

"I'm not talking to you, Timothy." Why did he have to interrupt my conversation?

"Send him back to his master," he said to Paul. "That is the right thing to do."

"We have spoken about this before. We will not mistreat

Onesimus."

"But what about his master being mistreated?"

"For the moment, we will do nothing, Timothy. Now is not the time."

"I don't understand you, Paul."

"In an empire of one hundred million and a city of a million, Onesimus arrives at my doorstep, just as I told you he would. It is not a coincidence. God sent him here for a reason."

"Maybe so we can do what is right for our fellow brother in Christ, Philemon. Onesimus is a slave. He should be treated as a slave. As a runaway, he should be returned to his master for justice."

"There is neither Jew nor Gentile, neither slave or free, for we are all one in Christ Jesus. I've told you this before, Timothy."

"Has he become one of us, that we treat him like a brother?"

I clenched my fists in anger. I wanted to hit him, but knew Paul would not like that. Timothy would use it against me.

"God sent him here for a reason. Accept that Timothy."

I did not want to hear any more. In anger, I left the house. Liberius was seated just outside the door, whittling on a piece of wood. He barely gave me a second glance as I ran away.

The Subura was crowded, like every day. I had to push my way through the crowd. People cursed at me and pushed back, but this was normal in this slum. The smell of the city filled my nose. Beggars sat against the walls, covered in the filth of the street, their hands outstretched, hoping for a scrap of bread or a sestertius. Dogs that were mostly bones nosed through the refuse, flinching in fear if someone swatted at them or came too close. Taverns were on every corner, but were so dirty, I could not imagine eating or drinking in them. Drunks lay outside them, covered in their own piss and vomit.

I pushed my way out of the Subura, only to find myself in the vicinity of the slaughter houses close to the river. Blood and excrement from the butchered animals filled the streets. The calls of terrified cattle, goats, and pigs filled my ears. Flies buzzed around the butchered carcasses. A swarm followed me, biting me on my neck and ears. The smell of death was stronger than the smells of the Subura. Above all the smells was the incessant smell of animals sacrificed on the altars of the many temples. Even the meat market had twin temples to Vulcan and Mercury, their altars billowing smoke into the streets. Was there ever an end to the death this empire demanded?

My eyes were burning as I entered the Campus Martius, a military camp just outside the pomerium, the sacred boundaries of Rome, but within the modern city walls. The crowds thinned out, as I passed the many barracks of soldiers. There were also taverns, but they were much cleaner than those in the Subura. No one gave me another thought as I walked to the bridge that led across the Tiber. I was just another man in a mass of humanity.

Across the river, the city continued, though officially it was not in the sacred boundaries of Rome, nor even within the modern city walls. Here were villas of the wealthy, nice homes of the middle class, clean streets, and clean markets. Augustus had built a villa here, but his descendants no longer lived here. Claudius, as a gesture of good will to the people of Rome, had the walls torn down, so the people could have access to the beautiful gardens. Flowers, fountains, and shaded pathways encircled a house that was no longer used. But this was a place where the wealthy wandered, not the poor, nor slaves. It was not for me.

I found a linden tree, already in full bloom. Its fragrance always reminded me of the home of my childhood, though I never remembered a linden tree in my forest or my village. I buried my face in my hands and started to weep. I had gone so far from the home of my birth. I no longer knew what that place looked like. The dream of my parents seemed like a cruel joke. I would never be free and never see that place again. I could not even escape in a place as big as the Roman Empire.

Why did Timothy hate me so much? What had I done to him? I had dared to be a man and say what I thought, when I knew his motives toward my master were not right. For that, he hated me to this day. From the day I met him, he had torn Philemon away from me, causing any semblance of brotherhood between us to be destroyed. He lied to my master and caused my innocent Rhoda to be sold. What horrors had she endured because of his jealousy, I could not imagine. I hated him for what he had done. I felt a pain in my stomach, the hatred was so great. The only answer I had for why he hated me was because I was a slave, someone who merited nothing.

I could not go back to Philemon. I would be mocked and treated with contempt. I would be ordered whipped again as Archippus had ordered so many years ago. The other slaves, even Zoe, would not look on me with pity, but with contempt. I could find nothing in the house of Philemon.

That man always called me a brother, but I was his slave. He did not mind me cleaning his filth every morning. He became angry when I proved I was better than him. For all the boasting he had done about being an educated man, I was better educated. If he wanted a poet, playwright, philosopher, or prophet quoted correctly, he came to me. I did not have to think, because it was written indelibly on my mind. He repeatedly called me his brother, yet the man treated his cousin more like a brother than he ever did me. I was not allowed to marry for fear that a child would take Zoe away from her duties. Even as he called Paul, Aquila, and

Apollos brothers in Christ, I was just his slave, someone who did not even merit learning about this Christ of his. It was his fault. He drove me to steal and run away. He caused me all this pain.

What did running away do for me? I had my first woman, but that left me feeling ashamed. What kind of man buys his love? Yet even that bought love was not love. Discovering she had robbed me, left me feeling empty. I wanted to be loved and she robbed me of that too.

I had never realized the protection I was accorded as a slave. As a free man, a senator and praetor tried to use me, something neither would have tried in Philemon's house. Both wanted me for the carnal pleasure I could bring them. My education did not give me the position I desired. Nobody cared. In reality, I had no purpose in life. At least as a slave I could eat and bathe. In my stupidity, I had destroyed even that. I could never go back to that life again. It would never be the same.

I looked up and noticed a lady staring at me. She was young and gripped the hand of a child. I couldn't tell if her look was one of fear or curiosity. I am sure she didn't often see a grown man crying in the park. The child, a boy, was no more than two or three years old. He looked at me and smiled. He didn't care if I was slave or free. She picked him up and began to walk briskly away, even as the little boy waved goodbye to me.

I stood and walked home. Paul, of all the people I had ever known, was the only one who accepted me.

"You were gone a long time, boy," Liberius said as I arrived back at Paul's house. He was sitting on a camp stool outside the door, again whittling a piece of wood. I could not see anything emerging from his effort. Maybe he did it to pass the time.

I crouched next to him, my back against the door.

“I hate him.”

“Timothy?”

“Yes.”

“Why are you here, Onesimus?”

“Because I don’t have anywhere else to go.”

“You’re not being honest to me or to yourself.”

“What do you mean?”

“If you are running away from your master, why would you stay in the house of his friend, with your master’s cousin staying here too?”

I avoided his question, because I didn’t have a reasonable answer.

“You are more like a friend of Paul, rather than his captor.”

“No man has ever been kinder to me. I was assigned to guard him almost two years ago. Never did I imagine that he would become my greatest friend.”

“What if he is sentenced to prison or death?”

“Paul and I have discussed that.” His countenance became thoughtful and sad. “He has decided and I will do as he wishes.” That sounded like Paul. “You are avoiding my question. Why are you here, Onesimus?”

“Paul has repeatedly said that God has a plan for my life.” I don’t know why I told him that. “So, I guess I am here to discover what that plan is.”

"For I know the plans I have for you," Liberius pointed at me with his knife. "Plans to prosper you and not to harm you. Plans to give you a hope and a future." It was from the prophet Jeremiah.

"Paul taught you that?"

"Yes, and much more. I know I am here, as his guard, for a specific purpose." He started whittling again, the shavings falling to the ground around his feet. "Have you heard the story of the Persian queen, Esther?"

I had read everything, so of course I knew it.

"The Jewish girl who saved her people. Yes, I have read it."

"What her uncle told her has become part of me. Do you know it? Paul says you can memorize anything you have read."

"If you remain silent," I quoted. "Deliverance will arise from another place, but what if you have come to this position for such a time as this?"

"That is the passage exactly."

I didn't respond, but watched him continue to whittle.

"I could simply be Paul's guard and do my job. But what if God assigned me this post for something greater."

"Like what?"

"I don't know yet."

"Do you want to know?"

"Of course, but this is where God has placed me at this moment. I could wonder and worry about why God has me here, or I could live in the moment, learning what I can from Paul and being ready when God sends me on my way." He looked at me. "Even sitting here whittling and talking to you is part of God's plan. I don't know what, but I know it is."

"Will you help him escape if it becomes necessary?"

"That isn't what he wants, so the answer is no."

"What will you do when this assignment is over?"

"I've dreamed of retiring to Thrace."

"Why there?" I almost laughed when I asked.

"I served with Claudius' legions when we took Thrace. I loved the place and the people. There is a settlement of soldiers on the river that acts as a boundary between Thrace and Dacia. I want to retire there. Maybe become a farmer."

"I was born in Dacia."

He looked at me and smiled. "Maybe I will go to Thrace and start a church among the retired soldiers."

"Paul has changed you then?"

"No," he looked out on the busy street. "Paul has introduced me to God. That is what changed me." He looked at me. "Just like God has changed you."

"Me?"

"Yes, God has changed you."

I was not sure that God had changed me. I stood.

"In answer to your question, I don't know why I'm here."

"You'll find your answer soon enough."

CHAPTER 17

STARS

"He determines the number of stars and calls them each my name." Psalm 147:4

Early on the morning of the first day of the week, the day after the Sabbath, what the Romans called the Day of the Sun, Paul was preparing for a group of believers to meet in his house. I wondered why they met on this day, rather than the Sabbath.

"If you are part of the Jewish religion, why do you not meet on the Sabbath, like the rest of the Jews?"

"For several reasons. First, most of the people who meet with me are not Jews. Many of those who are Jews, still meet at the synagogues on the Sabbath. Those who are not Jews, are not welcome. We could meet on the Sabbath, but our Jewish brothers would be left out. So meeting on the first day of the week, what the Romans call the Day of the Sun, is easier for Jews and Gentiles to meet together.

"Second, we are no longer bound by the Law and are not required to meet on the Sabbath. Yet we meet weekly to celebrate Christ's resurrection, which was the first day of the week."

"You obey many of the laws of the Jews."

"Yes, but for a different reason."

"What is that?"

"God wants us to produce fruits of righteousness, not out of fear of breaking the Law, but out of our love for Christ. Which leads me to the third reason. We meet to both honor God and to learn more about him."

The first who arrived was Lydia, the lady who cleaned the house, carrying a basket full of hot sweet bread she had baked early in the morning. Her son, Lucius, the boy who was healed by Paul was with her, carrying a sleeping girl named Patricia. Lucius was maybe twelve and the little girl just a toddler. Lucius put Patricia on Paul's bed and covered her with a blanket.

Demas, Aristarchus, and Epaphras arrived shortly thereafter. These were all men I knew from Ephesus and Colossae. They knew who I was. They knew I was a runaway. None brought up the subject. I assumed because of Paul.

Timothy engaged Aristarchus and Epaphras in conversation, but Demas came to talk to me.

"I heard you were here, Onesimus," Demas shook my hand. "It is good to see you."

"Thank you." I didn't know what else to say or do. I stood in the corner and watched. Demas stood beside me, smiling. I felt uncomfortable because I didn't know what to expect.

Luke arrived shortly after and introduced me to a man named Tychicus. He would be travelling to Ephesus with Timothy in a few weeks. Glaubus arrived with his wife and two teenaged sons, Glaubus and Julius. I later learned she was his second wife. His first wife died in childbirth. She was not much older than his sons.

Others arrived crowding the small room. There were two ladies who had shops nearby. I had already bought parchment from one. She remembered me and greeted me. There was an older man who ran the tavern on the corner. He brought a jar of wine with him.

There was a large man who reminded me of the stories of Hercules or Samson. He worked at the docks, so spent his life loading and unloading barges carrying supplies from Ostia. There was a quiet girl of about fifteen. A young Jewish scholar brought two of his friends from school, both sons of Senators. Liberius sat at the door as always, but when an elderly woman entered, he moved his chair beside Paul and guided her to sit.

"There are so many are here, Demas."

"Yes, there are."

"And they are all different."

"But they have a similar purpose." I looked at him, not asking for an explanation. "You have heard Paul say that in Christ we are all the same?"

"Yes. He says there is neither Jew or Gentile, Roman or Greek, slave or free."

"Exactly. Here you see it."

"I see two dozen people of different backgrounds."

"But with one purpose. They are all here to learn about Jesus and then share what they learn with those they meet."

"What do you mean?"

"The lady who brought the bread."

"Lydia."

"Yes, she learns what Paul says and then shares it with her customers throughout the week. The other two shopkeepers and the tavern owner do the same thing. The big man works at the dock. He is not well-educated, but when he has the midday meal with his coworkers, he tells them about Jesus and what he learned from Paul each week. The young Jewish scholar, whose name is Micah, goes home and checks what Paul has said, then discusses it with his rabbi and fellow students. Luke shares it with his patients at the clinic he volunteers in. And then there is Liberius."

I looked at the gruff soldier by the door. I was growing fond of him. "What about him?"

"He lives in the barracks. Every night he speaks about what he has learned to his fellow soldiers. Usually we have more soldiers than just Liberius here."

As he said that, two soldiers entered the house. One was as old as Liberius, but the other was a mere youth.

"Forgive us for being late, Paul," the older soldier said.

"I was waiting for you before I began."

"See what I mean?" Demas whispered.

"Tychicus, lead us in some songs to get us started."

Tychicus had a pleasant voice. He was not far into the psalm before his eyes were closed. He had a look of pure joy on his face. Lydia lifted her hands, as if she had a gift she was giving someone. Tears streamed down her face. As I looked around the room, all were like this, even Timothy. They were singing from their hearts and out of love. In Ephesus and in Colossae, they sang the songs of the synagogues. Here was something new.

I had a tingling down my spine. At first, I was afraid, but a sense of peace made me relax. I thought of all the pain in my life. A life without love. I wanted the peace these people had.

I felt a tug on my sleeve. The little girl, Patricia, had awoken and was looking up at me. She smiled shyly and I smiled back. Suddenly her arms reached up, asking me to pick her up. I looked across the room to see her mother, Lydia, looking at me. She nodded her head, indicating it was fine for me to pick her up. When I did, the girl wrapped her arms around me and put her head on my shoulder. She was comfortable in my arms.

So this is what it feels like, I told myself. This is what being loved feels like. This little girl did not even know me, but loved me. I could feel the tears on my cheek, but I didn't care. This felt good.

Timothy looked at me from across the room. There was something different about his look. It wasn't disdain for me being a slave. Nor was it anger at me for being a runaway. He held my eyes for a moment, then dropped his gaze to the floor.

"Today I want to talk to you about the stars," Paul said introducing his sermon.

There was a chuckle from a few. Luke, Timothy, and Micah were all seated at the table and began to write.

"On the fourth day of creation, God created the sun and the moon. These great lights are used to mark our days, our months, our times of festival, and our years. Moses also wrote, when describing the creation, five little words that mean much. 'He also made the stars.'" Paul was standing, slowing looking from one person to the next. He spoke slowly, wanting his words to sink in. "The stars seem so insignificant next to the sun and moon. The sun tells us it is day, but it also tells us our years. The moon is usually in the sky at night, but it does not tell us it is night, because sometimes we see it during the day. But the moon has a regular cycle of waxing and waning, that tell us our months. Both are important to our lives, even if most of the time we ignore their importance."

Paul had walked a little. He was now standing behind Timothy and put his hands on his shoulders. Timothy looked up at him. One thing I could say about Timothy, is that he loved Paul.

"But what about the stars?" Paul continued. "David, the psalmist, said,

> 'When I consider your heavens,
>
> The work of your fingers,
>
> The moon and the stars,

Which you have set in place,

What is mankind that you are mindful of them?'

"He set the stars in the heavens. Some seem to have a purpose according to men who study the stars. But most seem to have no purpose at all, unless it is to adorn the night sky with sparkling gems."

I remembered my night outside of Brindisium with the stars swirling over my head.

"He further says in a different psalm, 'By the word of the Lord, the heavens were made, their starry host by the breath of his mouth.' Have you seen the stars away from the city lights?" Paul asked the quiet girl, whose name I never learned.

"When we lived on the latifundia south of here, I often looked at the stars at night."

"How many are there?"

"I have no idea."

Paul turned to Luke. "You are the most learned man here, a true scientist. Tell us how many stars are in the sky. A thousand maybe?"

"More than that."

"There are about one hundred million people in the Empire. Do you think there are enough stars for there to be one for each person?"

"Yes, but I think there are many more."

"How many would you estimate?"

"A number greater than can be imagined."

"Did you know, Luke, that one of the last psalms talks about counting the stars."

"Oh?" He asked.

Paul looked at me. "Do you know what I am talking about, Onesimus?"

"Yes."

"Quote it for us."

"He counts the number of stars."

"And the next part."

The thought about the next part sent me into a quiet amazement. How was a god like this possible? Paul patiently waited for me. He knew that I knew the next part, but he didn't know that God had been speaking to me with that very same verse just days before.

"And he calls them each by name."

"Imagine this God for a moment."

He walked around the room, looking at each person. He loved them all. I could see it.

"We know from scripture that he created everything in existence. We know that he created us. He created the animals and the birds, the flowers and trees, and fish of the seas. He also created those tiny specks of light that we see in the night sky. We don't know yet what these are, but one day an astronomer will tell us. We don't know how big or small they are. We don't know how close or far away that they are. Yet on a clear night, far from the city, you can see a spectacular display of more stars than can be counted, according to our friend, Luke.

"Two things I want you to note about these stars. First, God spoke them into existence. 'By the word of the Lord.' 'By the breath of his mouth.' God spoke, and they were settled in the expanse of the heavens. A mere word and they were there. Second, he calls them each by name. God knows exactly how many stars are in the heavens. Not only could he tell you the exact number, but he has named them all, each and every one of them.

It makes that phrase 'he also made the stars' not seem insignificant anymore.

"Liberius, do you remember what we were talking about the other day? What Jesus said about the sparrow?"

"Are not two sparrows sold for a penny? Yet not one of them will fall to the ground apart from the will of your Father. So don't be afraid; you are worth more than many sparrows."

"Do you know where I am going from here?" Paul asked Glaubus.

"I think so."

"Tell me."

"God has created an amazing world for us, but to Him, we are so much more valuable." Glaubus reached for his wife's hand and held it tight.

"Then why did God spend so much of history, speaking only to the Jews? Why not the Greeks or Persians or one of the Barbarian nations?" It was the Roman friend of Micah, the young Jewish scholar. "Why did he wait so long to speak to the rest of us?"

"In God's eyes there is neither Jew or Greek, Barbarian or Roman, rich or poor, male or female, slave or free."

"But that doesn't answer my question."

"Because of Abraham's faith, God chose his ancestors, the Jews, to receive his revelation. They received the Law and the Temple. They received the words of his prophets. They also received his judgment when they strayed. And lastly, through the Jews, God gave us his Son, Jesus, who was born at the right time in history. Because they were given all these things, they have more responsibility to God. Now, though, God has given you the chance to know him."

"So what is my responsibility, as a Roman, a non-Jew?"

"To tell your own people about Jesus, because you, a Roman, can tell them better than I, a Jew."

I heard what sounded like a whisper in my ear. "There is a plan for your life." The man had said that to me many years ago when I was in the cage. I heard it again in my vision the night I fled from Brindisium. Paul had said that to me many times. Was I supposed to tell this to my people? I didn't even know them anymore. Was I supposed to talk to them about Jesus?

"Who better to tell them than you?" Paul was looking at me, as if he had heard the question. Did he address me, or the young man?

"God cares about you more than he does the stars. He loved you enough for Jesus to die in your place. Now it is your turn. You are to tell the people in your circle about Jesus."

Paul walked over to the dock worker and put his hand on his shoulder. "I don't know the men who work at the docks, but you do."

He turned to Liberius. "Nor do I know all the soldiers who served with you in Thrace."

He looked around the room, "Nor all the people you come in contact with every day." He looked back at the young man. "That is your responsibility."

Paul looked at me, but said nothing. He allowed the words to sink in. My responsibility. That was hard to imagine.

"So I end my little talk with this question. What are you going to do with Jesus?"

CHAPTER 18
REDEMPTION

"He did evil because he had not set his heart on seeking the Lord." 1 Chronicles 12:14

I was quiet the next few days, pondering Paul's sermon. What was I supposed to do with Jesus? Paul knew I was thinking, so he left me alone. I copied letters and organized his papers. I bought new quills and ink. I did little things like that. And I thought.

One afternoon, I think it was the Day of Jupiter, I was alone in the house with Paul. Timothy went with Luke after his visit. Liberius was outside the door, whittling as always. Paul was reading.

"What are you reading?" He was always reading. If he wasn't reading, he was writing.

I brought him the tea that Luke had recommended. If Luke were here, he would say he didn't need it, but with him gone, he drank it and seemed to enjoy it. Often, he added a little more honey or an extra slice of lemon.

"A passage from the prophet, Isaiah."

Paul took the cup and drank a little of the tea, before setting the cup on the table.

"Of course, you would be reading Isaiah. Who else would you be reading?"

He laughed.

"I was reading this passage and saw it differently for the first time. I was thinking I might share it with the others when we meet on the first day of the week."

"Read it to me." I said looking over his shoulder.

"Woe to those who go down to Egypt for help, who rely on horses, who trust in the multitude of their chariots and in the great strength of their horsemen, but do not look to the Holy One of Israel, or seek help from the Lord."

"What does it mean?" I sat next to him and reread the passage.

"What does it mean to you?" Paul was always doing that to me.

"Why do you do that?"

"Why do I do what?"

"I ask a question and you throw the question back at me."

"Because I see you as an intelligent man, Onesimus. You know more than you think. Now answer the question."

I pondered the meaning, and eventually answered. "I assume the Jews were involved in a war and were considering asking Egypt for chariots and horses. Isaiah is telling the people of Judah that they should not trust Egypt to save them, but their god."

"Exactly."

"But there is more to it than just that, right?"

"I have said before that the prophecies have multiple meanings in multiple layers."

I thought about how Paul would use this in teaching his congregation. He never told stories about the past, just to tell a story. Always he told a story to teach people how to live and how to believe in his god.

"This can apply to people today then." He nodded his head. "Then we are to be like the people of Judah and trust God."

"Yes, you understand. There are so many things in this world that people trust, but they don't trust God. They trust in their strength, or their wealth. People who are intelligent, like you, trust in their minds. Men, like Luke, trust in facts. The Jews trust in their traditions. The Romans trust in their power. Yet none of them trust in God."

"Does your friend Luke trust in God?"

"Yes, he does, but it took him a while to fully trust him. He has a Greek mind and wants infallible proof that he is not trusting in vain. But as the years have passed, he understands that there are things he must believe by faith and not just because he can prove it."

"That makes sense."

"And you, Onesimus, what do you trust?"

"If you are asking me if I am a believer in your god, then the answer is no. There are things I must do before I can ever be his follower."

"What things do you have to do?"

"I have to change who I am."

"That is not the way it is done."

"Paul, I am a slave. Nobody will want me to be part of their church as long as I am a slave."

"I've said before."

I interrupted him. "I know. You've said it doesn't matter if someone is a freeman or slave."

"So then what is it you have to do?"

There were things I had been thinking about for days. I didn't know how to reconcile them. I felt I had to get them out in the open and there was no one I could tell except Paul. I looked at the door, worried Timothy might return.

"Paul, I've done so much evil in my life. I must change who I am before I can come to him. I'm not ready yet."

I stood and walked to the window. The world was so busy outside. It seemed as if Rome never stopped moving, like an ant colony. Yet inside this house, the world seemed to stop.

"Explain to me what you mean."

"I've stolen from Philemon and ran away. And there are other things I've done." I hung my head, ashamed of my past. I couldn't tell him about the other things.

"Why?"

"Why did I steal? Because he took me from my home and robbed me of my freedom."

"Philemon did that to you? I thought he was a boy when you first entered his house."

"Yes, but you know what I mean." I looked back at him with

exasperation. "I was never free in his house."

"He always called you brother."

"He didn't understand what a brother should be like."

"Did you have a brother in Dacia? You never mentioned that before."

I thought for a moment. "No."

"Then how is a brother supposed to act?"

I thought again. I sat back down at the table. "Isn't it obvious? Be kind to each other. Help each other. Treat each other as equals, not one as a master and the other as a slave. That is how family acts, right?"

Paul laughed. "No, I am afraid that is not how families act. I had two brothers and a sister. My brothers and I used to roll on the floor fighting."

"Those are things that children do."

"Both of my brothers have rejected me. The older one has managed to take away my inheritance, because I follow Christ. My sister's husband, threw her out into the street, with her son, Benjamin, because they accepted Christ. Benjamin saved my life in Jerusalem. Except for her, I have no contact with my family. So tell me how families are supposed to act."

I was quiet considering his words. No one ever challenged me on how Philemon saw me.

"What about Philemon?" he asked. He took a sip of the tea, waiting patiently for my answer.

"What about him?"

"He was a boy raised by women. Until he was a man, his father had very little to do with him, correct?"

"Yes." I remembered how Archippus acted toward his family when I first entered the house. He ignored his son and daughters. He was rarely at home. When he was home he criticized his children for the slightest offence. Nothing seemed to please him. It took his illness to change him, but that was when Philemon was a man.

"It took both becoming believers before they ever got close to each other. Philemon and Archippus both told me that. Yet Philemon has lost two of his three sisters, both rejecting the family since they began following Christ. He reacted to his circumstances like any other man would."

Still I said nothing.

"He called you a brother, because he wanted a brother, but he did not understand what that meant. Did you teach him how a brother was supposed to be?"

"They beat me when I revealed I loved a girl in their house. Why should I teach him anything? He only saw me as his slave."

"Timothy told me once that Archippus beat you, but Philemon intervened on your behalf." He waited before continuing. "Isn't that what a brother would do?"

"I don't know."

"Why did you run away?"

"To be free."

"Did it make you free?'

"It didn't turn out the way I expected."

"Tell me about that."

"Why do you want to know everything, Paul? Am I so interesting that the tales of my failure will entertain you?"

"I only want to know so I can help you be truly free."

More than anything I longed to be free. I wanted to walk around with my head held high. Proud of who I was. Yet most of the time, I walked in fear.

"Tell me, Onesimus."

"I squandered money on a prostitute in Athens, because I had never been with a woman. Yet she repaid me by robbing me of half of my money. Two men, a senator in Athens and a praetor in Brindisium, tried to rape me. I beat the praetor. I ran so fast that I don't know if he is alive or dead. I lied to Christians in Corinth, wanting them to accept me. So you see, Paul, I am an evil man."

I looked at Paul, expecting him to look at me in disgust, but, as always, he looked at me with patience and love.

"Yet, God still chose you, Onesimus."

I shook my head, remembering the dream I had outside of Brindisium. "Why me, Paul?"

He laughed quietly. "Because God has a plan for your life."

"Why me? What plan could God have for a slave?"

"What plan did God have for me, a man who persecuted his people?"

"It's different."

"How is it different?"

"Look at you, Paul. You are well-educated, a man who can speak to crowds and sway them. You can take the scriptures of the Jews, like the one you just read from Isaiah, and see Jesus in every verse."

"Do you believe in the Jesus I teach?"

I was quiet. Did I believe in this Jesus? Yes, I told myself. I think I had believed in this Jesus for many years, but I thought because I was a slave, this Jesus would have nothing to do with me. It was to him I prayed in the temple near Colossae. It was to him I called out in despair outside of Brindisium.

"Yes, I do." I began to cry. "But look at me."

"It is not by anything you can do that will make you useful to Christ. It is him working in you." He stood and looked down at me. "Let me tell you what I see." He walked around my chair, much like he did when he preached. "I see one of the best educated men in the Province of Asia; probably one of the best educated in the Empire. Not many can say they have been taught by Tyrannus of Ephesus. You are fluent in three languages, both reading, writing, and speaking; and possibly a fourth, if you count the language of your birth. You have the gift of memorizing instantly every word set before you. You can quote or write every word you have ever seen."

"How does that benefit anyone?"

"You can return to Colossae and serve Philemon, thinking of him as the brother God gave you. Then you allow God to use you."

"All I ever wanted was to be free, Paul."

"It is for freedom that Christ has set us free."

"You are already a free man. You don't understand what it is to be a slave."

"I was not always free. Jesus has taught us that all have sinned and fallen short of the glory of God. What freedom is there in that? I was enslaved to my sin, my hatred, my pride. I was as much of a slave as any man that has ever been born. I more than any deserved eternal punishment."

"But you have done great things for God."

"There is no one righteous, not even one. I am not a righteous man. I will always recall what I did to Stephen and to other believers. Do you really think stealing money and sleeping with a prostitute is worse than being part of the death of men like Stephen? I am not any less guilty than the worst sinner you can think of."

He walked to the kitchen and poured more tea in his cup, then poured a second cup for me. He handed the fragrant concoction to me, then he sat back down. I drank the tea. It tasted good and relaxed me.

"When Adam sinned, death and sin entered the world. Every man that has ever lived has sinned and we are all guilty. Even something as trivial as being angry at Philemon for keeping you as a slave and not treating you as a brother, condemns you to suffer God's wrath. I am guilty. You are guilty. The payment for our sin is death."

"Then I am hopeless."

"No, because the gift of God is eternal life. God loves you so much, Onesimus, that he demonstrated his love for you, before you were even born, he died for you."

The words entered me. Was this the freedom I was always searching for?

"What is the answer for me, Paul?"

"That is the easy part, my son. Everyone who calls on the name of the Lord will be saved."

"Jesus," I whispered.

"Yes, exactly."

"Jesus," I said again.

"If you believe in your heart that he has redeemed you, you will never be a slave again."

"Are you saying, if I return to Colossae, that I will be a free man."

"I am not saying that you will be free from Philemon as your earthly master, but I am saying you will never be bound by the sin that destroyed your life." He reached across the table and gripped my hands tightly. "Onesimus, listen to me. It is your responsibility to accept Philemon for who he is, whether he does the same or not. You do this so you will be free from the bitterness and anger. You do this as your act of worship. Let God work on him."

"What do I do now?"

"What did Archippus do when he realized he needed Jesus?"

"He asked to be baptized."

"Do you remember what we did before I baptized Archippus and his family?"

"You prayed with them, making them repeat a prayer."

"Will you do the same with me now, Onesimus?"

"Yes," I said taking a deep breath. "I am ready to do that, Paul."

"Good," he said smiling at me. "Then repeat this after me. Father God."

"Father God."

"I have searched for freedom from slavery my whole life."

"I have searched for freedom from slavery my whole life." This was not the same prayer he said with Archippus. It made sense. If I was to know God personally, this prayer had to be personal.

"Now I have discovered that it is not slavery that has bound me."

"Now I have discovered that it is not slavery that has bound me." The weight of the chains now seemed heavier.

"I understand that it is the weight of my sins that has bound me."

"I understand that it is the weight of my sins that has bound me." I could feel shackles on my feet and arms weighing me. I wanted to fall to the ground and weep.

"You have shown me that Christ provided a way for me to be free from those chains."

"You have shown me that Christ provided a way for me to be free from those chains." I felt the shackles on my feet fall away.

"Christ died on the Cross, so I can be free."

"Christ died on the Cross, so I can be free." I laughed, because I felt the chains on my arms fall to the ground.

Paul ignored my laugh. "I ask you Christ, to redeem me, a slave bound by sin."

"I ask you Christ, to redeem me, a slave bound by sin." I could feel my limbs begin to tingle.

"In faith, I accept your gift of salvation."

"In faith, I accept your gift of salvation." The tingling sensation grew. Now it was covering my entire body.

"By faith, I will follow you the rest of my life."

"By faith, I will follow you the rest of my life." I now recognized it. The sensation was peace. I had finally found peace.

"Thank you for bearing my sins on the Cross and giving me the gift of eternal life."

"Thank you for bearing my sins on the Cross and giving me the gift of eternal life." This is what it felt like to be free.

"Come into my heart, Lord Jesus, and be my Savior, Amen."

"Come into my heart, Lord Jesus, and be my Savior, Amen." I did not realize I had been crying. There was one last thing I knew I needed to do. "Paul, will you baptize me?"

"Do you know what it means to be baptized?"

I thought about all the times I had heard Paul speak. "I'm not sure, though I know you encourage people to be baptized."

"Baptism is a symbolic gesture we make. We are sinners when we enter the water. Christ took upon himself all the sins of mankind, then he was buried. Entering the water says that we are buried with him. Christ did not stay buried, but he was resurrected. Likewise, when we come out of the water, we are resurrected to a new life."

"I think I understand." Paul could see the confusion on my face.

"Think of it this way. Baptism means you have turned from a life of sin to a new life in Jesus Christ. You are publicly identifying with the death, burial, and resurrection of Christ. And you are openly joining the family of those who believe in Christ."

"Now I understand. So will you baptize me?"

Later in the afternoon, when Timothy walked through the door, Paul stood and greeted him.

"Timothy, we are going to the bathhouse."

"Oh?" he asked. "What for?"

Paul put his hand on my shoulder and smiled proudly. "We are going to baptize our new brother in Christ."

Over the next few days, the reality of what I had done began to sink in. I was someone new. Even when Timothy looked at me with disdain, I was happy. He might not yet recognize that I was a believer, just like him, but I knew I was. Maybe he still saw me as his cousin's runaway slave, but I knew that I was free. I could walk outside and hold my head high. I felt proud of the decision I had made. When I left Colossae, I felt a giddiness that I thought was freedom. But now I felt a peace that I had never experienced before. It was like I had been reborn: a new man.

"Paul, when you are finished with this trial, where would you like to go?"

"I have always dreamed of going to Spain."

"Why?"

"Because it is the edge of the world. I want to bring Christ to that land."

"Then I am going with you to Spain." I was happy, thinking of my future life as Paul's companion to new and exciting places.

"No, you are not going to Spain."

"Am I to stay here in Rome?"

"You have a duty to make restitution to Philemon."

"What do you mean?" I could feel my heart beating rapidly in my chest.

"What does restitution mean?" Paul asked.

"You never answer my questions."

"That is the Socratic method. Didn't you learn that as a child?"

"Yes, but I prefer a straightforward answer."

"The reason I ask you in this way is for you to examine your mind. To explore what you already know. You have an amazing gift of memorizing everything you read. All of it is in your mind, waiting to be used." He paused to allow me to think. "I ask you again, what does restitution mean?"

"Restoring what was stolen to its proper owner."

"And that is what you must do."

"You mean going back to Philemon and being his slave again? I thought you didn't approve of slavery."

"I don't. I think it is evil."

"Yet you want me to go back to him and be his slave?"

"You were a valuable asset to him and you stole his money."

"I can work as a scribe or teacher. You can help me find work here in Rome. I can earn enough money to repay him what I took."

"That is not enough. As I said, you were a valuable asset. You are worth more than what was stolen."

"But if I return to Philemon, he could have me put to death for the crime of being a runaway slave."

"I realize that, but the Law is explicit. When one who has stolen from another man realizes his sin, he must make restitution in full."

"You have said before that we are no longer under the requirements of the Law."

"Jesus said, 'If you are offering your gift on the altar and there remember that your brother has something against you, leave your gift there in front of the altar. First go and be reconciled to him; then come and offer your gift.'"

"Paul, you are asking me to return to Colossae and face a death sentence."

"I don't think Philemon will have you put to death. But making things right with those we have wronged shows them we are serious about our walk with Christ."

"I could spend the rest of my days as a slave in his house."

"Was being a slave in his house worse than what you experienced being free?"

"I am afraid."

"What did God tell Joshua after Moses died?"

"I don't remember."

"You who remember every word you have ever read don't remember."

"Tell me."

"Have I not commanded you? Be strong and courageous. Do not be afraid; do not be discouraged, for the Lord your God will be with you wherever you go."

"I want to return to the land of my birth, but if I go to Colossae, that will never happen."

"I have told you many times…"

"Yes, I know. God has a plan for my life."

"Do you believe that?"

The answer that came to my mind was the vision I had outside of Brindisium.

"The night I escaped from Brindisium, I had a vision. I saw my mother and father, the way they were before I was captured and they died. I had forgotten what they looked like. I forgot the sound of their voices. Yet in that vision I could vividly recall how my mother smelled and the melody of her voice. I saw her eyes filled with love. And my father. I remembered him as stern, but in my vision, I saw a man who loved his family. I could see his scar and the tattoo on his chest. I had forgotten those things about him." I paused thinking about the other things I saw. Paul waited because he could tell that I had more to say. "In my vision, I was told that I would be useful to my people. But how will I be useful to them so far away?'

"I will ask again. Do you believe that God has a plan for your life?"

I thought about it. Was I supposed to return to my people? I could see this was the freedom I always wanted.

"Yes, I think I am supposed to return to my people."

"Then do what is right and then watch God perform a miracle."

CHAPTER 19
RUNNER

"For I know the plans I have for you," declares the Lord, "plans to prosper you and not to harm you, plans to give you a hope and a future." Jeremiah 29:11

Timothy had his hand on the door, about to leave for his morning run.

"Timothy, may I run with you today?"

He looked from me to Paul.

"Don't look at me," Paul said.

"Do you mind him running with me?" Timothy asked. I knew he was thinking I was just a slave. What would a slave know about running races? Why would a slave want to run if not to flee? I don't think he believed that I now was a Christian. That didn't matter. I had something I needed to do and only Timothy could help me.

"He does not belong to me," Paul said, turning back to his writing. From where I stood, I could see a smirk on his face. He was enjoying this.

"But what if?" He didn't finish the question.

"What if I run away?" I asked, finishing the thought. Paul turned to look at us. The tension between us was always strong. I was the runaway slave of his cousin. But Paul could see that I had a plan. Maybe he had even figured out what that plan was. Knowing Paul as I did, he probably had somehow put the idea into my head when I was sleeping. I looked at Paul and smiled.

"Yes, I guess that is what I meant."

"What is to stop me from running now?" I could sense the tension building. I was sure he would start another argument. "I have walked freely through the streets of Rome this last month. You could go on your run and when you return, I could be across the Tiber." I let that sink in. "So I will ask you again. May I run with you today?"

"Try to keep up," he said gruffly exiting the door. Liberius laughed as we passed by him.

We left the house and trotted through the crowded streets of the Subura. Though early morning, some of the taverns were already full with those who worked night shifts at the docks or cleaned the streets of the wealthier parts of the town. There was a line of grouchy people outside of the latrines. Some did not wait to get inside. You could not run through this part of the city, because there was always a crowd and the Subura was filthy with the rubbish people threw out of their windows at night or other unmentionable filth. The stench of the streets and the unwashed bodies surrounding us was almost unbearable. But Timothy ignored it and ran through the crowd at a slow trot. He never looked back, as if he did not care if I was there or not.

As we started the climb out of the Subura, up the Esquiline, the air became cleaner and the neighborhood less crowded. There were still tenements, but also homes of the rich, public squares, imposing public buildings, and temples. The streets were wider and there was less traffic crowding them. Timothy began to run faster, sometimes weaving between pedestrians, but always careful not to touch anyone.

I bumped into a man as I tried to catch up, only to have him curse me. Ahead I saw the gate. Timothy looked back. Smiling he said, "Don't lose sight of me once we are out of the gate."

That moment he looked back allowed me the chance to catch up.

"Only a fool looks back to see who is following him," I said panting at his side.

Timothy laughed and darted ahead of me. He was through the gate and moments later I was behind him. I was panting. I needed to stop to catch my breath. But Timothy was far ahead of me. I could not stop.

"It is for freedom, that Christ has set us free." Paul's words rang in my ears. Freedom. Christ. Set free. I felt the words rise in me. They were real. I had only known this Christ for a few days. The years of listening to what others said about him no longer mattered. He was becoming real to me.

But there was one more thing I needed to do, so today, I would run.

Timothy was ahead of me and was not looking back. He had the good, steady pace of someone accustomed to running long distances.

Fatigue left me. I wanted to run beside him, my new brother in Christ. I pushed harder and felt my legs burn.

Timothy turned off the road to run through the fields of freshly harvested hay. A horse tethered to a tree, stopped munching on the hay and stamped and snorted. He longed to be free to race with us. I wanted to run beside the horse too, but now I had to catch this man ahead of me.

Timothy jumped a log and seemed to soar across a small stream. I strained to get closer.

"It is for freedom, that Christ has set us free."

I was free. I laughed. I had not felt free my entire life. I had been chained. Chained as a captive in real chains. Chained as a slave in Ephesus and Colossae to a good family, but still separated as a slave. And chained by the sins of bitterness and debauchery. Now I was free. Christ had set me free. Never again would the chains of slavery bind me, even if I remained a slave my entire life. Never again would I go back to the hatred that bound me worse than chains. Never again would I return to the debauchery that drove me into pain. I was free.

Suddenly, I felt the chains fall off my feet. My legs were no longer bound by my slavery.

So, I ran.

I jumped a log, just moments after Timothy. He heard me, but this time he did not look back. He knew I was behind him. He was running toward a forest.

I ran seeing the trees ahead. I wanted to be in this forest. I wanted to feel the trees speak to me. I wanted the freedom of the forest.

So, I ran. Faster and stronger. I ran.

At my side was Timothy. I had caught up to him. I did not turn to look at his face, but I could sense his surprise. He laughed. His joy was infectious. He enjoyed running and I had caught up to him.

"You know how to run!" he shouted. He was running faster.

"I haven't run since I was a child." I felt joy grow with every stride.

He started to push faster, straining past his normal pace, so he could pass me. I could sense the tension growing in him. It was not anger, but the tension of the race.

I pushed harder. I was faster. I was free.

I no longer had to prove to anybody that I was the fastest. I didn't have to race the deer or wolf. I didn't have to outrun the slavers. I ran because I was free. I could run past Timothy, because I was as free as he was free.

It felt good to feel the wind in my hair. It felt good to feel the burn in my legs. It felt good to be free.

Timothy shouted, "Wait. Stop."

By the sound of his voice, I knew he was far behind.

I stopped, the forest in front of me. I bent panting, my hands on my knees. I was not tired, but more refreshed than I had ever been. I could smell the forest beckoning me. I wanted to run in this forest, but there was something more important I had to do, so I could forever be free. I would not live another day as a slave.

"You know how to run," Timothy repeated as he stopped beside me.

"I am free." I said.

"What?"

He was panting and looked confused. I am sure he thought I was about to run away.

"It is for freedom that Christ has set us free."

"Paul taught you that?"

"Yes, Brother."

I had never called anybody brother before. I had no brother or sister when I was a child. Philemon had wanted his slave to be his little brother, but he also wanted his slave to serve him. A brother does not enslave his brother. I had never known what it was to have a brother. This runner standing next to me was my brother in Christ. We both had the same father in Paul, who taught us both to be believers in Christ.

"What are you going to do, Onesimus?"

I had been plagued with this question for weeks. It was known I, the runaway slave, was living in Rome, in the house of Paul. Probably Philemon knew by now. Maybe Timothy had even told him. Even from this far away, he could summon the authorities to take me.

"I am never going to be a slave again, Timothy."

I had thought long about this. I could not be a slave any longer, no matter the consequences.

"I don't know what to say, Onesimus."

I knew Timothy was perplexed in how to handle me. He thought I was about to run away.

"Am I your brother, Timothy?"

He felt like a brother to me now. We both were Christians. We both were runners. We both were free.

"I am not sure how to answer you."

"Paul says repeatedly that we are all brothers in Christ if we believe. He says there is no difference in someone being a Gentile or Jew, a Greek or Roman. He says to me often that Christ does not look at me as a slave. He says there is no difference between you, a Roman citizen, and me, a slave."

Timothy bent his head and looked at the ground.

"So, I ask you, Timothy, am I your brother in Christ?"

"I cannot help you escape, Onesimus. Philemon is my cousin. I must do right by him."

"I am not asking you to help me escape, Timothy. I could run now if I wanted to. No one would notice and no one would care, except you. I could be far away before you could summon the authorities." I took a deep breath and looked around at the beautiful countryside so close to the crowded noisy city of Rome. "But I want to know if I am your brother."

"You are my brother in Christ." Timothy said it without hesitation. "I have watched you change over the years, especially in these weeks here in Rome. I have listened to your words. I have heard your answers to Paul. I believe you are a Christian, like me. I have believed that for a very long time and that disturbed me. How was I supposed to act toward you, my brother in Christ, who is also my cousin's slave? Yes, Onesimus, I believe you are my brother in Christ."

"Then I need your help to be permanently free, my brother."

"I told you, I won't help you escape." He looked at the ground. I knew the battle was real inside him.

I grabbed him by the shoulders, making him look at me. "Brother, I want to go with you when you return to Ephesus, and then on to Colossae."

"What?" he asked confused.

"I need to return to Philemon." Suddenly what I needed to do made more sense than anything I had ever done in my life. I was afraid, but I also felt at peace. "I need to ask his forgiveness for stealing from him and running from him." I could not control the tears that started to flow.

"What?"

"I must have his forgiveness to be completely free. Even if he sells me to the mines or to the oars of a ship, or even if he orders me killed in the arena, I must return to him. I must ask his forgiveness. I need to do this to be complete."

Timothy breathed a sigh of relief. "I understand."

"So, I ask if you are my brother and if you will help me."

Timothy hugged me. "I will do all I can to help you, Brother." I wept as my brother embraced me.

We walked back, not speaking. I could see that Timothy wanted to say something further, but he couldn't get the words out. Maybe it was my duty to speak.

"I'm not afraid to go back." He looked at me. In the past, he had never looked me in the eye, considering me less than he was.

"It is Philemon's right to do to you whatever he wishes."

"I know." I picked up a rock and threw it down the road, watching it skip and bounce.

"Then why go back?"

"You who have been saying I should go back are now asking me why I want to go back?"

"Yes. I never thought you would willingly go back. But I do ask. Why go back?"

"I am a believer like you. I know that my heart has been changed. But I can't live my life with the guilt of my crimes. Paul has been teaching me about restitution. I have to make things right with Philemon."

"I think I understand."

"You were correct in one thing. Philemon always treated me well and even told people I was a brother to him, even though I don't think he understood the concept of brotherhood. I hated him for many years. I stole from him. And I ran away. Whether he accepts it or not, I have to make peace with him."

Timothy didn't answer that. A few times over the next few minutes he made a sound like he was clearing his throat. He wanted to say something more.

"What is it you want to say, Timothy?"

He cleared his throat again. "I'm sorry, Onesimus."

We both stopped. He looked like he was in pain.

"I'm sorry for what I did to you."

I didn't speak. What was he apologizing for?

"That girl, I don't even know her name. I…"

"Her name was Rhoda."

"I am sorry for what I did. I hated you because you were so intelligent. Philemon talked about his amazing brother over and over. I didn't want a slave being more important to him than me. I saw, everyone saw, that you cared for her. I wanted to hurt you."

I didn't know how to respond. For years, I wanted to tell Timothy how much I hated him for what he did. Every time I looked at him, I wanted to hit him or worse. She was innocent.

"What happened to her?"

"All I know is that she was sold. They never told me anything else. I am sorry, Onesimus."

I thought about what Paul had been teaching me about making things right. That is what I wanted to do with Philemon. Even if he hated me, I wanted to do what was right. This was no different. I had to forgive Timothy. He was making things right with me.

"I forgive you," my voice cracked as I said it. Even as I said it, I prayed silently that God would teach me how to forgive.

We started walking, again silent. A cart passed us and a man waved a greeting. Two women, carrying fresh vegetables, joined the road in front us. A farmer was moving the horse we had earlier passed to a greener part of the pasture. I put my hand on Timothy's shoulder. It felt right to forgive him. He put his arm around my shoulder. I had found my brother.

CHAPTER 20
CAESAR

Then Jesus said to them, "Give back to Caesar what is Caesar's and to God what is God's." And they were amazed at him. Mark 12:17

I was awakened by the smell of smoke. It filled the air, making my throat raw and scratchy. My eyes were burning. I went in the kitchen and wetted a rag to wash my face. The kitchen hearth was burning, but the smoke wasn't coming from it. I lit a lamp so I could see better.

Paul coughed, not his regular cough, but something deeper. I was still holding the wet rag, so I took it to him. I placed the lamp on the table by his bed and started washing his face with the rag.

"What is burning?" Paul coughed.

"Nothing in the house."

He took the rag from me and coughed into it. "Go and find out."

Janus, the night guard, was not sleeping on his cot in front of the door which was slightly ajar. That is when I saw the orange light outlining the door. Fear gripped me as I slowly opened it.

Janus was standing a few feet from the door with a look of shock on his face. The city was engulfed in flames. The wind was blowing it away from us, in the direction of the Tiber, but half a mile away tenement houses were burning. I watched as one collapsed. Above the sound of the fire, were the screams of the dying.

"What is happening?"

"The city is burning."

Out of the smoke, Liberius suddenly emerged, covered in soot and sweat. He stopped in front of us and doubled over, his hands on his knees. Through his coughs he ordered, "Get inside, Janus, and guard Paul." He coughed again. "Be prepared to move him at any moment." There was terror in Janus' eyes. He didn't move as he continued to gawk at the fire. "Do you hear me, man?" Liberius screamed. "Do your job and protect Paul."

Janus ran to do as ordered.

"He did it." Liberius looked at the hellish scene before our eyes and then repeated, "He did it. He burned the city."

A moment later, Timothy came outside. He gasped at the scene, then ran in direction of the fire. I started to run after him, but Liberius grabbed my arm tightly.

"No, you must stay here with Paul."

Lucius Domitius Ahenobarbus was the grandson of Marcus Antonius and great nephew of Caesar Augustus on his father's side, and the great, great grandson of Caesar Augustus on his mother's side. His mother, Agrippina, was the sister of Caligula, still hated by the people of Rome. Caligula was assassinated while he was still young and his uncle, Claudius became emperor, though most of Rome thought he was unfit for that office, because he stammered and stuttered. Claudius proved his detractors wrong by being an efficient administrator for the vast Empire. Though already old when he became Emperor, he added Britain, Thrace, and Mauretania to the Empire, even participating in the campaign for

Britain. He built much needed aqueducts for the burgeoning city of Rome, as well as roads and canals throughout Italy, and a highway from Dyrrachium on the Adriatic Coast to Byzantium on the Black Sea. If something was inefficient, he ordered it made more efficient, no matter the cost. He passed laws that protected slaves from being abandoned by their masters or thrown out onto the streets if they became ill or old. By the end of his reign, the man who most thought was incompetent, was beloved throughout the Empire, even more than Augustus.

Agrippina used her feminine charms to convince Claudius to marry her, even though he was her uncle. She then plotted his demise, because she wanted her son, Lucius, to be emperor. Old Claudius was poisoned.

Just a few weeks shy of his seventeenth birthday, Lucius became the fifth emperor of Rome, taking the name of Nero Claudius Caesar Augustus Germanicus. He became known to history as Nero. For a short while, Agrippina tried to rule Rome for her son. He resented that and refused to listen to her advice. She turned on him by promoting Claudius' son, Britannicus to be emperor, but the poor boy of only fourteen was discovered poisoned just a few days later. A year into Nero's reign, Agrippina also died of poisoning, leaving the boy to rule Rome alone.

Nero was jealous. Nothing he did could sway the people's love for his uncle, the old emperor who stammered and stuttered. The Senate thought Nero was too young and too inexperienced, and were constantly instructing him how to rule more effectively. The people enjoyed when he gave them gladiator fights or chariot races, but they still talked about the good years under his Uncle Claudius.

That is when Nero came up with the idea of creating a palace so beautiful that future generations would be in awe of its creator. It would be called the Domus Aurea or House of Gold. This palace would be the largest palace in the Empire, even larger than Cleopatra's palace in Alexandria. It was to be a complex of sumptuous buildings with domed ceilings, elaborate frescos, granite pillars, and gilded chandeliers. There would be marble, ivory, and golden statues of the gods and nymphs. Fountains would grace the courtyards, including a waterfall on a wall of crystal. Here Nero would display the finest art of the Empire in his glorious palace. There would be dramas and comedies in his theater. Music would fill the ears, because Nero loved music. It would be a palace of beauty and art unprecedented in the history of the world, and Nero would be its creator.

The plan was to build in in the heart of the city, close to the Capitoline Hill so it would be viewed from anywhere in the city. The only problem was that there were villas of senators and wealthy merchants, and neighborhoods of profitable tenements where he wanted to build. Some of these tenements were as much as eight stories high, filled with occupants who paid dearly to be in the center of the city. The landlords depended on these rents. When Nero's agents offered to buy the properties, almost all turned him down. It would be too expensive to build a new villa in the suburbs or across the Tiber, the Senators said. The landlords said it would be impossible to build such profitable tenements somewhere else. Those who entertained his offer, demanded more than Nero was willing to pay. Several suggested he build his palace across the Tiber, but Nero wanted it in the heart of Rome so everyone would see it every day.

One hot, windy summer night, it happened. One hundred city guards marched from the Campus Martius, each carrying a torch. There was nothing strange about that in itself. The city guard patrolled the streets of Rome at night to protect the city against crime. Even in the dark alleys of the Subura, crime was controlled by the night patrols. What was out of the ordinary about this group is that they stayed together as a group, not breaking up into patrols of two to five as was normal.

When they arrived on the edge of the Subura, they began to light piles of rubbish and anything that was burnable. Piles of wood outside a tavern. Canopies over shops. They upturned jars and urns of oil and set them on fire. They kicked open the door of a shop that sold parchment and set it ablaze. Also, a shop that wove rugs, another that sold lamp oil, and a warehouse of wood for cooking and heating homes.

The first tenement burst into flames before anyone screamed a warning. It was eight stories high, on a street crowded with similar tenements, most built next to each other with only the gap of a narrow alley. They were all made of wood and housed dozens of people. This one had a ground floor occupied by an oil distribution warehouse. It had only one exit onto the street. The first scream came from within the tenement, but by then it was too late.

The oil exploded into a torch that lit up the night sky. A dozen other tenements were set ablaze as the tenement collapsed into the street. Hundreds died in the flames or jumped to their deaths to keep from being burned to death. Before dawn, not just the tenements, but villas were on fire. People found themselves surrounded by walls of flame. The fire raged all that day, burning a swath all the way to the Campus Martius, where the soldiers worked feverishly to stop the flames from spreading.

Close to where we lived, brigades of men were able to keep the fire from coming in our direction. The wind helped by never changing direction. Janus left before the night was over to help the fire brigade. Timothy didn't return. To ease Paul's worry, I went looking for him. I found him after an hour, blackened by smoke and soot.

"Timothy, come with me," I begged.

There was a burn on his hand that needed attention and his clothes had been singed.

"I can't leave." He said. As he looked at me, he began to cry. "Hundreds have died and even more are dying."

"Come with me." I took his arm and pulled him in my direction. His body was weak. He collapsed in my arms and began to weep.

"So many died."

"Come, Timothy, we are going home." I almost carried him. He was weak and distraught.

"Thank you, Brother," he whispered as I helped him into bed.

I washed his face and put ointment on his burn, then watched him as he slept. Never did I expect to find a brother in him. The hatred and resentment was gone. It was as if nothing bad had ever happened between us. That was the joy I had discovered becoming a believer. As Christ had forgiven me, and I forgave others, peace enveloped me.

The fire burned for two more days, but it did not spread. The same men who had started the fire were now employed getting it under control. When rumor spread that Nero started the fire, he opened a family palace to be used as an infirmary. Twice he visited the sight of the devastation. One time he openly wept before a group of homeless widows and promised to give them relief. Though the second time, he was seen with his architect, Severus, discussing plans for the building of his Domus Aurea.

A week after the fire, Glaubus arrived. He was white as if recently frightened. Nervously he sat at the table and accepted a cup of wine.

"Thank you," he told me, then downed the cup. He held the cup to me, indicating he wanted more.

"What is happening, Glaubus?" Timothy asked sitting next to Paul. Liberius came from the door and stood behind him.

"I have just been to see the Emperor's secretary. I received a message before dawn ordering me to the palace."

He took another deep drink of wine. I started to refill the cup, but Liberius put his hand on my arm and shook his head to indicate I should not.

"You are ordered to the palace at dawn tomorrow for your trial."

"That is a good thing, my friend," Paul said quietly.

"It is what the secretary said next that frightened me."

I sat down in the one empty seat.

"Tell me." Paul seemed very calm.

"The secretary spit out a curse at me. He said, 'How can you Christians commit such an atrocity?'"

"What atrocity?" I asked.

"He said Christians burned the city. Already there are dozens of arrests. I met Luke on my way here. He was with Epaphras when he was arrested. Aristarchus and Demas have been taken."

"Go back to Luke and send him to me," Paul stood and went to his desk.

"Paul, I came here to get you out of the city."

Nobody moved, but Paul continued to sort through his letters. Liberius gripped his sword, but the look on his face was of sorrow.

"I'm not escaping, Liberius." Tears coursed down the guard's cheeks.

"Paul, you must flee." Timothy stood.

"Onesimus, come and help me sort through these letters. I want copies for Luke as well as for Timothy." When I came to the desk I realized I was crying too.

"I don't think you understand," Glaubus said.

"I understand clearly. Nero is going to blame the fire on Christians. I am known to be the leader of the Christians in Rome and to many churches throughout the Mediterranean. I will be put on trial that will be a farce. False witnesses will claim I was ordering my followers to burn the city. I will be publicly executed, with many of our brothers."

Glaubus put his face in his hands and began to weep.

"That's why we must get you out of here," Timothy said. I looked at him and realized that he too was crying. He brushed the tears away with the back of his hand, still wrapped in a bandage.

"All of you, sit down." Timothy and I returned to the table. Liberius had not moved. "You too, my friend." Liberius sat and tried to control his tears.

"When Jesus sent his disciples out into the villages of Judea he told them that a day like this would come. He said he was sending them out as sheep into a pack of wolves. He told them that they would be handed over to local councils and flogged in synagogues. And he said because of him that they would be brought before governors and kings to be a witness before the Gentiles. I have always known this. That is why I came to Rome. I knew it when I first stepped on the ship in Crete bound for Rome. I knew I would stand before Caesar and tell him about Jesus."

"Caesar is a mad man," Glaubus said through his tears. "You will never convert him."

"There will be others there when I am tried. Someone will hear my words and seek the Lord."

"Hundreds more could hear your words if you were to leave the city." Timothy added desperately.

"And if I flee, Nero will take it out on Christians across Italy and the Empire. I will be labeled a coward and my testimony will be worthless. No, Timothy, I will not flee."

He looked around the table.

"Here is my plan. Liberius will not leave me, even though he knows I won't flee. I will not have his life taken because of me. His witness among the soldiers is vital. Glaubus, I want you to take Timothy with you. Find Luke and Tychicus and bring them here as quickly as possible. They must leave today. Onesimus will help me order the letters I want sent to the churches."

Nobody moved. Paul looked around at the sad faces.

"I'm staying with you," Timothy said.

"We have discussed this. You are returning to Ephesus to complete the work there." I watched the struggle written on Timothy's face. "You are needed Timothy. My time is at an end. It is now your time to lead the Church until the day that God calls you to stand as a martyr for your faith in Jesus."

Finally, Liberius stood. "You heard the man, do what he commanded." He pushed Glaubus' chair. The lawyer stood.

"After you find them," Paul instructed, "Go home and get your family out of the city."

"I will go with you to the palace tomorrow, Paul." Glaubus said.

"I understand, but get your family to safety today." Paul went to his room and brought out a small bag with coins.

"No." Glaubus refused the coins. "God has provided for me and will provide for my family."

In a few minutes, I was alone with Paul. We barely spoke as he looked over letters, signing a few or adding a last-minute note.

"Pack your bags," he finally ordered me.

"I'm staying with you, Paul."

He sat down and took out a new parchment. "I am writing a letter to Philemon. Remember our conversation? You have unfinished business with him. Now go pack while I finish this letter, and pack a bag for Timothy too."

Reluctantly, I did as he asked. When I returned, he was sealing the letter.

"This letter, along with the ones for the churches in Colossae and Laodicea, are yours to deliver personally. I want you to read all three in the churches."

Timothy returned with Tychicus and Luke. Glaubus did not return that day. After hurried instructions, Luke and Tychicus left. Timothy waited at the door for me.

"Hurry, you have to go." Paul commanded, handing me the three letters.

"I'm staying here with you," I couldn't help my tears.

"No, you have to go."

"Paul, I can't leave you." I buried my head in his chest crying.

"You have a job to do in Colossae. You know that."

"I know." The weight was too heavy. I couldn't bear it. "But I want to stay with you."

"And the people of Dacia wait for you too."

I could see my mother and father, and the old man who sat by the well, those who had died when I was taken; Zoltes, Duras, and Teudila, children, like me, who did not survive being taken captive; and old Agata, who had died as a slave in the house of Philemon. They never knew Jesus.

"They will kill you."

"I know. I am ready to die." His face showed peace. He looked beyond me as he spoke.

"Tell me, Paul. What do you see?"

He looked at me as if in surprise. Then he smiled. "The grayness of this world vanishes like a mist and I see a green field as vast as the Sea. The sun is breaking over the horizon and it all becomes clear. Fragrant flowers are blooming and the trees are full of fruit. Birds fly overhead. They are calling me to follow them."

He paused, enraptured by his vision.

"And I see it."

"What do you see?"

"A city with so much light coming from it that there are no shadows. It has walls of the brightest white marble, crystal, and precious gems. There are people I know coming to greet me." A tear rolled down his cheek.

"I've seen it before."

"You have?" He looked at me and smiled.

"I saw it in a dream once. A place with no shadows."

"I can't make out his face yet, but He is approaching."

"Who?"

"Jesus." I didn't realize until that moment that his hand was squeezing mine. "Since He blinded me, all I have ever seen was Him. Do you understand me, Onesimus?" He looked at me.

"I understand you."

"There is nothing that matters. All the preaching, teaching, and writing doesn't matter. All that matters is Jesus."

"But the rest matters too. Your preaching, teaching, and writing have guided people to Jesus. They have guided me to Jesus."

He hugged me tightly. I began to sob. "Son, you have to go. My work is finished, but you have a job to do."

I pried myself loose and stood. "I will never forget you, Paul."

I took my satchel and walked out the door. Timothy was by my side as we walked out into the street. We walked for several blocks and turned onto the road that leads to the Esquiline and out of the city. Timothy put his arm around my shoulder, like a brother.

"Let's run," I said to Timothy.

CHAPTER 21
BROTHER

No longer as a slave, but better than a slave, as a dear brother. Philemon 16

The wine dark sea accepted the spark of gold off the mountains to the east. Slowly the sea turned from deep purple, to orange splashed with gold. Finally, as the sun came over the mountains, it became the azure for which the Aegean is famed. As the world awoke, on this warm summer day, I could now see the white and gold of the temple, standing above the city of Ephesus, the city of Artemis the Great, the city now a center of Christianity. As we drew closer, the rumble of a city awakening grew louder.

The *Triton*, the ship in which we traveled from Corinth, arrived shortly after sunrise. Timothy stood beside me as we watched the shore draw closer.

"It feels good to be home," Timothy said.

I didn't answer. I was afraid. I was unsure about this return.

"You are awfully quiet."

"I am terrified."

"Of Philemon?"

"Yes."

"Then stay with me for a few weeks in Ephesus. I will write a letter to him and say you are here. Maybe he will come."

"You know I can't do that."

"Yes, I know." Timothy and I had talked about my return to Colossae many times. "Then what are you going to do?"

The ship was drawing near to the dock. The breeze was cool, but I was sweating. I truly was terrified about what I needed to do.

"When we disembark, I am going to continue down the Sacred Way to the eastern gate. I will go back to Colossae today."

"You won't even stay with me a night and greet the church here in Ephesus?"

"No, Timothy. I can't."

We stepped off the ship and began the walk down the Sacred Way. Timothy didn't say a word as we walked.

"You should be going down that street," I said as we approached the street where Aquila and Priscilla lived.

"I'm going to walk with you to the gate."

"You don't have to do that."

"I am a free man and I can do as I please."

I laughed.

"Say goodbye to me here." I stopped where we were.

Timothy dropped his satchel and hugged me tightly. "Hurry back, Brother. I need you here in Ephesus."

I pulled away from him, not wanting to cry here. I had cried too much in my life. I did not look back as I continued down the street. Would I ever see him again? I had no answer to that.

I passed through the gate a few minutes later, feeling a pull inside me to get home to Colossae, as quickly as possible. I had new clothes, bought by Paul before I left Rome and money to stay in inns and for food. I had a small satchel over my shoulder with my things and three letters.

One letter was for the church in Colossae and another for the nearby church of Laodicea. My instructions were to deliver them to the leaders of these churches, and if Philemon would permit, read them to the congregation. I knew every word of those letters and could recite them if I had to. I had seen Paul write those letters and he discussed them with me. I recited them in my head as I walked along the road going east.

The third letter was addressed to Philemon. I knew not one word of its contents. A dozen times on the journey from Rome I had looked at it, my thumb caressing the seal, knowing it was one of the last things Paul had touched. His letters did not say he was dead, but I was to relay that message, just as Timothy would relay the message to Ephesus. This letter was the last thing Paul wrote the morning we left.

Paul was dead. I had no evidence to present, as Luke would require, but I knew in my heart that he was dead. I could tell the story of the last days, the fire, the imprisonment of many Christians, and the order for Paul to go to Nero's palace. On the road south through Italy, in Brindisium, in Patras, and Corinth, we traveled faster than the news of what was happening in Rome. Rumors of a fire were known, but nothing more than that. It would be my duty to inform the church of Colossae that Paul was dead. His letter to them did not say that, but they needed to know.

I arrived at my little, ruined temple. It was exactly the same. It seemed like I had been here just days before. I sat on the steps eating the bread and cheese I had bought at the inn. I listened to the birds sing and the breeze rustle the leaves. Everything was the brown of late summer, except that in the cool shadows on the edge of a wooded area there were flowers.

I had never once counted the money Paul gave me. I paid my own way at every inn. I paid passage on two ships; one from Brindisium and one from Corinth. I bought my own food. I looked at the packet of gold and silver coins. Nobody was around to see me. I dumped the coins out on the step I was sitting on and stacked them in neat piles. It couldn't be right. I counted again. It was the exact amount I had stolen from Philemon.

"What does restitution mean?" Paul had asked me.

"Restoring what was stolen to its proper owner." That was my answer.

"That is what you must do." He had said to me reassuringly. "Do what is right and then watch God perform a miracle."

Did you plan to do your own miracle, Paul? I laughed, because that was the kind of thing Paul would do.

I gathered the money, put it back in the bag, and continued on my way. God would provide. I did not know his answer, but I felt at peace and no longer terror.

Soon the town of Colossae was in front of me. I saw familiar faces, people I didn't know by name, but whom I had seen repeatedly in this tiny town. Just inside the gate I stopped to pray, not for my rescue from slavery, but that Philemon would forgive me.

"There is a plan for your life."

It was not a memory of Paul speaking to me, but further back to when I was in a cage on the coast of my land.

"For I know the plans I have for you," declares the Lord, "plans to prosper you and not to harm you, plans to give you a hope and a future."

"Is this what you have been saying to me all this time?"

I looked up to see a man dressed in white walking down the street in the direction of Philemon's villa. He turned and looked at me. I knew he was the same man I had seen that night in the cage. There was a smile on his face. He turned away from me and continued on the street. I got off my knees and followed him. He was too far away, for me to catch up. As I turned the corner, he was gone.

I was standing in front of Philemon's villa. Now was the moment.

"Today, this is my plan," I told the door, touching it with a loving caress. "Tomorrow I do not know my plan, but today it is here."

Suddenly the door opened, startling me. Thestius stood there, staring at me.

"Thestius, why are you here and not in Ephesus?"

"What does it matter why I am here. Why are you here? Are you insane?" Thestius closed the door behind him and looked nervously around him. "He rants about you almost every day, especially after he heard you were in Rome."

"I must see him, no matter the cost." I reached into my satchel. "I have letters to deliver to him from Paul."

"Give them to me." He tried to snatch them away from me.

"I was ordered to give them from my hand to his."

"You must get out of here as quickly as you can." He held out his hand for me to give him the letters. "Give them to me and I will give them to him."

"And how you would explain these letters? He would have you beaten for not telling him I am here. Open the door for me Thestius and tell Philemon I am here."

"You never learned your place did you."

"Yes, I have recently learned my place. That is why I am here, Thestius."

He reluctantly allowed me in. "Wait here."

I took a deep breath and waited. I was doing the right thing. Suddenly, I felt a love for Philemon I never had before. He has always wanted a brother and I denied him that. Even if I was his slave again, I would love him like a brother. Even if he had me sentenced to death, I would love him like a brother. I would give him what he always wanted. I would learn to be his brother, as I had learned to be Timothy's brother.

I heard shouting and curses, but also the calming voice of Apphia.

"Why should I speak to that ingrate?" The sound of his feet told me of his approach.

"Calm down," Apphia repeated. "He came back of his own accord. Hear what he has to say first."

Philemon entered. His face was red with anger. He had aged since I last saw him, though it was not so very long ago. He had put on weight and there were dark circles under his eyes. His hair had begun to fall out. I couldn't hate him for enslaving me, when I realized what I had done to him. Philemon had a whip in his hand. I would not resist. I would not back away. I fell on my face in front of him.

"I have letters from Paul." I held the letters out in front of me. "One is for the church here in Colossae and another for the church in Laodicea. Paul has also sent you a personal letter, just for you."

The whip did not come down on my back, as I expected. I could only see his feet, but I could hear his uneasy breathing.

"Take the letters, Philemon," I heard Apphia say.

The uneasy breathing continued. He dropped the whip and took the letters. I heard him walk away.

"I'm glad you are back, Onesimus." I felt her hand on my head. "He has missed you so much."

I did not lift my face, but said softly, "Thank you, Mistress."

I heard something break and curses coming from Philemon again. I looked up to see him returning with Archippus following, using a cane to steady himself.

"I have always treated you well and trusted you with everything I owned."

"That is true, Master."

"You stole from me and made me look the fool to everybody, my friends and my slaves."

"I have returned to ask your forgiveness and make whatever restitution you require." I opened my satchel and handed him the bag of money. He took it and threw it on the ground behind him. I heard the coins scatter across the atrium.

"That's not good enough. I want an explanation."

"Everything you said is true. I don't ask that you restore me to the house. I don't ask that you save me from death or serving in the mines. I ask no favors of you. Do with me what you think is right. I only ask that you forgive me, so I can be right with God."

"Did I not treat you like a brother?" Philemon asked. His voice was no longer angry but filled with hurt and desperation. "Answer me, please."

"Is a brother told to clean the night water pot for the other brother?" He wanted the truth from me. I would give him the truth. "Is a brother refused the right to marry? Is a brother denied the chance to learn about Jesus with the rest of the family?"

"Onesimus…"

Tears were streaming down his face. Apphia stood next to him. She didn't touch him, but I could tell she wanted to protect him.

"You told me and everyone that I was your brother, but I was never treated like one."

"Onesimus."

"But neither of us knew how a brother was supposed to be. We both stumbled along, never helping the other learn how to do the right thing."

"Onesimus."

"When I was in Rome, I was introduced to Jesus by Paul, your friend and mine. I learned what it means to have a brother. I have returned to make things right. I hated you. I resented that you could discuss philosophy and religion with Paul and Timothy, but not with me, the man you called your brother. I resented that I wanted to marry, like you did, but you refused me, even as you called me your brother. I wanted to be free, never realizing it was my hatred and resentment that enslaved me."

"Onesimus." I could see that Philemon had broken. He was shaking.

"I don't care what punishment you inflict on me. I don't care if you sentence me to death. I only came to do what is right in God's eyes so I can have peace. I come here as your slave or as your brother, however you will have me."

Apphia was weeping.

Philemon reached down and helped me to stand. He looked me in the eye. I saw the hazel eyes with the green ring around the iris, just like his mother had. But he looked tired.

"I ask your forgiveness, Philemon."

He embraced me and began to cry. When I started to pull away, he drew me tighter to him. His body was shaking from his crying.

"Please forgive me, Philemon."

"I forgive you."

"Paul, an apostle of Christ Jesus by the will of God and Timothy our brother," I began to read the letter Paul had written to the church. Philemon had sent word to the believers in Colossae that I had arrived and that I had a message from Paul for them.

"To the holy and faithful brothers in Christ at Colossae: Grace and peace to you from God our Father." I could feel the tears growing in me. I tried to go on, but the words on the paper grew blurry. I didn't need to read it. I knew it by heart. I handed the letter to Philemon and continued.

The letter began with greetings and a word of thanksgiving, and reminding them that the gospel message was growing everywhere it was shared, just like it was in Colossae. I told them about the supremacy of Christ, how he was the perfect image of the invisible God and how all things were created by him. I shared about Paul's labor for the church, how everything he did was for the spiritual welfare of the believers, like the people in Colossae. I told them about the freedom they had in Christ, as they were no longer bound by the regulations of the law, and warned them to beware of false teachers that would try to force them back under the slavery of the law. And lastly, I told them how to live holy lives.

This is what Paul had written to the small congregation of Colossae. This letter was written for me. I had copied it many times, but I had never noticed how Paul had addressed me in this letter. Though equally I knew it was addressed to every man, woman, and child seated before me.

"After this letter has been read to you, see that it is also read to the church in Laodicea and that you in turn read the letter from Laodicea."

I looked at Archippus as I quoted the next part. "Tell Archippus: 'See to it that you complete the work you have received in the Lord.'" He shook his head, remembering Paul's command.

I took the letter from Philemon and held it up to the congregation as I quoted the last part. The tears rolled down my cheeks. "I, Paul, write this greeting in my own hand. Remember my chains. Grace be with you."

I handed the letter to Philemon.

"Tell us what happened to Paul? Why is he imprisoned?" A man asked.

"Will he be coming here soon?" Another asked.

"No, Paul is not coming." I answered.

"Tell us, Onesimus." Archippus begged.

I took a deep breath. "Paul is dead." There were groans. "He died sharing his love for Christ with Emperor Nero. He was true to the end. He could have escaped but he refused. He wanted Timothy and me to return. Timothy is in Ephesus."

"Don't hold anything back," Apphia said. "We want to know."

"Nero burned a large area of Rome. Thousands died. He blamed the Christians. I only know that Paul was to be blamed as the ringleader and killed. More than that, I don't know."

I looked around the room, realizing I was the one who had to heal the sorrow.

"Paul knew what he was doing. His love of Christ could not be quenched. You know that. For me, he will always be an example of what a true Christian should be like. I am proud that I can call him friend, and am even more proud that he called me son. And that is what I am. Though a slave, Paul loved me enough to share his faith with me. I became his son in the faith. No matter what my future holds, I will serve Christ and encourage those I encounter to do the same."

"What is the last thing he said to you, Onesimus?" Philemon asked.

"My work is finished, but you have a job to do."

I looked around the room.

"And likewise, you have a job to do. You can sit here and weep, or you can rejoice that our brother Paul is in Heaven. You will be there with him one day. Until that time, we have work to do."

CHAPTER 22
SINGIDAVA GETAE

All authority in heaven and on earth has been given to me. Therefore, go and make disciples of all nations, baptizing them in the name of the Father and of the Son and of the Holy Spirit, teaching them to obey everything I have commanded you. And surely, I am with you always unto the very end of the age. Matthew 28:18-20

The next days were quiet. Without ceremony, I was given a room in the villa. Not a slave room, but one for the family. The next morning, Apphia herself, not a slave, invited me to breakfast.

It was a little tense when I sat, but Alyx reached over and patted my hand. "I enjoyed what you said yesterday."

"Onesimus," Archippus asked. "Will you sit with me today and tell me about Paul?"

"I would be honored, Master."

Philemon cleared his throat. "You will no longer address him as master."

"If that is what you wish."

Little else was said at the meal. I was uncomfortable. Except with Paul, I had never eaten with free men and women before. I didn't know how to respond. After breakfast, I didn't know what to do either.

"Philemon," I asked standing outside his library. "May I speak with you?"

"Please, Onesimus." He stood and offered me a seat.

"I am not sure how to respond." I didn't sit either. "What are to be my duties now?"

"I wanted to talk to you about that." He opened a small chest on his desk and rummaged through some documents. He pulled one out that was sealed. "Please sit, Onesimus."

He handed me the document as I sat.

"What is this?" I took it and examined the seal.

"When you left, I intended to free you when you returned. These are your manumission papers."

"What?"

"I had them drawn up months before you left, but I couldn't bear the thought of you leaving. Apphia and I discussed it often. She urged me to set you free if I was going to continually call you brother. When you thought it was Zoe who got pregnant, I told her about it. She said it was time we change how we treat our slaves. We are going to free them all eventually, but I don't know how to do this. If I allow them to walk out the door, some might find themselves as beggars in a few months. I don't want that for any of them. Apphia suggested I free you first and ask for your help."

"You were going to free me?" I looked at the paper as if it were made of gold and precious gems. I was afraid to touch it.

"It is official. You are a free man and have been for a long time."

There was a long silence as I looked at the paper. Slowly I broke the seal and read it to myself. I would always remember every word.

"So instead of you asking me what your duties are, I will ask you."

"I don't know."

"I have a favor to ask of you."

"Anything, Philemon."

"I am sick; you can see that. I don't know how many years I have. Apphia, it seems, is barren. So I have no heir. When I die, who will care for my wife or my sister? If my father outlives me, who will care for him in his old age?"

"I will stay and do whatever you need." I thought of Dacia at that moment, and wondered if I would ever get there.

"I think there are other plans now. You and Paul surely discussed those. Years ago, he told me that he felt God had something special for you."

"Paul spoke to you about that? What did he say?"

"Just that, nothing more. I always wondered about that and how to talk to you about it. God gave you an amazing gift. I have seen that most of my life and you frightened me." He paused. "In the future, not just yet, I want you to return here and care for my family. Will you do that for me?"

"I will do that."

He handed me another document. It was not yet sealed. "I wrote this one this morning. It makes you my heir and legally declares you my brother. Upon my death, all I have is yours, but I ask for you to care for my family. Can you do that for me?"

"Since I was taken captive, I have dreamed about returning to the land of my people. I am not even sure where that is, but I want to go to Byzantium to find out. I was hoping you would allow me to go and find them." Philemon looked sad. "Paul spoke in Rome about sharing the news about Jesus to the people in our circle. When he said that, I thought about the people of my land. I knew I must find them, if possible, and tell them about Jesus."

"I understand."

"But Colossae and Ephesus are also my circle. If you will give me leave for a year, maybe two, and allow me to search for them, then I will return and serve your house, either as your friend or as your brother."

Philemon's face lit up with joy. He reached across the desk and gripped my hand. "Thank you, Brother."

I stood, both letters in my hand.

"You are a free man now. What will your call yourself?"

I didn't hesitate to answer. "Onesimus."

The next few weeks were busy as I made my preparations. I was now a member of the family and Philemon spared no expense for my journey. I was provided with money, new clothes, a cloak because of the cold further north, new sandals, and copies of Paul's letters.

Timothy greeted me warmly when I arrived in Ephesus and laughed when I showed him my papers.

"So, there was no need to run after all?"

"It has new meaning now. It would not have meant the same a year ago."

"And I guess that means you are now my cousin."

"No, I am always your brother."

I stayed a week in Ephesus. Instead of being in terror of being caught, I was surrounded by people who I never realized loved me.

Twenty members of the church in Ephesus prayed for me at the dock, including Timothy, Aquila, and Priscilla. Zoe was also there, now a member of the church too. It was sad, because I did not know how long I would be gone or even if I would return, but I had a vision of a boy running through the forest. I had to find him.

Nothing was familiar in Byzantium. I did not know if the city had grown so much that I no longer recognized it, or if somehow, I was mistaken that I had lived there with the cloth dyer. But I heard singing my first morning there and knew there were Christians here. When I found them, I asked about Dacia and how to get there, none of them knew the answer. When I told them I had been with Paul, they begged me to stay a while. I had six of his letters with me and promised to make copies of each for them. So, I was there for almost a month copying Paul's letters and teaching the elders of the church what I had learned from Paul.

One morning, I went to the dock. There was a ship that among its cargo of goods, were letters being delivered to Asia Province. I wanted to include a letter I had written to Timothy and another to Philemon. I had just finished delivering my letters when I heard children crying.

On the dock nearby, were children in chains. I stared at the children for several minutes, hearing their cries and their whispers. They were Dacian, Getae like me. Here were children destined to become slaves like I had been. How could I help them? I didn't have enough money to buy one, let alone all of them.

Nearby I noticed a woman selling bread. Her basket was full. I bought the entire basket and started handing bread to the children.

"It will be alright," I told one in Getae as I handed him a loaf of bread.

"God has a plan for your life," I told a second one.

"Don't despair," I told another as he wept.

"What are you doing?" the captain shouted at me. His whip was raised.

"I am a free man of Asia Province." I pointed at his whip. "Hit me with that and I will own you and that ship."

He lowered his whip. "What are you doing to my property?"

"They are hungry. I am giving them bread." I pointed to the children. "How can you carry them in the bottom of your ship and not feed them? I am only doing what is right in God's eyes and giving them bread."

He was silent as I continued to feed and offer them comfort.

"How do you speak, Dacian?"

"I am from Dacia a very long time ago."

He grunted.

"I have a proposition for you."

"There are twenty-five of them. I won't give you a discount for buying them all."

"I don't want to buy them. I want to return to Dacia."

And so, the next morning, I found myself on a ship heading north to Dacia, only this time I was on the deck of the ship, not in the cargo hold below. The cold winds on the Black Sea were invigorating to me. I wrapped myself in my cloak and watched anxiously as we sailed near the shore. I was expecting every day to see the wide mouth of the river, only I had never seen where the river emptied into the sea. The captain told me a few days into the journey, that the river emptied into a swamp. I didn't remember that, but then I was in the bottom of a boat, so how did I know for sure?

Eight days later, we arrived at Halmyris, a busy but little port at the mouth of the river. It was not exactly as I remembered, but there were cages, much like mine, by the docks filled with boys. I found an inn quickly. It was not like what I had seen in Greece, but nothing was like Greece. Most of the buildings were low wooden structures, with thatched roofs. None even had real doors, only an animal skin or rug across the opening where the door should be.

"How do I find a boat going upriver?" I asked at the inn.

My knowledge of Getae was weak, but every time I spoke, I imagined the answers I was given written on parchment, just like Luke had suggested. That helped me remember the words and most importantly, how they said words and constructed sentences. I could relearn my language, I decided.

"Why do you want to go upriver?" The innkeeper asked. His wife, standing at his side, looked at me suspiciously.

"I was born in the territory of the Singidava. I have been gone most of my life and want to return to my people."

"I have never heard of the Singidava."

"They lived near the mountains."

"There are no regular boats. They come when they come. Stay here for a few weeks and wait."

"If I don't want to wait, then what would you suggest?"

"Walk and hope a boat comes by."

So, I would walk. I felt an urgency to find my tribe, but I also felt a quiet peace to be in the land of the Getae. I wanted to learn about my country and my people, since I had been denied that as a child.

The road from Halmyris led to a village half a day away. Several huts were sprawled along the shore and near the road, but many more were just offshore on stilts. I could see men mending nets at these huts. Further out, there were men in canoes fishing in small groups of two or three. From the people I could see and guess from the number of huts, there were maybe fifty people in this village.

A woman was turning fish on a rack that allowed the fish to dry in the warm summer sun. She reminded me of Agata, the slave that had first greeted me in Philemon's house. She eyed me with the same look of disgust that Agata had.

"Peace to you," I greeted.

"What do you want?" she asked brushing a lock of hair out of her face.

"I am travelling your land. I'm hoping to find a place to sleep for the night."

"You can ask the elder." She pointed to one of the huts in the water. "I have nothing for you."

"Thank you," I smiled and inclined my head. I was still relearning the language and knew I struggled over a few phrases. I could tell she took me for an idiot from Halmyris out to explore the country.

The hut of the elder was not far, but it was in the water. He saw me, but went back to work mending his nets. I walked into the murky water, until my knees were in the water, but I was only halfway to his hut.

"In the name of Jesus, I greet you."

He stopped what he was doing and stared at me in confusion. I knew this was a time for boldness, much like Paul had done repeatedly. If I failed today, I would fail throughout the land of the Getae.

"I am here to tell you that the Kingdom of God has come to you this day." I walked closer, but the water was not any deeper.

"Why should I listen to you, a foreigner?"

The head of a woman poked out from the door of the hut.

"I am not a foreigner. I am of the Singidava Getae. When I was a boy, my village was destroyed by slavers and I was taken as a slave. I learned to hate the Greeks and Romans who did this to me." I had arrived at the hut and looked up at him.

"But then I met the one true God."

I reached my hand for him to help me up. He took my hand and pulled me up to the porch of his hut. The woman stepped out of the hut, followed by two boys. Out of the corner of my eye, I saw I was being watched by people on the nearby huts, some in canoes, and even the woman on shore. I took a deep breath and continued.

"The God I am preaching created all things. He created the sun and the moon, the seas and the mountains. He created you and everything that has the breath of life. This God has shown you His eternal power and divine nature. It is clearly seen, so all men are without excuse. But I am here to reveal to you that God sent His very own Son to earth, so that you may be with Him when you die."

The elder looked at me. I wondered if he would laugh or order the men to kill me. His face was expressionless.

"I invite you to tell us more about this god of yours."

That evening, as the sun set, I told them my story. I told them of how I was taken and my village murdered. I told them meeting a man in white at the port of Halmyris. I left nothing out about my humiliation as a slave. Then I told them about Paul and how he taught me about Jesus. I told about how he healed the sick and drove out demons in Ephesus.

"This man healed the sick?" one man asked. He was holding a little girl of about five years of age. The girl looked hungry.

"He did not have that power in himself, but Jesus, through him did this."

"My wife is dying," the man said desperately. "I can't live without her. Will you visit my wife and pray for her?"

I swallowed nervously. This was not what I expected on my first day in the land of the Getae. Healing the sick and driving out demons was something that Paul did. I started to decline with an excuse.

I heard a voice that whispered, "Go to her."

I stood. "Take me to her."

He handed his little girl to a woman sitting nearby. We walked to the shore and stepped into his canoe. Almost the entire village followed in their own canoes.

His hut was dimly lit by a fire. It had the smell of death that I remembered from Abigail's death. Terror seized me. I was just a man. I could not heal this woman.

"Go into all the world and preach the good news to all creation. Whoever believes will be saved. These signs will accompany those who believe: in my name, they will place their hands on sick people and they will be healed."

The voice was as clear as the crickets and the crackle of the fire. I looked around to see if others had heard it. They stared at me in anticipation.

"Who is this man, Tiati?" A woman was lying in the bed, covered in sweat, obviously in great pain.

"He says his god heals."

"I am dying, Tiati." She said weakly. "Don't bother this man."

At the door, one man sniggered. "Does any god care enough to heal?"

I took a deep breath and said clearly so all inside and outside the hut could hear. "I came to tell you about Jesus. He healed the sick and He still does through his followers."

I placed my hand on the woman's forehead. I could feel the heat of her fever, then a tingling all over my body. I heard words, but did not think they came from me.

"In the name of Jesus Christ of Nazareth, rise and be healed."

She looked in shock at me and stood. Gasps filled the room. Tiati fell on his knees, quickly followed by everyone but the woman. I heard someone shout out of the hut that the woman was healed.

"A god has come among us," one man said. They began to fall on their faces.

"Do not worship me," I said forcing Tiati to rise. "I am just a man. Worship God, who has come to you this day."

I stayed a full cycle of the moon, teaching the village and baptizing every man and woman, beginning with Tiati and his wife. He became my disciple, learning every story and parable I could think of about Jesus, while we fished or mended the nets together. Every night I had him tell the stories I taught him to his village.

One day a group of men arrived.

"Is it true that you teach a god who heals the sick?"

And thus, it began. I said goodbye to the village, with the old woman crying on my shoulder. My journey began for real that day. I went from village to village, staying a week or a month. News preceded me and I was usually asked to pray for the sick. I saw miracles that I still am in awe of to this day.

In some villages, there were men who could read and write Greek. In these places I stayed longer, writing out the letters of Paul in Getae, while teaching young men to share the faith with their own people. I always asked that they go back to the villages I visited, sharing the letters with them.

I wintered in a town by the Great River, teaching a dozen young men about Jesus. When travelers came through the town, I asked them about the Singidava tribe, but none knew who they were.

One day a group of Romans, who lived at a town across the river, in the province of Thrace, came to the town I was living in. They had heard rumors that someone was teaching about Jesus among the Getae and they came to investigate. That is how I stood face to face with Liberius.

I wept into his shoulder as he caressed my head like a little boy. "Come now, Onesimus, is that how you greet a friend?"

"I have wondered many days if you and the others in Rome were alive or not."

"I am alive and doing what Paul wanted. I already had my discharge papers when I went into service guarding Paul. I could have left at any moment, but I wanted to stay. The day I turned Paul over to the palace, was also the day I handed my discharge papers to my commanding officer."

"What happened?"

"Paul gave a splendid defense. Never once did he waver. He was made for that moment. But you know Paul; you know what he would have said."

"When I left Asia, I had not heard yet if Paul was dead or not. I assumed he was and told that to the church in Colossae." We sat at a table in the tavern, drinking a warm mulled wine. "Tell me about his last days."

"Three days after the trial, Nero put on a horrific spectacle. Four hundred men, women, and children were crucified in the Circus Maximus. You could hear their screams of pain all over the city. Paul was in chains forced to listen to them. But he did not weep. He stood boldly and proclaimed the message of Christ. Nero could stand it no longer, so he ordered his head removed. After that, Nero was bored, so he ordered those on the crosses to be soaked in oil, then he set them on fire, as torches to light the night sky."

I could not say anything, imagining the horror. Liberius was calm. He smiled.

"You are wondering how I can be so calm?"

"I am trying to put my thoughts into words, but basically, yes."

"Because this was what Paul was meant to do. He knew it. I knew it. I will see him one day and I will not be ashamed when I do."

"What are you doing now?"

"I live across the river. Claudius founded the town with retired soldiers so we would be a buffer in case the Getae were to invade Roman territory. But we are just happy to be away from the evil of that man Nero. We trade with the Getae and they trade with us. We are friends. I think I would be more inclined to defend them against the Romans than fight them. And as for me, I have built a little church. Paul left me with his writings. I don't know if you knew that. And I collected all the scrolls he had left in his possession. They all tell the story of Jesus."

I laughed.

"I grow my own food and I tell the people about Jesus. You should come visit the church."

"Maybe I will, but first I have to find my people."

"I know you will find your people."

I never saw him again after that day.

In the spring, I worked side by side with the men, plowing the fields. I was invigorated experiencing the life of my homeland, learning what made them laugh and what made them sad. They were my people and daily I felt my kinship with them revived.

In the summer, I hunted with fierce tattooed warriors, with bare chests and blonde braids. I felt like I was learning from my father. Even a people so fierce had a desire to know the one true God.

When autumn came, I was in a village under the shadow of the mountains. While helping with the harvest, I taught the people about Jesus.

Again, I asked, "Have you heard of the Singidava Getae?"

"Yes," a woman answered.

"You have?" I could barely contain my excitement.

"I was Singidava before I married." When she smiled, I saw the face of my mother.

"How do I get to them?"

"They are three days walk from here," a man pointed to the west.

"I can take you there," a young man offered.

"I would like that very much."

Early the next morning, before sunrise, four men set out with me to discover the land of my birth. I couldn't contain my excitement. I wanted to run, but the others took a more measured pace. The first day I didn't speak. I was excited, but nervous.

Before sunset, we stopped by a stream. Two of the men left to look for food. The other two began to clear a place to sleep and to make a fire.

I went to a nearby hill and looked at the mountains in the distance. They were gray and heavily forested. But to me they didn't look quite right. This was not my home.

As we sat around the fire that night, they asked me why I was making this journey. I told them about my village being destroyed, being sold into slavery, and living as a slave in the Roman Empire.

"Holy man," one of the men asked. That was my title among many of the Getae, because they had heard about what I had done across the land, healing people and teaching them about God. "Holy man, you are free now? So why not live in that land of amazing wealth?"

"Because in that land, I came to know the one true God. I returned to tell my people, you and others, about him. What a selfish man I would be if I came to know Him, but did not share Him with the people of my birth."

"Tell us about this god."

Late into the night and all the next day, I answered all the questions they had about God. I was amazed that my memory could recall every story in such detail. I could hear Paul in my answers and this made me bolder. The fear I had lived in so much of my life vanished.

That was it. For years, I had wondered why God had given me the gift of memorizing everything I saw written. It was for this moment. I knew every story about Jesus. I knew all the prophecies and psalms written about him. I could recall every word that Paul wrote to the churches. My gift was for this. So I could tell my people about Jesus.

That night I sat alone, away from the fire and prayed. I looked up at the stars, the Milky Way brighter than I had ever seen it in my life. Truly, as Luke said, the number of the stars was greater than could be imagined. I laughed as I realized there were so many, and yet, God had a name for each.

"God," I prayed with my arms outstretched. "Thank you for the beauty of the heavens. Thank you for my salvation. Thank you for bringing me home. Thank you for healing my broken heart. And give me a boldness to share your message to my people."

The next morning was cold. There was a mist in the air, not thick like a fog. There was clear sky beyond it. As the day warmed, the mist would dissipate. It promised to be a beautiful autumn day.

We walked through a forested land that morning. I could smell decaying leaves around me as we walked under the shadow of oak, locust, and pine. Leaves danced in the air, falling in reds and oranges from the trees.

We entered a clearing, with a small hill. From there, I could see the mountains. I stopped and studied them. They looked right.

"Why are you stopping, holy man?"

I looked around and studied the place. I knew that off to my left was a stream.

"This is it," I said confidently.

All four men looked at me. They knew I was seeking my home.

"Are you sure, holy man?"

"Follow me."

I walked to where I knew the stream to be. There was a clearing not far away. The sun had broken through and the mist was dissipating. In that clearing, my stream flowed, slow and cold. I looked around. It all looked the same.

My guides looked at me in astonishment. I knew they were asking if I were insane, but soon they would see that I was not.

I bent down and took a drink. A man looked back at me, welcoming me home. I smiled at him.

We continued to walk. The oaks thinned and gave way to fir, beech, and alders. They were dancing in the late morning breeze, welcoming me home. Soon even these trees disappeared as we walked into a field, freshly harvested of its wheat. Cattle were grazing contentedly, being watched by a boy with blonde hair and blue eyes. He was sitting on a rock with his dog asleep at his side. He eyed me curiously, so I waved at him. He waved back.

There was a village, not exactly where my village had been, but when I left it had been burned to the ground. We walked into the village and were greeted by curious faces.

“Welcome,” a man greeted me. He was tall and his chest was bare. He had a tattoo on his chest. His black hair was braided and hung almost to his waist.

“Peace to you,” I said extending my hand to the man.

A group of men surrounded him. Any one of them could have been my father. I felt safe in their midst. I was home. I could fulfill my purpose and tell my people about Jesus.

I held out my hands, as if offering a gift. “I am here to tell you that the Kingdom of God has come to you this day.”

EPILOGUE
ONESIMUS

"Onesimus, our dear and faithful brother, who is one of you." Colossians 4:9

I had not moved during the entire story. Could it be true?

The bishop handed me a letter, too small to be in a scroll. I opened it and read the letter from Paul to Philemon, asking that Onesimus be restored.

"So, all this is true?" I asked as I put the letter down. I examined this man in a new light. He had suffered, but the joy of Christ was evident in his every move and every word.

"Yes, all of it is true."

Sophia returned. "Would you like me to serve dinner?"

"Not yet, child. Come and sit with us."

"Is she your slave?" I asked.

"Before Philemon died, he freed all of his slaves. Those who are here were slaves once. They have nowhere to go. I give them food and a place to stay. In gratitude, they continue the work they did before." The girl stood next to him and took his hand.

"Sophia was born free, but her mother died just hours after her birth."

"Your mother was a slave?" I asked.

"Yes, she was. Onesimus tells me she was beautiful. Her name was Zoe. When she was freed, she married another slave in the house, but he left to find other work. He never knew that my mother was with child."

"I'm so sorry."

"Don't grieve for me," she smiled. "I have never known my father or mother, but Onesimus has raised me as his own. He is the only father I have ever known."

This was the daughter of Zoe, the woman Onesimus wanted to marry. I smiled. Onesimus understood and returned the smile.

"Why did you return from Dacia? Why didn't you stay with your people?"

"I stayed the winter and spring with the Singidava. I taught them about Jesus. But one morning I woke up and knew I was supposed to return. God had more work for me."

Sophia poured some water for him. Onesimus took a deep drink.

"Thank you, my child."

"Is that the end of the story?" I wanted to know it all.

"Yes and no. I returned to find Philemon on his deathbed. No one, neither Archippus or Timothy, disputed my inheritance. Apphia wanted to stay in Colossae. The villa was in her name, so she stayed there with Archippus, who died a few months later. Alyx returned with me to Ephesus. She is still here with me."

"She is, as always," Sophia added, "Feeding the poor and caring for the sick. A day rarely goes by that she is not out in the streets looking for someone in need. She should be returning soon."

"I told you about Timothy. I was there to see his death. And I told you about John. So yes, that is the end of my story."

"But you also said there is a no. So that means there is a part of the story that has not ended. Tell me, please."

"No, the story is not over, because you are here."

"What do you mean?"

"As long as there is someone to tell the story of Jesus, the story is not over."

I thought about what he said. All my fears and struggles seemed meaningless. He watched me as I pondered what to say.

"What are you going to do with Jesus?"

MESSAGE TO THE READER

Dear reader,

Thank you for taking the time to read about the life of Onesimus. Before you close this book, I must ask you if you have given your heart to God. If not, it is such an easy thing to do. Say aloud the following prayer:

Father God. I have searched for freedom from slavery my whole life. Now I have discovered that it is not slavery that has bound me, but my own sins. You have shown me that Christ provided a way for me to be free from my sins. Christ died on the Cross, so I can be free. I ask you, Lord Jesus, to redeem me, a slave bound by sin. In faith, I accept your gift of salvation. By faith, I will follow you the rest of my life. Thank you for bearing my sins on the Cross and giving me the gift of eternal life. Come into my heart, Lord Jesus, and be my Savior, Amen.

If you prayed this prayer, don't keep it a secret. Talk to your pastor or a friend that is a Christian. Like Onesimus, don't stop with just the prayer. God has a plan for your life too.

If you feel the message in this book would be beneficial to someone else, someone who needs Christ, or someone who needs to grow in faith, then please share this book.

Thank you from the bottom of my heart,

Mark Potter

BIBLIOGRAPHY

All quotes and paraphrases of the Bible are from the NIV version of the Holy Bible.

The Holy Bible, New International Version. Grand Rapids: Zondervan House, 1984. Print.

1. "A Quote from the Oresteia Trilogy." *Goodreads.* Wednesday, 15 Dec. 2016 http://www.goodreads.com/quotes/10573-oh-the-torment-bred-in-the-race-the-grinding-scream

2. Dubnoff, Julia. "Poems of Sappho." *POEMS OF SAPPHO.* 1 February 2017 http://www.uh.edu/~cldue/texts/sappho.html

3. Epicurus, "Letter to Menoeceus." From "Epicureanism." *Wikipedia.* Wikimedia Foundation. 10 March 2017. < https://en.wikipedia.org/wiki/Epicureanism

4. "The Birds (play)." Wikipedia. Wikimedia Foundation. 15 April 2017. https://en.wikipedia.org/wiki/The_Birds_(play)

ABOUT THE AUTHOR

Mark Potter is an avid student of history, with a Bachelor's Degree in education, literature, and history from Dallas Baptist University in Dallas, Texas. He is a retired educator with over thirty years' of experience as a classroom teacher of reading, math, and social studies. Twenty-four of those years were at Nash Intermediate in Kaufman, Texas. He has traveled extensively to various countries in Europe and Latin America. Currently he is living and travelling in Bolivia. He is a relatively new author of two previous books – The Spartan Sisters, a different look at the Trojan War, and Mojón con Cara, a love story set in Santa Cruz, Bolivia. His love for travel, history, and the arts has given him an extraordinary gift for writing. Onesimus is a book you will enjoy, but will also be inspired to live a more forgiving life.

11823893R00210

Made in the USA
San Bernardino, CA
07 December 2018